A GENTLEMAN'S TOUCH

"Tell me, Miss Armstrong, will you have the choosing of your husband?"

Amy glanced at him, then looked hastily away. "If he meets my uncle's approval."

"Ahh. That means if he is sufficiently wealthy. Perhaps titled?"

"Just so. I am exactly what you fear me to be, Lord Maxbridge. A fortune hunter. A scheming fortune hunter." She tilted her chin up defiantly.

"I understand. I wish you well, little schemer." He drew up at the front steps and took the small gloved hand she offered him.

"And I you, my lord." She withdrew her hand reluctantly, something in her heart turning over at the look in his eyes, a look in which the masculine admiration she always received was mingled with something else. Could it be tenderness? Surely not. Maxbridge did not even like her, did he?

Abducting Amy

June Calvin

A SIGNET BOOK

SIGNET
Published by New American Library, a division of
Penguin Group (USA) Inc., 375 Hudson Street,
New York, New York 10014, U.S.A.
Penguin Books Ltd, 80 Strand,
London WC2R 0RL, England
Penguin Books Australia Ltd, 250 Camberwell Road,
Camberwell, Victoria 3124, Australia
Penguin Books Canada Ltd, 10 Alcorn Avenue,
Toronto, Ontario, Canada M4V 3B2
Penguin Books (N.Z.) Ltd, Cnr Rosedale and Airborne Roads,
Albany, Auckland 1310, New Zealand

Penguin Books Ltd, Registered Offices:
80 Strand, London WC2R 0RL, England

First published by Signet, an imprint of New American Library,
a division of Penguin Group (USA) Inc.

First Printing, July 2003
10   9   8   7   6   5   4   3   2   1

Chapter One

"*H*e is a disgusting brute of a man, and you should not ask Amabel to marry him."

"He is a prosperous farmer willing to take a girl with no dowry and a dependent mother, and I say she shall marry him! You expect me to take the pair of you in, don't you? Why should I take the sister who destroyed our family's hopes, and her misbegotten brat?"

"Amabel is not misbegotten, nor a brat," Delia Armstrong declared, then grasped her chest and fell back against the ancient chair on which she sat.

"And enact me no Cheltenham tragedies, ma'am. You are fortunate indeed to have this opportunity open to you, else the pair of you will be out on the streets!" Victor Colbourne, Lord Brinker, loomed over his sister, fists clenched. "Now, send for the chit and let us get this unpleasant interview over."

At that moment the door opened. "I am here, Uncle. I pray you will not distress my mother further. I will marry Mr. Stennup."

"Listening at keyholes, eh?" Lord Brinker whirled around. The sight that greeted his narrowed eyes caused his fists to unclench, his jutting jaw to drop open, and an audible gasp to escape his mouth. "Wh-why, are you my niece, then?"

Amabel Armstrong curtsied, head bowed and eyes lowered, as her mother rallied to make a proper introduction. Lord Brinker barely seemed to hear her. He stood transfixed, staring at the astonishing creature before him. She was tall for a female, and slender, yet even the shapeless black bombazine mourning dress she wore could not hide her womanly curves. Almost blue-black curls frothed around a face as near to classical as could be imagined, perfectly oval with delicately high-arched brows above large, well-opened eyes of dark green, framed in dark lashes so heavy it seemed improbable that she could lift her lids without effort. In profile the classic mold was broken, but not in an unattractive way, as her narrow nose arched slightly in an echo of the Roman profile of the males of her family. Her sweetly spoken words of submission, and her demeanor, suggested to her uncle that she was not stubborn, as her mother had been.

When the trio was seated and Lord Brinker had gathered his wits about him, he tested this theory. "So, missy. You are prepared to do your duty and marry as your uncle wishes?"

"I am prepared to save my mother from being plunged into abject poverty," she replied, with a gentle lift of her chin.

All he could think of was how her head rested on a neck every bit as swanlike as that of the accredited beauty who had taken the *ton* by storm the year before. He could not recall the damsel's name then, but now she was Lady Prenderbottom, though she had been as lacking in dowry as his niece.

Lord Brinker, formerly General Colbourne, had never led his troops in any action that helped to carry a major battle in the Peninsula, but he was an expert on regrouping, and now he smiled at his niece.

"That is a relief to hear. But now I have seen you, Amabel, I think your mother quite right about the proposed marriage to Mr. Stennup. Indeed, I think you might be worth a London Season, under certain conditions."

"The Lord be praised," Mrs. Armstrong gasped, and slid down into her chair in a faint.

Amy and Mary McDonald, their one remaining servant, helped Mrs. Armstrong upstairs to her bed. "Hurry, dearest," her mother urged her as Amy tucked the covers aound her. "Don't keep your uncle waiting."

"Let him wait. How are you?"

"I am much better now. Only think! A Season! My parsimonious brother is to give you a Season."

Amy chuckled. "He almost swallowed his teeth when he saw me. You should have been there, Mary. It was quite comical. One minute he was raging at mother that I should marry Mr. Stennup. The next he was goggling at me like a country bumpkin."

"Men be men," Mary said with a grim smile, "whether they be plowboys or parsons, farmers or fine lords."

"Or hard-hearted uncles, it seems." Amy stroked her mother's forehead. "Now don't worry, Mama. You said once he saw me he'd come around, and he has."

Her mother clutched at the coverlet, hands working nervously. "Oh, yes, he was knocked back on his heels by you, as all men are, but this is no laughing matter. Your uncle is not a charitable man. If he wants to give you a Season, you may be sure he means to benefit from it. Realizing you are beautiful did not suddenly turn him benevolent."

Amy nodded. "I know you are right. But few things could be as objectionable to either of us as my marrying Mr. Stennup, could they?" She shuddered at the thought of the bad-tempered farmer who had offered for her, and grudgingly allowed that her mother could make her home with them.

"No. No indeed. I only wish I were well enough to deal with your uncle as I should."

"You must not be excited any more this evening. I will go down to him and be all that is charming. Perhaps I can warm that hard heart of his."

Her mother's hands relaxed, and she stroked her daughter's face lovingly. "If anyone can do it, you can. Very well, then. Go to your uncle, my darling. Wrap him around your pretty little finger if you can, but if you cannot, bargain with him. Be sure he agrees that you must at least like and respect the husband he will find you."

*   *   *

Lord Brinker gave every appearance of being willing to be charmed by Amabel. He talked enthusiastically to her of her two young cousins, whom she had never seen. He listened with apparent sympathy to her account of her father's last difficult year and early death, overworked as a country curate often is.

"Out in all weather, no doubt," his lordship said with a knowing nod of his head.

"Indeed, and at all hours of the day and night. And it is a large parish, though sparsely populated. The Yorkshire climate did not suit him, or Mama."

"What is the nature of her illness, my dear?"

"I cannot say, Uncle, for we have no physician nearby, nor means for consulting one. Certainly she has had problems with her lungs since she took a terrible fever two years ago, but I also think her heart is involved. And the loss of my father has very nearly broken what was already a weak instrument."

"Hmmm. You love her very much, I believe."

"Very much indeed. I would do anything for her."

"Even marry Stennup. Brave girl. Well, as I have said, you need worry about that no longer. But we have certain things to discuss regarding this Season I have promised you, for it will cost the earth, you know, and I am not a wealthy man."

"I have been thinking about that, Uncle. I do not need a London Season, do I? Please do not think me proud, but I know men take notice of me. Surely a few weeks in Brighton or Bath, or . . ."

Her uncle leaned forward and took her hands in his. "Hush, child. You do not yet know your own worth. I hope you do not become spoiled when you realize it, and will be grateful and dutiful to your uncle who makes it possible for you to come into your own. When you have captured the heart of some nabob or wealthy, titled lord, you will doubtless remember your two little cousins, my daughters. I am said to be a hard man, Amabel, and so I have been, of necessity, in most things. But those two little girls can turn my heart from stone into mush in an instant with their sweet little prattling and trusting, loving kisses. For them I would do anything, and I know you will feel for them, too, once you come to meet them."

From the tone of his voice and the look on his face, Amabel could not doubt the sincerity of his affection for his daughters. "I look forward to getting to know them, Uncle," she said with equal sincerity.

"Indeed, it was the way you remind me of them, not in appearance, but in your youthfulness, that made me ashamed of my willingness to marry you to a farmer such as Stennup, just to be rid of the responsibility for you. 'No, no,' said I to myself. I could not do it to my own daughters, could I? No more can I to this sweet young innocent."

"You are very good, Uncle. My cousins are fortunate to have you for their father." Amy laid her hand on his arm and gazed at him appealingly. "I hope you will be like a father to me."

Brinker's eyes widened, and he drew in a deep breath. "Well, now, you *are* a darling, aren't you? Be sure I shall take good care of you. Now we must make our plans carefully, for I doubt not you will need some polishing in regards to etiquette, dancing, and such, before you go among the *haute ton*. While you are yet in mourning, I must see to such matters. Fortunately, the Season does not begin for several months. This winter you will spend in preparation, and next spring you will take the *ton* by storm."

"In the end, Mama, I am not sure who was charming whom."

"But you knew his game, and so surely had the best of him."

"I sadly fear he knew my game, too. Though he spoke very kindly, and enlarged endlessly on his fondness for me and determination to see me well married, he made it clear he expects to reap some benefit from the time and money he will spend on my presentation and Season. In short, he not only expects me to marry well, he expects my husband to compensate him for what he spends on me."

"That I can believe." Mrs. Armstrong fell back on the pillows, worry permeating her features. "Oh!" She put her hand to her chest in a despairing gesture. "To think I would live to see my daughter put up for sale like a beast at a county fair."

"An expensive beast, too, I think. He mentioned his daughters needing dowries. Is it possible, Mother, to get a husband to not only marry me but to pay for the privilege?"

"Possible, but unlikely he would be the sort of husband you would wish for. Very likely old, or repulsive, or from the merchant class, or all three."

"I don't mind if he is old, or a merchant. But repulsive—I draw the line there." Amy sat on the bed beside her mother, and smoothed her furrowed brow. "Do not look so sad, Mama. When the day began, we feared I must marry George Stennup or be thrown into the street. This evening we have hope of much more."

"It may be very difficult to 'draw the line' with your uncle. You do not perfectly understand the kind of man you have to deal with." Mrs. Armstrong sat up a little bit higher in bed. "Amabel, fetch me that casket in which I keep some of your father's personal papers."

Amabel did as she was told. They had already winnowed their belongings down to the barest minimum, selling anything that had value to keep them in food since her father had died, and culling the rest so that they would have very little to pack when they left the vicarage, as they must do in the next few days to make room for the new curate. But this little casket had survived the severe pruning, for it contained, among other things, her mother's marriage lines, from a Gretna Green marriage that had scandalized the *ton* and infuriated her father and brothers.

"My older brothers were both the brutal, bullying sort, with never a kind word to say to me, so much younger than they. Worse even than my father, who was bad enough. So hard, all of them, turning their back on me because I married a younger son meant for the clergy rather than the dissolute old lord they had arranged for me to marry. A dreadful man he was, too." Mrs. Armstrong shuddered.

"Victor went into the military very young, so I have seen little of him as an adult, but I have evidence that he did not change for the better there. Ah, here it is." She lifted a yellowed bit of newspaper from the box and held it out to her daughter. "I'm not sure why Michael kept this—perhaps to remind himself that in giving up my family for him, I had not given up so very much."

Amabel read the clipping through, chuckling a little.

"You find it funny?"

"This line about the closest General Victor Colbourne ever got to victory was his first name."

"Yes, Michael loved that. And felt so sorry for that young lieutenant who so rashly challenged his superior officer for excessive flogging of his troops. He went so far as to ask for a court-martial for Victor."

"Lieutenant Maximilian Follett," Amy read aloud. "That was the end of his military career, it seems, for this article criticizes the army roundly for cashiering Follett instead of punishing my uncle for the brutal floggings he inflicted on his soldiers. I wonder what ever became of the young man."

"I have no idea. The point is, this 'flogging general' is the man we have to deal with. He has no pity, and is not particularly competent. That is a bad combination. I intend to talk to Victor myself tomorrow, when I am feeling stronger, to see that we reach an understanding about what sort of husband you must accept."

"Now, Mother, you mustn't come to cuffs with him. It will only make you ill without accomplishing anything."

Her mother sighed despairingly. "I only wish I may live to see you well established. After that I shall be glad to join my beloved husband."

"Now, I won't hear such talk. The very first thing my benevolent uncle is going to do for us is to get you to the best doctor London holds. I will make him agree to that."

"Amabel, dearest, promise me you will never let an eligible *parti* see that particular look of fierce determination on your face. It would frighten off all but the strongest minded of gentlemen." Amy quickly schooled her features, and mother and daughter laughed as she produced the look of perfect submissiveness with which she had first greeted her uncle.

"That's better. I could wish you might always be honest in demeanor as well as word and deed, but it is not always wise." Her mother touched her cheek gently. "Though I wish for you to marry a man like my Michael, who would admire your intelligence, strength, and determination, I sadly fear most gentlemen prize submissiveness above all."

To amuse her mother, Amabel took up the mirror from her dresser and practiced a variety of poses. "Is this insipid enough?" she asked. "Does this make me look sufficiently vacuous?"

Mrs. Armstrong laughed. "Minx! You can never look either insipid or vacuous."

"Then I shall just have to hope for that strong-minded man to come along, shan't I?"

"Uncle! What do you think of this Waterfall I have tied?" Christopher Ponselle bounded eagerly into the dressing room of the Earl of Maxbridge, as the latter was completing a simple, elegant, knot of his own devising.

"It seems a great deal of cloth for so small a space," Maxbridge observed dryly, his left eyebrow lifted in a cynical expression so well-known in the *ton* it was called the Maxbridge brow. "Doesn't it crowd you a bit? And with those shirt points, I am at a loss to know how you can see what is anywhere but directly in front of you." He shrugged into the elegant evening coat his valet held out for him.

"Oh." Christopher tested his range of neck motion. "I daresay I look a quiz."

The cynical eyebrow lowered, and a kinder look swept Maxbridge's chiseled features. "No, I am sure you are all the crack. It is I who am getting a bit old-fashioned." He adjusted his sleeves.

"What rot. You set the fashion. You are a nonesuch, a prime-goer, top of the trees . . ." The eyebrow was up again, causing Christopher to stammer a bit. "P-perhaps I shall tie mine as you tie yours. Will you show me how?"

"Both with identical ties? Make of us a bit of a raree-show, don't you think?" Maxbridge picked up his gloves. "Smith, I think a *trone d'amour*?"

The valet nodded. "The very thing, m'lord. If you will allow me, Master Christopher?"

To have his neckcloth tied by his uncle's toplofty and accomplished valet was almost as overwhelming an honor as to have his uncle teach him his own special style. Christopher submitted humbly and gratefully to the operation, and caught for just a moment in the mirror an expression on his uncle's face that might be interpreted as a fond look. This gave him courage to open a topic dear to his heart.

"I am glad we are ready a little early. I must arrive in time to secure a dance from Miss Armstrong."

It was not the first time Maxbridge had heard that name. He smiled. "The Season's diamond? By all means, let us depart immediately, then. Perhaps I shall find fortune smiles on me, too."

Christopher's expression grew anxious. "Oh, you won't ask her to dance, will you? I pray you will not."

Maxbridge frowned. "I am not to approach the beauty?"

"Once she meets you, what chance shall I have? Why would she smile upon a presumptive heir to an earl when the earl himself is in the running?"

The frown deepened. "Title-mad, is she? I wasn't planning to propose to the chit."

"Once you see her, you will change her mind." All the wind had gone out of Christopher's sails. Head hanging, he stalked from the room.

"Oh, in that case, I had better stay away," Maxbridge said, following upon the boy's heels. "I'm not ready for parson's mousetrap just yet."

His volatile nephew turned a beaming smile on his uncle. "Just what I thought. You plan to remain a bachelor, don't you, Uncle? So I am a bit more than a presumptive heir, aren't I?" And he bounded down the stairs, leaving Maxbridge feeling that more had been understood than had been meant, and yet not willing to once again crush the boy's mood.

Christopher was indeed his heir, at least until he married and had a son, since the Maxbridge title could descend through the female line in the absence of male heirs. The boy had been his ward less than a year, since the death of his mother, who had raised him in the country alongside three older sisters. It was to this female influence, he supposed, that the boy owed his emotional outbursts and rather delicate sensibilities, so unusual in a young man nearing his nineteenth birthday. When first Christopher had come to live with him, he had been the greenest of halflings, and Maxbridge had almost feared he was effeminate, so little awareness had he of the usual masculine pursuits. But the boy desired his uncle's approval so much that he eagerly embraced every such experience to which Maxbridge had exposed him, even if he had seemed a bit green about the gills after his first cockfight. Since Maxbridge himself had no great fondness for this sport, there had not been a repeat visit to the pits. But they had taken in the best prize-fights and races, gone yachting, and fenced with Angelo.

He still had a lot of work to do to teach Christopher the finer points of tooling a curricle along the busy streets of London and shooting pistols at Manton's, but the boy had the makings of a fine fencer and even showed a great deal of grit at Gentleman Jackson's. There was a man in that slender boyish body, Maxbridge knew, and he had set himself the task of guiding his nephew through the difficult passage from boy to man; though playing bear leader to a youth would have been the last thing any of his enemies, his friends, indeed he himself, would ever have expected of the taciturn, some even said cold-hearted, Earl of Maxbridge. As he climbed into the coach after Christopher, Maxbridge could not forbear to tweak him a bit. "Last week you were wishing for a military career. This week it is a female. What next week, I wonder?"

Christopher scowled. "Since you wouldn't buy me my colors, what else is left?"

"Oh, so easily world-weary. And I didn't say I wouldn't purchase a commission for you, only that you need to learn a bit more of the world first."

"Not to mention how to handle a saber." Chris relaxed. "I know I've a great deal of ground to make up, Uncle. But I shall."

"I know you will, bantling. Just don't put too many more gray hairs on my head in the process, if you please. Now, about this diamond . . ."

"Miss Armstrong outshines all the stars in the sky!"

"Save your poetry for her. But you are taking your first love too seriously, particularly since she is a marriageable female. You are far too young to marry."

"Still, I mean to marry her if I can. A man could look his whole life and not find her like."

Maxbridge digested this for a moment. "What happens to the army then?"

"She's the only one I'd give it up for. Not that she'd ask me to, likely. She'd want me to be happy. But if she crooks her finger, I'll be whatever she wishes—country squire, diplomat, politician—oh, anything, only to have her by my side."

Max frowned at his volatile ward. "Going to volunteer for the ring through your nose, eh?"

Chris flushed. "She's not the sort to ride rough. Wait until you meet her. Sweetest, dearest creature imaginable, in addition to being the most beautiful."

"What I wish you to consider is that if you must trot out your status as my heir presumptive to attract her, she may not be worth the effort. You have a considerable estate, you know, and are of old aristocratic families on both sides. You are a fine-looking young man. If she won't consider you with all of that, she is a fortune hunter, and would make you a very poor wife."

Chris scowled mightily. "She isn't a fortune hunter. But *she* is being hunted, by all the most eligible men in London from eighteen to eighty. Once she knows me, falls in love with me, my status won't matter to her, I am sure."

"I hope it may be so," Maxbridge muttered, and looked out the carriage window at the wet pavement. Spring of 1816 had been the coldest, darkest one of his memory, yet darker still was the memory of a love lost long ago.

Chapter Two

"*D*id I not tell you she was magnificent? Now, don't for-get, Uncle Max, she's mine."

"Is she?" Maxbridge lifted that skeptical eyebrow. "A goodly number of young cubs don't appear to know that."

Indeed, the lovely young girl they were discussing was sur-rounded by men, so that she resembled a deer at bay.

"They don't know it yet. Well, she don't, either. But she will. I will have her. I *must* have her. So you mustn't charm her, Uncle Max. With a nonesuch like you in the race . . . and indeed, how could I bear to see her *your* wife?"

"Pax, Chris. I'll not poach. But wife is the important word here. This beautiful creature is ripe for marrying."

"Mean to marry her."

"So you said." Maxbridge felt helpless in the face of Chris's enthusiasm. *Absurd for a boy of his age to think of marriage!* He schooled his features not to show his disapproval, knowing full well how that would tend to make his nephew dig in his heels.

"Excuse me, sir. Must secure a dance with her." And Chris hurried off, leaving his uncle to contemplate the latest start of his ward and heir. Of all the things he might have suspected of the boy, marriage-madness was the last. He'd shown very little interest in females of any variety before now, preferring to apply himself to acquiring the manly arts he'd missed under his mother's protective eye.

Maxbridge watched with appreciation as Chris managed to outmaneuver his rivals somehow and lead the dark-haired beauty out for the first set. *The boy has good taste, I'll give him that,* he mused as Miss Amabel Armstrong moved energetically through the figures of a country-dance. She danced with more enthusiasm than finesse, he noticed. She was tall, by no means dwarfed by his gangly six-foot-three nephew, and her black curls whirled wildly about her face, bouncing as she danced.

The true impact of Miss Armstrong did not strike Maxbridge until Christopher drew her over to introduce her. She was simply stunning. He had never seen such skin on an adult. Hers was not the vapid beauty of cameo-perfect features, either. Her narrow nose had a slight Roman arch and flared out at the nostrils, hinting at a sensual nature. Certainly a man felt an instinctive urge to see them flutter with desire. Her deep green eyes, fringed with dark lashes, sparkled with intelligence and an expression that hinted at strength of character, an impression enhanced by her firm chin and strong jawline.

As Chris introduced her to him, Maxbridge was satisfied, though not surprised, that she showed a feminine awareness of him, as suddenly widened eyes enticingly demonstrated. She looked down and away, whether in true modesty or a carefully choreographed display of same, he couldn't have said, but when she raised those huge emerald eyes to him again, something unexpected was there—unexpected but unambiguous, and it wasn't admiration or flirtation, but laughter. She looked him full in the face, eyes dancing with mirth, then turned to his nephew.

"Christopher Ponselle," she said in an accusing tone. "*This* is your uncle?"

Christopher fidgeted with his neckcloth. "Just said so."

She cut her eyes back to Maxbridge for a moment, then turned to Chris, one hand on her hip. "Your *elderly* bachelor uncle?"

Chris choked. "Never said that, exactly."

Max chortled at his discomfiture. "Nor ever called me odious, either, I'll vow."

She laughed, a low, throaty laugh. "As to that, my lips are sealed."

The laugh was Maxbridge's undoing. Now it was his turn to be enchanted with the young woman his nephew had introduced to him—enchanted, and wary. That dance she had given to Chris in the teeth of so many rivals had very likely been granted to the heir to a doddering earl. With a cynicism nourished by experience, he doubted Chris had a chance with her now. And under other circumstances Maxbridge might, for once, have welcomed the edge his title and wealth gave him with eligible females. *So much for learning from my mistakes,* he thought ruefully, as he suppressed all signs of interest under a veil of cool *politesse*. Even if he were inclined to repeat the folly of falling for a coldhearted fortune hunter again, he could not court this beauty, not with his nephew head over heels in love with her. So with inward regret but outward indifference, he allowed Christopher to lead her away rather than soliciting a dance with her.

He watched as Christopher returned her to her chaperon, an anxious-looking woman who seemed older than her years. She looked vaguely familiar to him. *Not the beauty's mother, for certain,* he thought, noting the total lack of resemblance.

Maxbridge danced with the wife of a friend, then went to the card room. After half an hour he returned to the ballroom, fully expecting the lovely Miss Armstrong to find some excuse to seek him out, now that she had digested the fact that Christopher's elderly uncle was in fact a young man in his prime. He found her easily enough. She was surrounded by excited suitors just as before, but this time there was another young girl at her side, whom he recognized as Miss Puckett, the daughter of a friend. Both girls were quickly claimed by partners. To his surprise, Miss Armstrong never looked his way, danced a second time with Chris, and appeared completely oblivious to his presence. He tried to ignore her, even going so far as to dance with a young girl, very much against his usual practice, but he could not keep his eyes from seeking out Miss Armstrong. He supposed he was intrigued that she did not do as he expected and throw herself in his way. *Surrounded as she is by eager young men, perhaps she merely cannot manage it. Or perhaps she knows ignoring me will intrigue me.*

At length he grew bored with the waiting game and tired of fending off matchmaking mothers, so he took himself off to White's, telling Chris he would send the carriage back for him.

"So she is a diamond of the first water, eh?" Mason Markingham looked up from dealing the cards. "Funny, that, your nephew telling her you were elderly! Though it comes to the same thing, I suppose, confirmed bachelor that you are."

"I am not a confirmed bachelor." Maxbridge gathered up his cards and began arranging them.

"Hunh. One of the worst misogynists I know. Why would you ever marry, thinking of the sex as you do?"

"I don't think ill of the sex. Just"—he paused, then grinned reluctantly—"just the penniless unmarried ones. When I marry, it will be to a woman of birth, with a fortune to match my own. That way I'll know she's not simply after my money or my title."

"Wonder if this new diamond has a fortune?" Mason tapped his chin with his cards. "A beauty with a fortune. Now that is just what I need."

That possibility had not occurred to Maxbridge. "If she does, too bad Christopher has already declared her off-limits to me."

"Gad. Christopher is too young to be in the Marriage Mart."

"And so I told him. But he is so smitten with this chit, he thinks to wed her." Both men laughed at the absurdity.

"Not to worry, Max. If she is as wealthy as she is beautiful, I'll cut him out." Mason toasted Max and then turned his attention to his cards.

"Please do give over crying, Miss Puckett." Feeling overwhelmed by the attention she was receiving, Amabel had come to the withdrawing room to catch her breath, and now found herself confronted with a sad young woman sitting on a sofa sobbing into a tiny dab of a handkerchief. She sat beside the miserable creature. "What has overset you so?"

Lifting red eyes to Amabel's face, the girl shrank back as if from a loathsome object. "You!"

"Me?"

"You have stolen my beau. My intended."

"I am very sorry to hear it indeed. Who is your intended?"

"Was. And it's no wonder you should ask, since you have so many men dancing attendance on you, you can hardly be expected to notice any of them in particular. Nor do I blame them, for why should anyone look at ugly little me, after all, with such a beauty as you on the scene?"

"Ugly! That is ridiculous. You are quite a pretty girl."

"I am not! I have a snub nose, no-color hair and . . . and . . . freckles!" Miss Puckett fell into a new bout of tears.

Amabel wanted to put her arms around the girl, but knew it would only add insult to injury. Instead, she burst into tears herself. Miss Puckett left off her weeping to stare at her.

"What are *you* crying for?"

"Wh-wh-why can't I just be ordinary looking? None of the other young girls will have anything to do with me. I haven't a friend in the world."

"What need do you have of friends, when you have all the beaux?"

"Of what use are beaux, really? I can't marry them all. I can't really talk to them about anything that interests me. And they talk so foolishly of me, writing odes to my eyelashes and other such nonsense, that I think I shall go mad." Big tears rolled down her cheeks.

"You're even pretty when you cry," the other girl exclaimed, though her tone was less hostile. "You're eyes don't get all red like mine do."

Amy put her head in her hands and sobbed loudly.

"Now, don't take on so. I know you can't help it."

"N-no, I can't." Amabel peeked out from between her fingers. "I didn't ask for all of this masculine attention. It is quite overpowering. I feel like a freak in a fair."

"That's silly! Every girl wishes to be admired by gentlemen."

Amy scrubbed at her tears and took a deep breath. "Not so excessively. Though in fact, I doubt they truly admire me at all. For instance, you really are pretty, as are many of the other young girls. It is just that I am in fashion now. All of these men circling round me are doing it because all of the others are doing it. It is quite vexing."

Miss Puckett clearly did not know how to respond to this, so she patted Amabel's back sympathetically.

"Oh, I do wish I had a female friend I could talk to about it all," Amabel lamented, dabbing at her wet cheeks with a tiny lace handkerchief she had pulled from her reticule. "I am so confused."

"Why? What confuses you?"

"Well, I have never been around men much. I don't understand them. I don't know which one might make a good husband and which one would not. I don't know which ones are even serious about me and which ones are merely following the others, dashing after the Season's diamond. I must choose a husband, and soon, and I just can't get to know these creatures, because they behave so . . . so unnaturally around me."

Miss Puckett had lost all hint of hostility now, but looked very puzzled. "If you think it would help, you can talk to me about it, but I don't see how it would."

"Oh, but it would, you see. You, for instance, have brothers."

"Yes, and my youngest brother is one of your admirers."

"Well, surely you know something about men? About how to judge a man's sincerity? How to talk to them?"

"Well, I suppose I do, but much good it does me, for no one wants to talk to me or dance with me, at least until your dances are all promised."

"And that is another thing." Amy squeezed out another pair of tears. "I can't dance! I've seen you dashing through the figures of a reel or cotillion like thistledown. I am forever mistaking the steps or tripping up my partner. It is mortifying. I only just learned, you know."

"No, I didn't." It hadn't occurred to Miss Puckett before, but now she realized that Amabel Armstrong had in fact turned a recent country-dance into something of a rout.

"Well, I did. Learned this winter from an old Frenchman and had little time to practice before being pitchforked into society. I'm expecting any day now to be given some nasty sobriquet from someone like Mr. Lansdowne."

"Oh, dear, yes. He would delight in it."

"I can just hear it now. 'The clumsy country bumpkin.' "

" 'The clumsy diamond' is more like." Miss Puckett laughed a little.

"Yes, that. Or something worse. Complete with rhyming verse. Perhaps I shall be pictured in a cartoon."

"Oh, don't cry again! Perhaps—perhaps I can be your friend, and you mine."

"Oh, I should like that ever so much," Amy said on a breathy sigh. "It feels so good to be able to talk things over. I can't with my aunt; she just starts worrying that she has somehow failed me."

"I know! You shall come to my house some morning soon, and we'll practice some of the dances."

"Oh! Could I? Would you?"

"Indeed, yes! My sisters can help, and my brothers would doubtless be glad to join us." Miss Puckett sighed. "And Dorwin, too."

"Dorwin? Oh, Dorwin Smythe-Amhurst."

"Yes. Do you . . . do you favor him, Miss Armstrong?"

"Oh, please call me Amy."

"If you will call me Esmée. Pronounced in the French manner. That is not my name, but I have decided that is what I shall be called. I hate Esmerelda!"

"Esmée is lovely."

"Do you?"

Amabel wrinkled her forehead. "Do I what?"

"Favor Mr. Smythe-Amhurst?"

"I am not entirely sure who he is."

Esmée drew back, astonished. "But you just danced with him! It was to be our dance, but he danced with you instead."

"Oh. Dear me. *That* young man. Is he your intended?"

"He was until recently. Don't you like him? I find him very dear, and quite handsome."

Treacherous ground, Amy told herself. *I must assure her I don't want him without saying something that insults him, and therefore her.*

"He is very handsome; that is true enough. And as for being dear, how would I know? As I told you, they all act so silly and unnatural around me. All except for Christopher Ponselle, who treats me as a sister. As for favoring Mr. Smythe-Amhurst, now that you are my friend, I won't even notice him, will I?"

She smiled, and after a moment Miss Puckett laughed. "Oh, I see. Being your friend will definitely have its rewards!"

"A dancing party! Why should you go to a dancing party? You know how to dance. Didn't I hire that French dancing master for you? You need to start looking for men, not go dancing with a bunch of children." Thus her uncle greeted her news after the ball. He had not wished to accompany her and Aunt Edwina, but he waited for their return and pounced on her immediately for an account of the evening's conquests.

"I don't really dance well, but that is not my main purpose. I need to make some female friends, someone more *au fait* with the *ton* than myself or Aunt Edwina. I received invitations to the three parties I have been to so far through acquaintances of my mother. But she has been out of society for so long that few remember her and fewer still will invite me, because of the old scandal. If I do not widen my circle soon, I shall find myself sitting at home.

"The Pucketts are very good *ton,* and her mother is very knowledgeable of the aristocracy, with a wide circle of acquaintances. Also, I need someone who can tell me who is eligible and who is not. Miss Puckett has brothers. They have friends. She will have been warned by them to avoid certain young men. If Esmée and I become fast friends, she and her mother can advise me in ways that dear Aunt Edwina cannot."

" 'Dear Aunt Edwina.' " Victor's tone was mocking. "Your dear Aunt Edwina is a fool."

Amy lifted her chin. "She hasn't the background Mrs. Puckett has. One isn't born knowing how to maneuver in the *ton*."

Victor ran his hand through his hair. "Lud, don't I know it. I'm all at sea. M'brother was raised to be the heir. Knew everyone and everyone knew him. What was I, but a younger brother, sent away to be cannon fodder. I sometimes think that Wellington got rid of me because I couldn't dance beautifully, like his young aides. No hand at doing the pretty with the ladies. Just a crude old soldier, that's all I was. If I'd known I was going to inherit, wouldn't have married Edwina. Pretty girl, you'd hardly believe it to see her now, but then, just a perfect English rose, in India. Came out to find a husband there because without a dowry she'd no chance in England. Oh, that mother of hers was a wily one. Set a trap for me, she did, and I walked right into it. Old fool that I am."

"Uncle! You are not an old fool. Aunt Edwina is a wonderful woman." *More than you deserve,* she thought.

"Yes, yes. Well, she was wonderful for an old bachelor with no future in his chosen profession. Thirty years her senior, and lonely, I was. Fifty and with little prospects, thought myself dashed lucky to have her. Didn't know I'd inherit. She's country bred, barely has pretensions to the gentry, no knowledge of society. Who's to introduce my daughters into the *ton*? Who's to show them the way to go on?"

Amy stood up and went to her uncle, where he paced in front of the fireplace. "I am, Uncle," she said in a soft voice. "I shall be well established by the time they are of an age to marry."

"Yes." He brightened a bit. "Yes. Well. Got a good head on your shoulders. Can't say you haven't the right of it. Very well, then, go to your dancing party. Just don't fall for some younger son or boy who won't inherit for years."

"I won't." Amy gave Victor the kiss on the cheek he always expected and dashed up to her room. There she wrote a letter to her mother in which she told what she had not told her uncle: she had met a man at the ball who made her heart flutter. A wealthy earl, he was perfect in every way but one.

Amy lifted her pen from the paper and stroked her lip with the feather as she remembered Lord Maxbridge's deep chocolate brown hair and vivid blue eyes, his chiseled features and strong jaw. *Tall,* she thought. *Taller even than his nephew, and broad-shouldered, too. And such warmth in his eyes when first we were introduced.*

But immediately his warmth had turned to coldness. This was why she had not included the meeting with Lord Maxbridge in her report to her uncle. The only man who both made her yearn for his regard and could meet her uncle's need for wealth, had thus far been the only man who had taken no interest in her at all.

Chapter Three

The next morning, nearer to noon than dawn, Christopher entered his uncle's study as directed by their butler. Maxbridge looked up from some sums he was doing.

"Don't look as if I am going to eat you," he said, indicating the chair by his desk.

"I know I was in late. After the dance, some of the other fellows and I . . ."

"Spare me the details. Glad you are making some friends and kicking up some larks. Just remember what I said about not wishing to be gray by the age of thirty."

Christopher laughed. "We didn't box the watch or anything. Just went to the pantomime."

Maxbridge templed his hands. "Something you said last night has been gnawing at me. It is clear to me that you gained Miss Armstrong's attention by letting her think I am a confirmed bachelor . . ."

"But you are!" Chris sat forward in his seat, staring at his uncle anxiously.

"No, I am not. At the age of twenty-eight, I can by no means be considered out of the Marriage Mart."

"Then why did you leave the ball early last night, instead of dancing with the marriageable young ladies?"

"I didn't say I am actively pursuing marriage, just that I have by no means forsworn it. I have been very busy the last few years repairing the damage done to the Maxbridge estates

by my older brother, or rather by his delightful countess, far
too busy even to look for a wife, much less give a family the
attention it deserves."

"But why should you marry, Uncle? You don't lack for female companionship, and you have an heir. I'll be a good one,
too. I know I've shown no interest in your business matters as
yet, but I will. My mother made sure I know how to oversee
my own property, and you'll teach me even more, I don't
doubt. You can just relax and enjoy the company of the latest
delectable opera dancer, and let me worry about perpetuating
the Maxbridge title."

"Very decent of you, you young chub! I thank you very
much for offering to see that I never have a family of my own,
children to dandle on my knee and comfort me in my old age."

Chris chortled. "I can't imagine you dandling a brat on your
knee! But if you should ever feel the urge, I'll be glad to provide you one of mine and Amabel's."

"Amabel? On first name basis already?" Maxbridge
scowled.

"No, no indeed. Miss Armstrong is far too proper for that.
But I overheard her aunt referring to her in conversation with a
friend. I've found that hanging about chaperons is an excellent
way to gather information and ingratiate yourself."

Maxbridge lifted his eyebrow. "Indeed. I see I shall be going
to school of you soon."

Chris shrank back in his chair. "Never! Pardon me, sir, I
never meant . . ."

Maxbridge gestured brusquely with his hand. "It was a jest.
Only consider yourself warned. I make no undertaking to
avoid parson's mousetrap."

"Very well," Chris replied reluctantly. "Understood. But you
won't . . . that is . . ."

"Tell Amabel Armstrong? Let her marry you under false pre-
tenses? You need some character molding, my lad. Even if she is
a fortune hunter, she deserves truthful dealings from you."

"No, of course I couldn't do that." Chris looked down at his
hands. "I don't think she is a fortune hunter. Not really.

Only . . . a young woman must marry as well as she can, mustn't she?"

"Many think so. I hold it to be despicable if there is no affection in the match."

"Well, naturally." Chris glared indignantly at his uncle. "I don't think Amabel would consider such a thing! But she is simply surrounded by suitors, and I sought some means of standing out from the crowd. However, I have another strategy, too. The others buzz about her with florid compliments, stupid poems, and boring braggadocio about their various exploits. I know it drives her nearly mad. I'm just treating her like a friend, like one of my sisters, in fact. She finds it refreshing. She told me so. Once she knows me, I am sure that love will soon follow. Didn't she dance with me a second time last night, quite eagerly?"

Max had to admit that she had. He had thought the chit would lose interest once she learned Chris's "elderly" uncle was a man in his prime. He wondered why knowing he had been mistaken felt more like disappointment than relief. *Doubtless it is Chris's strategy,* he thought. *He's succeeded too well. She thinks of him as a friend; therefore, she continues the friendship even knowing he is unlikely to inherit.* Then his suspicions reasserted themselves. *She plans to use him to further her acquaintance with me, like any resilient fortune hunter. I must be on my guard.*

He did not want Chris to suffer the pain he had suffered when a beautiful young girl had used him in the same way to get to his older brother. Besides, the boy was too young to consider marrying. Maxbridge decided he must come up with a strategy of his own. If she was wealthy, Mason could be the solution. A man of his looks and address must surely be able to edge out a callow youth such as Chris.

And if she is not wealthy? He would find a way to expose her for what she was. He smiled, the kind of sardonic smile that had caused enemies to tremble. His nephew left the room in a disquieted mood.

*   *   *

"I never thought to see so many eligible young men attend a morning dancing party," Mrs. Puckett said, beaming down at her daughter.

"It is because of Amy, of course." Esmerelda Puckett smiled at her new friend. "I can scarce believe it, but my own brothers were actually eager to attend."

Aunt Edwina looked around the room, somewhat astonished. "I thought you said it would be a family party, Amabel, with one or two other couples."

"That is what I thought, Aunt. Did you invite so many, Esmée? Do they *all* know I cannot dance?" She felt her face redden at the thought.

"I told no one but my brothers the purpose of the dance. And as for so many being here, most of them just came. Very naughty of them, but one can forgive them, since they are all so eligible."

"All?" This was the kind of information Amy needed.

"Well, I cannot say that Royden Deburgh is so eligible." Mrs. Puckett frowned. "Did you invite him, Amy?"

"Certainly not!"

"Nor I, Mama."

"And that Gabriel Carleton! What is that rake doing here!"

"The same as all the others, Mama. Seeking to dance with Amy."

Aunt Edwina looked quite alarmed. "I did not know he was not acceptable. Such a prettily behaved young man."

"Pretty is as pretty does," Mrs. Puckett said, primming her lips. "Likely I should ask him to leave, but I shall just keep my eye on him."

Aunt Edwina sighed. "I am very grateful for your guidance, Mrs. Puckett. I haven't the acquaintance in the *ton* that you do, and sometimes I fear I am all but useless to my dear little niece."

"Of course you are not useless." Amy gave her a quick hug, then turned appealing eyes to Mrs. Puckett. "I hope you will guide me, ma'am. I do not know any of them. I want to encourage only those who might meet my uncle's rather strict notions of eligibility."

"Which are?"

Amy felt a little flushed at Mrs. Puckett's raised eyebrows and speculative tone of voice. "Well, he naturally hopes for the best possible match, ma'am, consistent with a true gentleman who will treat me considerately."

"I am glad he is not merely looking for the richest gentleman of the *ton*."

"So Mr. Carleton is a rake? I am so glad you told me that. I danced with him at the Merckles' ball. He wanted to take me for a carriage ride, but I didn't know whether to accept."

"Better not," Mrs. Puckett advised. "Now, Mr. Holmes might suit you. He is quite his own master, and a gentleman to the core."

"Would you point him out to me, ma'am?"

"I shall do better than that. It is time to get things started. I shall present him to you for a partner. However shall we manage, I wonder, with so many more gentlemen than ladies? An unusual dilemma, but a pleasant one, I suppose."

The Pucketts' drawing room, a long, narrow room in their long, narrow town house, had been converted into an impromptu ballroom by the simple expedient of pushing the furniture to the wall and rolling up the carpet. A governessy matron sat at the piano at the bottom of the room. Four young ladies, in addition to Amy and Esmée, stood giggling around them, waiting for the dancing to begin.

Mrs. Puckett beckoned Mr. Holmes to her, and presented him to Amy as her partner. He turned out to be a little shorter than Amy, with a premature tendency to baldness. If Amy was disappointed in Mr. Holmes's appearance, however, she soon realized he was an agreeable and gentle young man. He danced quite well, more than making up for her own deficiencies in the subject. Before she went to her next partner, she had agreed to a drive in the park with him.

Christopher Ponselle was there, of course, and eagerly sought a dance with her. As he guided her through a quadrille, he teased. "I thought you wished to learn to dance before everyone figured out that you couldn't. But everyone is here." He winked at her.

"Oh, surely not everyone. But I think you are right. It is an open secret now." But Amy couldn't regret the outcome of this impromptu party. She now had five female friends, a much wider acquaintance among eligible young men, and her aunt had a helpful guide in Mrs. Puckett, who seemed willing to assist.

Vauxhall was everything Amy had been led to expect. It was a pity the evening was so cool. She shivered in her gauzy muslin dress as she looked around her at the fairy lanterns decking the walkways. She had a gentleman on each arm as she strolled the Grand Walk. Behind them Esmée giggled with her escort and Miss Georgianna Wilcombe. After they viewed the cascade at nine o'clock, they returned to their hostess's box. Aunt Edwina and Mrs. Puckett were in conversation and seemed to be getting along well, which warmed Amy's heart, for Edwina had few friends in the *ton* and always seemed very ill at ease.

Her titular hostess was Mrs. Wilcombe, the mother of Georgianna Wilcombe, one of Amy's new friends from the dancing party the day before. But the woman presiding over the excellent supper, complete with Vauxhall's famous thinly shaved ham, was Lady Phinea Marchant, Georgianna's grandmother, who easily dominated her daughter and all others in her vicinity. She commanded Amy to sit by her for a spell, and questioned her closely about her mother. She knew of the old scandal, but did not appear to be too disapproving of it, instead animadverting on the mercenary natures of the Colbournes.

"Hard to say which one was the worst, the third Lord Brinker or his son John, so briefly but disastrously the fourth lord. I don't suppose you ever knew either?"

"No, Lady Marchant. Only what my mother told me of them." Amy did not quite succeed in suppressing a shudder.

"Well, Victor Colbourne did not exactly show himself to be

a humanitarian as a general. I don't suppose he is any improvement as Lord Brinker, is he?" The formidable old woman eyed Amy shrewdly.

"Actually, I think he is, ma'am. He has taken a great interest in improving the estates his predecessors left in such shambles."

"Hmmm. And will he treat his women any better? The only women the other Colbournes ever treated decently were their mistresses. That estate where your mother is staying just outside London was built for Lord John Brinker's favorite *femme de joie*, you know."

Amy shook her head mutely.

"Oh, pish tosh, girl. Don't blush. T'isn't your fault. Nor all that unusual, come to think of it. Now, what I really want to know is if your uncle means to sell you as his father tried to sell your mother."

This was plain speaking indeed. Amy looked around, seeking some diversion, and found it in the approach of two of the handsomest men she had seen all evening. One of them she already knew, and had even dared to dream about, Lord Maxbridge. The other she had not met, but he was looking at her in a way that told her it wouldn't be long.

"Oh! There is Lord Maxbridge. He is Christopher Ponselle's uncle, you know." She lifted her hand in greeting, for Maxbridge had his eyes fixed on her.

"Yes, I certainly do know," Lady Marchant said. "Well, go along with you, girl. We'll continue this discussion another time." She turned to her daughter, announcing loudly, "Prettily behaved, and even lovelier than her mother. Doubt not she'll make a good match, if that horrid uncle of hers don't play her wrong."

Maxbridge could not take his eyes off the dark-haired beauty sitting next to his Aunt Phinea. He had not expected her at the Vauxhall outing, and was intrigued to see her in deep conversation with his aunt. *Now how had she come to be there, instead of cavorting with the other young people?* he wondered. *Laying her plans with some subtlety, perhaps? Ingrati-*

ating herself with my family? He could not help the rush of desire that thrilled through him at the sight of her, but he could control his behavior toward her, so he nodded to her coolly when she caught his eye. He turned to his companion.

"Mason, you remember the beauty I told you about?"

Mason was instantly alert. "Here?"

"Even so. Come, I'll introduce you."

"Is she wealthy, then?"

"I haven't had time to inquire."

"Oh, well, may as well have a look at her." Mason allowed himself to be steered to Lady Marchant's table.

"Miss Armstrong." Maxbridge bowed. "My friend here would like to make your acquaintance." He indicated Mason and made the introductions.

Amy looked with interest at the man Maxbridge had presented to her. He was not so tall as the earl, nor so elegant, but his golden hair, large hazel eyes, and boyishly handsome face were such as could only please. He executed a magnificent bow.

"Report did not lie, Miss Armstrong. You are truly the loveliest creature to come among us in many years."

Amy suppressed a sigh. Her father had impressed upon her that God had given her beauty. It was not something for which she deserved compliments, so she took little pleasure in them. She smiled slightly, and when he asked if she would honor him with a dance, she agreed. She would have preferred that the Earl of Maxbridge invite her, but he seemed quite oblivious to her. Having presented her to his friend, he had quickly bowed and left.

Mason Markingham was a truly charming man, and she enjoyed her dance with him. But once he learned her family name, she could feel a withdrawing in him. "So, you are Brinker's niece," he said in a disappointed tone. "Maxbridge did not tell me that."

"I don't suppose he knows," she said.

"No." Markingham sighed and looked away. When the figures of the dance brought them together again, he had recovered his charming manner, but made no attempt to stay by her side or learn where she might next be seen, as most young men did. Instead he delivered her back to the box and bowed over her hand with an air of regret.

"A true delight," he said. "Alas." And was gone.

Puzzled, Amy took her place next to Lady Marchant again.

"No use to hanker after Markingham," that grande dame pronounced, her bosom shaking with silent laughter. "He has to marry a fortune. Smoked you out right away, didn't he? Never one to waste his time on pointless pursuits, my girl, and you might think to do likewise. Pity you, I do. Hope that uncle of yours means to give you at least some say."

"He does," Amy said, lifting her chin.

"Good, good. Expect it will be some arch-Tory, though."

"Oh, I hope not," Amy said emphatically.

"Ah?" Lady Marchant's eyes opened wide. "Have political opinions, do you? That father of yours. Now, let's see. No, his family is Tory, too."

"He was a Tory, but he held some notions that my uncle and his arch-Tory friends would deplore. Not that I am incapable of forming independent ideas."

"Excellent." Lady Marchant nodded approvingly. "Here is another dance partner come to claim you. Why don't you and your aunt call on me soon? We can discuss politics to our heart's content. You'd be surprised how much power a woman can wield in our country's politics if she only knows how."

Fascinated, Amy quickly agreed, then allowed herself to be carried away by Mr. Ingleworth, a wealthy young man who already bid fair to be an ardent suitor.

The next evening Maxbridge and his nephew attended the opera in the company of Chris's oldest sister, Mary, in town so that her husband could complete the purchase of some land. Chris lost no time singing the praises of Miss Armstrong to his sister, who listened in astonishment.

"Marriage! At nineteen! Uncle Max, what can you be thinking, to let him contemplate such a thing."

"He didn't ask my permission. Toppled head over heels for her at a dinner party before I knew the trap had been laid."

"Trap!" Chris bounced on the carriage seat in restless indignation. "She's not out to trap me, I say. She's the acknowledged beauty of the Season. Of any Season! To win her would be an amazing honor."

"Hmmmpf!" Mary had seven years on Chris, and regarded him as almost her child rather than her brother. "She's a scheming minx, no doubt, setting up to ensnare a young, naive man just because he's an earl's heir. Who is her family, anyway? Armstrong is such a common name. A little country nobody, hoping to marry on her looks, I don't doubt."

Mary took the same pride her entire family did in their heritage, both on the Maxbridge side and their father's side. Their mother, Maxbridge's older sister, had married an impoverished but noble Frenchman, the Compte de Ponselle, whose title and lands had been lost in the maelstrom of the French Revolution. Chris's father had died fighting the revolutionaries, fully intending someday to regain the title and land for his son. Negotiations to restore them were underway with the new French king, though their success was by no means assured. To smooth the restoration, many of the families newly enriched under Napoleon were being allowed to retain their properties rather than automatically returning them to the previous owners.

Maxbridge had not yet inquired into Miss Armstrong's family. That Mason had not remained by her side last night, but had left the park without so much as a farewell, told him the girl was unlikely to be wealthy. Now he folded his arms across his chest and waited with interest to hear his nephew's account of her family background.

"She's not a country nobody. Her uncle is a lord. Lord Blinkett, I think."

"I am not familiar with that title." Mary, though she had married a country squire herself, continued to take a great interest in the aristocracy.

"Neither am I," Maxbridge growled. "Can't be a new creation, I'd have heard of it. And doubtful if it's an old one, for Mary has DeBrett's almost memorized, don't you, my girl?"

"I do, Uncle," she said with pride in her voice. "I can trace my ancestors on both sides back to the Norman conquest. On father's side, even farther."

"Well, he does have a title, so there! And so shall I, some-day."

"When I stick my spoon in the wall. Something tells me I'd better watch my back. No, Chris, don't fly up into the boughs. It is a jest." Maxbridge regarded his nephew fondly. "You take life too seriously."

"I meant my French title," Chris grumbled, then returned his uncle's smile.

Once settled in their box, they amused themselves like the rest of the *ton* in studying the crowd and gossiping about who wore what and who escorted whom. Chris's avid eyes searched the boxes as they talked, and Max knew just when his inamorata arrived, by the joy on his face. He followed the boy's gaze, as did Mary.

"Is that her?" Mary asked, raising her opera glass. "You did not exaggerate her attractions, brother. Who is that with her?"

"General Colbourne," Max exploded. "By all that is holy, it is the flogging general leading your diamond into the box."

"The f-flogging general?" Chris shuddered at his uncle's disgusted tone.

"Just so. The man who had more than a dozen soldiers beaten to death in one month, and got me cashiered from the army when I objected."

"Oh, no! Well, surely he can't be a relative of hers, or a suitor. J-just a friend of the family, likely."

"No, for I recognize her chaperon now. That poor, martyred woman. I am surprised she is still alive after several years with such a brute of a husband."

"That can't be his wife. That is Lady Blinkett, her aunt," Chris responded uneasily.

"Not Blinkett," Mary corrected him. "Brinker. That is the Colbourne title."

Max turned stern eyes on his nephew and pronounced an awful sentence upon him. "We will never ally ourselves with that family. Never! Do you understand me?"

"You can't mean it. You can't punish Amabel and me for what happened between you and her uncle a hundred years ago."

"I can! When you marry someone, you marry their family, too. I could not bear it. Nor will he wish the connection, mark my words."

"Hush, both of you. You are attracting attention. And the best scene in the first act is beginning. I do beg you to be still. Perhaps the rest of your audience will follow your example." Mary turned toward the stage, hoping her brother and uncle would do likewise. The two men continued to glare at one another for a few moments, then Chris stood up. "I find I have no taste for music this evening. I'll find my own way home." He left the box, and Mary put her hand on Max's arm to keep him beside her.

"Let him cool off," she counseled. "And you, too. Don't you know the quickest way to drive him into that girl's arms is to forbid him?"

Max passed his hand over his face and sighed. "You have the right of it, Mary. Not well-done of me, though I meant every word."

"And justly so. She is utterly penniless as well as connected to that nasty man."

"How do you know so much about them?"

Forgetting her stated interest in the opera, Mary proceeded to enlighten him about the old scandal of Miss Delia Colbourne eloping with a clergyman, the youngest son of a prosperous but stern country squire, with the result that both families cast them off entirely. "She was a famous beauty, and stood to marry a duke, who would have paid well for the privilege. The previous two Lords Brinker were rakes and profligates, so this one has inherited a bankrupt estate. He has turned her out rather smartly, I must say, considering his finances." Mary glanced once again at the beautifully gowned young girl sitting quietly in her uncle's box, her attention on the stage.

"Probably sees it as an investment. I doubt not they plan a rich marriage for her." Though the information confirmed his suspicion that Miss Armstrong was a fortune hunter, Max could not help but wonder how willing the beautiful young woman was to sell herself to enrich her uncle. Would she, like her mother, kick over the traces and marry for love? Or had she indeed set herself to ensnare the wealthiest man she could?

He began to chuckle.

"What on earth? Max, will you be quiet? I see nothing funny in the situation. Christopher is top over tail in love with a penniless girl from a family you despise."

"I was just thinking. I introduced her to Mason last night."

Mary saw the joke at once. "I wish I could have seen his face when he learned what her expectations were!"

"I am surprised that Christopher Ponselle did not come to our box tonight," Lady Brinker observed as they settled in the carriage to return home from the opera.

"Christopher Ponselle? Why worry about him, when she was visited by almost every other eligible young man in the *ton*?" Lord Brinker smiled smugly, delighted with the success of his niece. Intermission had brought a considerable crowd of suitors to their box, clamoring for Amabel's attention.

"Oh, just that he has shown such a marked interest in her, and is heir to a wealthy earl. When he left their box tonight I was sure it was to come sit by her."

"Aunt Edwina, I have told you Christopher is not a suitor. He is more like a brother, all fun and frolic. And far too young to be thinking of marriage."

But her uncle's ears had pricked up at the thought of such a promising suitor courting his niece. "If such an eligible young man shows interest in you, I make no doubt you can turn him into a suitor if you wish. Whose heir is he?"

"The Earl of Maxbridge, an elderly, confirmed bachelor,"

Lady Brinker said eagerly. To please, or at least placate, her husband occupied almost all of her time and attention.

"Not so elderly, I fear, and I wonder if he is in fact a confirmed . . ." Amy began. She still remembered the jolt that had gone through her when first she beheld Lord Maxbridge. Something about that lean, sharply cut face and those brilliant blue eyes had done astonishing things to her insides. She had, in fact, been bowled over by him. Alas, at Vauxhall the other evening he had continued behaving quite coolly toward her.

Her uncle suddenly exploded, cutting her off with a foul oath. "Maxbridge? Maxbridge? You've been letting my niece be courted by the heir to the Earl of Maxbridge? You ninny! You idiot! I knew I should not have let you chaperon her."

"Uncle!" Amabel put her hand on his arm, partly to distract, and partly to restrain him, for it looked as if he would strike his wife then and there.

Her aunt cringed back against the squabs. "W-why . . . ?"

Toning down his voice only marginally, Brinker growled, "Why? Why? Because Maxbridge is none other than Maximilian Follett, that cursed young pup who cost me my command with his maudlin squeamishness over my disciplinary methods, that's why!"

"Oh!" Lady Brinker put both her hands over her face. "I didn't know. The boy's last name isn't Follett. I thought . . ."

"You thought! You thought! Females are incapable of thinking! You!" He addressed himself to his niece, holding up a warning finger in her face. "You will cease to have anything to do with this young cub, this . . . what was his name? Why isn't it Follett, if he is Maxbridge's heir?"

Neither woman knew the answer to this question. Fortunately for them, the carriage had completed the short journey from King's Theatre to their rented home in Curzon Street. Lord Brinker exited first, rocking the carriage with the violence of his egress and leaving the two women looking at one another in mutual alarm.

Chapter Four

"Go upstairs, Aunt Edwina. I'll talk to him." Amy had no intention of letting her aunt face her uncle when he was in such a temper. For some reason—whether because he was truly fond of her, as he claimed, or because he dared not damage his "investment"—her uncle had never hit her. He had made feints in that direction once or twice, but instead of cringing as her aunt did, she had jutted her chin out and glared at him. Perhaps that signaled to him that she had determined, whatever the consequences, she would not allow him to physically abuse her. Still, she tried not to defy him, wishing to keep their relationship as pleasant as possible, to nurture what little affection he might have for her.

She followed him into the drawing room, where she found him pouring himself a generous libation of brandy, as expected. She put on a woeful countenance and approached him slowly.

"Oh, Uncle Victor. I am so sorry."

"It isn't you needs to be sorry, m'dear. 'Tis that fool of a wife of mine. If only your mother had been strong enough to endure the Season. She at least has some knowledge of the *ton*. Though of course, it wouldn't serve. She is too romantical, might encourage you to be unwise as she was. Fortunately, you don't take after her in that sense, do you, child?"

Amy opened her eyes wide. "Not at all, Uncle. I feel quite as you do about the importance of a good marriage. But I hope you can forgive poor Aunt Edwina, for how could she have guessed, with Chris . . . Mr. Ponselle using a different last name than his uncle."

Victor frowned thoughtfully. "Do you suppose the boy is running some sort of rig? Imposing on you by telling you he is an earl's heir? Because if he is, I shall find him and horsewhip him."

Amy suppressed a shudder. She knew all too well her uncle was capable of such a thing, for hadn't she seen him beat a stable hand senseless? "I don't think so. At least, if he is, he has help, for he introduced me to someone as the earl. And he was in that man's box for a while tonight."

"I'll horsewhip him, too, if he is posing as a nobleman."

"I seriously doubt such an imposture is possible in the midst of the cream of the *ton*. Still, the gentleman Mr. Ponselle introduced as his uncle was not old, as Aunt Edwina and I had been led to believe." She added to herself, *And I think he might be a rather more dangerous person to horsewhip than young Christopher.* Knowing her uncle's temper, she did not speak this thought aloud.

"How old? Describe him."

"Thirty, or close to it, I should think." She paused, choosing her words carefully so as not to let her uncle see how attractive she found Maxbridge. "Dark hair, blue eyes. Tall. Chiseled features."

"Sounds very like Follett, all right. You could cut yourself on those cheekbones of his. He was a younger son, like me. Inherited, too, damn him. I hoped I'd ruined him, as he did me."

"How did he ruin you, Uncle?" Amy made her voice sympathetic and sat down, patting the seat beside her.

"Tried to have me court-martialed. Oh, I beat him, right enough. Enough others determined not to see corporal punishment done away with, in spite of those fools the dukes of York and Gloucester. Instead of trying me, they expelled him for insubordination. But soon after that I lost my command on the Peninsula, was sent to India to a pointless bureaucratic post. Wellington pretended it was for military reasons, because I failed to heed a command to bring my troops up at such a time as I would have been a fool to risk them! But I know it was because he, like Maxbridge, is weak and lily-livered when it comes to discipline."

Amy wondered about this. She had not heard that Wellington opposed flogging per se. She suspected her uncle had been a rather poor soldier, and that he had, in fact, been rejected by the great general for that reason rather than the conflict with Maxbridge.

Victor continued berating those who advocated abolishing flogging. "Women and soldiers! Beat 'em or they're worth nothing."

Amy stiffened, and he looked at her shrewdly. "Now, don't you go pokering up. Never did I beat a good soldier, and never will I beat a dutiful niece. But as I said, you're not to have anything more to do with this Christopher Ponselle, or with his uncle. However eligible he may be, I will not tolerate such a connection."

"No, of course not, Uncle. Though it will be difficult to cut him entirely, you know. Either of them, for that matter. They are met everywhere, and have many friends. It would look decidedly odd, and start talk among the *ton*."

She forbore to look shrewdly at him in her turn, but it was a home hit, and she knew it. He had kept in the background thus far because while he had officially won his dispute with Maxbridge, his excessive thirst for strict discipline had been scorned and mocked in times past. Some, she knew, supported flogging, but others pointed out that the Germans forbade it, and had troops who were better disciplined than the English soldiers. Renewing the controversy might make the *ton* a less-than-comfortable place for him, and thus for her. He did not want to begin hearing her referred to as the "flogging general's niece." For this reason, as well as because he was truly uncomfortable in elegant society, he had sent her and her aunt unaccompanied to such parties as they had attended thus far.

"No, not cut him, I suppose," Victor at last agreed. "But not encourage him, either."

"Definitely not. Though as I said, he doesn't seem to be courting me. Just a kind young man. He has many friends who are very well connected, so he is a good one to know. I'll just continue the present line with him, shall I, and treat his uncle as coolly as I can and still not cause comment?" She looked at him appealingly.

Lord Brinker smiled. "That's the ticket. Clever girl. Knew I'd done right to bring you out. How are things progressing with Lord Vendercroft?"

It took all of Amy's excellent control of her facial expressions to keep the wave of loathing this name inspired in her from marring her submissive look. The Marquess of Vendercroft was an aging roué with a reputation that made more careful relatives draw their unmarried daughters aside when he came near. "Well enough, Uncle. He seemed pleased when I agreed to promenade with him in lieu of a dance last night."

"Good, good. Getting on in years to do all that hopping about. But what are a few years in his dish in a man who has ten thousand pounds a year?"

She smiled back at him, though her teeth were clenched. "What indeed? I'll bid you good night, then, Uncle." She kissed him on the cheek and then whisked herself out of the room.

"A few years in his dish," she muttered to herself as she climbed the stairs. "There is a good deal more wrong with Lord Vendercroft than age, as you well know, dearest Uncle Victor!" He had already been widowed twice, which was enough in itself to make her less than eager to be his third wife. The man had made himself notorious as a rake. His arrogance and rudeness were legend. That he was received at all in the *ton* was a testament to the power of those ten thousand pounds a year. However, Amy's chief objection to him lay in his odd behavior. He never looked her in the eyes when speaking to her, but stared fixedly at her mouth. She had the impression he would like to grasp her jaw and open it to minutely examine her teeth.

She doubted hints about Vendercroft were much more than a

threat her uncle used toward her, as she had so many more socially acceptable suitors. Didn't he want his little daughters' future marriage chances to be enhanced by her choice of husbands, after all? Surely he would not wish such a dubious connection as Vendercroft for them?

To Amy's pleased surprise, Lady Marchant sent her a note urging her to call on her, giving her at-home days and hours. Such an explicit invitation could not be ignored, nor did she wish to do so. Not only were the Marchants well placed in the *ton*, she had been intrigued by the older woman's reference to women's political power. Not that she hankered after power, but she took an avid interest in politics, and had often been frustrated to think that women had no vote and no voice in the political process.

Aunt Edwina went hesitantly, for while she had liked Mrs. Wilcombe, she found Lady Marchant intimidating. To her relief Mrs. Wilcombe and Georgianna were present also. The three of them poured over the latest issue of *La Belle Assemblée* while the older woman and Amy held a long discussion about such issues as the correct measures to be taken in France to ensure that no further eruption of war occurred, the harsh poor laws, and, dearest to Lady Marchant's heart, Catholic emancipation. They found themselves in agreement on most things.

"A great pity you are not in Paris now, my dear," Lady Marchant said. "You would surely be a great hit among the politically active aristocrats who are there. You would make a great political hostess. I could provide you references, recommendations . . ."

"Oh, Grandmother," Georgianna chimed in. "That is a wonderful idea. Do say you will go, Amy. Mother and I plan to leave for Paris in May. *Tout le monde* will be there! Just think—dresses from real Parisian mantua makers!"

Lady Marchant rolled her eyes. "Hush, Georgie. Miss Armstrong is that rare young woman who has a mind. Go back to your fashion plates and let us talk."

Georgiana shrugged her shoulders and rolled her eyes in an exact imitation of her grandmother, and turned back to her magazine.

"I should like to go to Paris, ma'am," Amy said, "but I do not think my uncle wishes me to do so."

"Well, perhaps I can do something for you here. I have someone in mind, but he will have to be approached carefully. He was once the victim of a fortune hunter, and seems disinclined to marry."

Amy was intrigued but could see that Lady Marchant intended to say no more, so she asked her what she thought of Mary Wollstonecraft's writings. This launched a lively discussion that found the two of them often at odds, yet the discussion was without acrimony.

"You must call on me again, my dear," Lady Marchant said. "It is a pleasure to match wits with you. How did you acquire so much knowledge of matters which are generally thought to be the province of men?"

"My father encouraged my interests. We were wont to discuss everything—politics, women's rights, religion, art, literature. He had few peers in our remote corner of Yorkshire, you know, so he turned to my mother and me for intellectual companionship in a way that I suppose many men do not."

"Some do, though. You must look for that one. It would be a great waste for you to marry a man who sees only your beauty."

Amy looked down at her hands. "I hope to do so, but to tell the truth, I shall be very happy simply to find a man who is kind and considerate, and will care for my mother."

Lady Marchant made a throaty sound almost like a growl. "Indeed, indeed. A dutiful daughter."

Amy took leave of her hostess reluctantly, for she felt more alive, more real, more like herself in the presence of the dowager than she had done since coming to London.

"And so I have two friends and allies now. Though Lady Marchant's ambitions for me seem unattainable, still it is nice to know someone thinks me of worth for something beside my beauty."

"How sad that you should ever doubt it." Her mother patted Amy's hand. "Your father often said he almost wished you weren't so pretty, so that you wouldn't be treated like an object rather than a person."

Seeing tears welling in her mother's eyes, Amy decided to distract her. "As for my friendship with Esmée Puckett, it is a rather uneasy alliance, to be sure, as she still watches me with Mr. Smythe-Amhurst as if I were a dog about to steal a juicy bone."

"It was very naughty of you to turn on those crocodile tears," her mother said. Her laugh spoiled the admonitory effect of her words.

"Well, if I were the sort to cry easily, I *would* have cried just then, for I told her only the truth. None of the young girls were friendly with me, the boys were driving me crazy, and I didn't know any of them well enough to know whom to encourage."

"Your aunt can't be of any help to you, either, can she?"

"Of course not, poor dear. She has spent most of her adult life in India. She is as intimidated by the *ton* as she is by Uncle Victor, and that is saying a great deal."

Delia grew serious. "How do you get along with my dear brother?"

"Aside from the occasional veiled threat, he hasn't done anything untoward. He wisely stays out of the drawing rooms and ballrooms as much as possible, for he knows he is both uncouth and not well regarded."

"Oh, Amy, I do wish I could be there with you. Perhaps I could . . ."

"No, Mama." Amy put her hand on her mother's arm and patted her comfortingly. "All the activity would wear you out and fret you terribly. You are looking much more the thing, thanks to Dr. Gantry's heart medication and lots of rest and good food. You stay here at Wayside. I will come out to see you as often as possible. There is no lack of young men willing to drive me here!"

"Write me often, too." Her mother reached over and hugged her. "By the way, tell me about your handsome earl, the one you mentioned in your letter."

"Oh, dear. Sadly, there is nothing to say. You'll never guess who he is!" She explained that her earl was none other than the young man mentioned in the ancient newspaper clipping. "So you see, he is quite out of reach, not that he ever showed the least interest in me anyway."

Delia shook her head. "So unfortunate. Well, you will find someone soon. You are in looks, darling. I must say Victor has come down handsomely in the matter of your wardrobe."

Amabel nodded her head. She did not voice the thought, so constantly on her mind, that Victor expected a handsome return on his investment. Let her mother be easy in her mind, at least as long as possible, about this business of finding a husband.

"Now I expect I had better pay some attention to Mr. Ingleworth, since he has taken the trouble to drive me over here." Amy stood and walked to where her swain was feeding the ducks, which swam close to the banks of Wayside's garden pond.

"Thank you for giving me some time alone with mother, Mr. Ingleworth. You have been most kind. Will you have some refreshments now?"

Ingleworth turned eagerly toward her. "Of course. Any food or drink served by your divine hand must be as nectar from the gods."

Amy smiled demurely. "That is good, since all we really have to offer is lemonade and cakes."

"And strawberries," he exclaimed enthusiastically. "Your mother said we were to have fresh strawberries."

"Alas, I cannot eat them," Amy sighed. "They make me break out in spots."

Ingleworth looked askance at the thought of his adored beauty breaking out in spots. She led him back to her mother, and served him his nectar as gracefully and soberly as possible while suppressing the mirth that threatened to overwhelm her.

Mr. Ingleworth was one of the few young men she knew sufficiently well to know that he would meet all of Victor's requirements. He had money to throw away, if his plethora of carriages and horses was any guide. Orphaned at ten, he had obviously already come into his inheritance. He seemed well accepted in the *ton*. He showed every indication of adoring Amy sufficiently to offer almost any sum to wed her.

From Amy's perspective he was not quite so ideal. Shorter than she, he had very little in the way of a chin. More importantly, he had very little in his brain box, either. How could she respect such a man? Would it not be a large risk to trust her life, and her children's lives, to him? She hoped to keep him from coming to the point right away. Surely among his many rivals she would find someone better.

As Amy folded her napkin after delicately patting her mouth free of crumbs, she swallowed a small sigh. Truth to tell, none of her suitors interested her very much.

There was but one man of all she had met thus far to whom her thoughts turned constantly as iron filings to a lodestone. But the Earl of Maxbridge was strictly off-limits, even if he had shown the least interest in her. He was coolly polite to her when they met, a tone which she, obedient to her uncle's dictum, had maintained in her turn. She had been a little surprised that he continued to let Christopher pay her so much attention. She supposed it was because he knew that the boy regarded her merely as a sister. She found being with Chris enjoyable for this reason, and felt grateful that her uncle had let her continue the association.

"Miss Armstrong?"

"Oh, I am sorry, Mr. Ingleworth. I was woolgathering."

"It is time that we headed back to London, I think."

"Indeed!" Amy took her leave of her mother, kissing her and hugging her tightly. She waved to her two little cousins, who after looking over her beau and filling their hands with cakes had run back to their beckoning governess.

Mr. Ingleworth handed her up into his high-perch phaeton. He was inordinately proud of it, and Amy had enjoyed his skillful handling of the ribbons. She had no fear that he would overset them, so sat back and enjoyed the scenery while listening with half her attention to Ingleworth extolling the virtues of his cattle. She had no idea exactly how far they had gone before she realized the scenery was unfamiliar.

"Are we going back to London by another route?" she asked him.

He looked down at her and smiled that fatuous, adoring smile that annoyed her so. "Yes, my goddess. I thought this direction might afford you some pleasure, as you seem to enjoy pastoral beauty so much."

Something about his manner made her a little uneasy. She looked about her. "It is a less well-traveled road, though, isn't it? Rather bumpy, too."

"We'll hit the Highgate road in about a mile," he assured her. Instead of slowing his cattle to allow for the rough road, he flicked his whip at his leader's ear.

Amy held on tightly, but said nothing. She did not wish to be a complaining, vaporous female. In a few minutes they reached an intersection, and she saw with relief that it was, in fact, the smooth, level turnpike. Her relief was short-lived, however.

"Mr. Ingleworth, I sadly fear you have turned the wrong way."

Chapter Five

"Won't you call me George?" Mr. Ingleworth glanced at her eagerly. "Surely now we are alone, you can allow a greater degree of intimacy."

"Did you not hear what I said, Mr. Ingleworth? You have taken the wrong turn."

"Nonsense. You are the one who is turned around. It was that winding country road, I expect. Your first name is Amabel, I believe. May I call you that?"

Amy looked around her, trying to calculate their direction from the position of the sun. "I think you had best stop at this farmhouse and inquire, Mr. Ingleworth. I believe we are heading north rather than south."

For answer, Mr. Ingleworth lifted his reins and again flicked his leader's ear with his whip.

"Please, Mr. Ingleworth. I am beginning to be frightened by your behavior. What can you mean by it, sir?"

His mouth set in a grim line; he made no answer.

"Stop this carriage at once," Amy said in a firm, loud voice. "I will not go another inch with you until you explain yourself."

After a moment, he slowed his team down and looked at her with eyes feverish with excitement. "But once I do, you *will* go with me, won't you? Willingly! I knew it! But how can you need explanation, my dear Amabel, my goddess, my . . ."

"Cut line, if you please." Amy frowned at him. "Explain yourself."

"We are eloping, my love. That is the explanation. I am mad about you, and must have you. It is that simple."

"You are certainly mad! Eloping! Why would you do such a thing?"

"I . . . thought it would be romantic."

"Romantic? Fustian! Do you plan to go to Gretna Green in a phaeton? Without luggage? Your cattle are tiring already, sir. Have you a change of horses arranged?"

"No, I . . ." If the situation had not been so serious, Amy would have laughed at the look of chagrin on his face. "I shall take job horses in a few miles, of course."

"So you do mean to go to Scotland in an open carriage, without luggage?"

"We . . . we can take a post chaise and purchase what we need on the way."

"You must have a huge purse on you, then. May I be permitted to count your coins, to see if you have brought enough?"

He put his hand to his coat; Amy thought for a moment he would really hand her his money. But he pulled it away. "I haven't enough in coin, actually. But I can write a check."

Amy snorted. "How will you convince people who do not know you, far from London, to cash a check while your passenger is protesting and asking to be rescued?"

"But . . . but why should you protest? I love you. I know we shall suit. Amabel, my darling, you could not hope for a more devoted husband." He pulled the horses to a standstill and put his arms around her. "You know I am rich as Croesus. I shall take the greatest pleasure in draping you in diamonds and rubies. I have thought since first I saw those ripe red lips that rubies would suit you." He leaned forward, obviously hoping for a kiss from those ruby red lips.

Amy turned her head, pushing hard against his chest. "Please, Mr. Ingleworth, you must turn this carriage around. It is getting late. We shall have a difficult time making it back to London in the daylight as it is. If you wish to marry me, you must court me and then ask my uncle for permission to marry you."

"Your uncle won't give permission." Ingleworth pulled away and took up the reins again. She put her hand out to stop him before he could give the horses the office to start.

"Why not? You are an eligible *parti*, or else I could not have accepted your offer to drive me out to visit my mother. My uncle vets all my beaux carefully." And so he had, since learning of her association with Christopher. He did his vetting at a distance, as it were, asking his solicitor to look into the background and finances of all the young men who had been courting her. He had already insisted that she cease encouraging some who did not meet his requirements.

"Your uncle doubtless does not know my situation perfectly. He probably thinks I am in control of my fortune, as my parents are dead. But I have trustees, you see. They have control of it until I am twenty-five. They give me a generous allowance, but will never hear of me marrying so young, not even to the most beautiful woman London has ever seen."

"How old are you?"

"Three and twenty. Only two years to go, my darling."

Amabel thought furiously. She must dissuade him from abducting her somehow, without letting him know how hopeless his suit was, for if she ever would have considered marrying him, this hare-brained and inconsiderate scheme had put paid to any such notion. "You can surely convince them of your deep love for me?"

"And of yours for me?" He took her hands eagerly. "Say you love me as much as I love you, do!"

"I cannot say, for I do not know. Certainly I find you an agreeable . . ."

"Agreeable!"

"Eligible . . ."

"Do you feel no affection for me at all?"

"I do not know you well enough. Now, please, let us return to London and resume our friendship. If it should ripen into something more, I am sure our guardians can come to some sort of agreement."

"No! I know them. Especially as you have no dowry. You

haven't, have you? My uncle, Sir Tristram Abernathy, said you haven't. Said, in fact, your uncle would expect a tidy sum for you. I call that unconscionable, to sell you like a beast at the fair."

For once, Amy was in agreement with him, but she could not say so. "How dare you insult my uncle so! He has been all that is good and kind to me since my father's death. I tell you, turn this carriage around or I shall get out and walk back to London." She realized she had made a strategic error when his left arm shot out and encircled her waist.

"No, you will not. I must have you!" As best he could with one hand, he urged his team forward.

Amy thought furiously. She must find some way to influence him. "Tell me, George. You did say I could call you George?"

He looked down at her with a relieved smile. "Indeed, I beg that you will."

"Will your trustees continue your allowance if you marry against their wishes?"

"I . . . I don't know. It doesn't matter."

"Doesn't it? What shall we live on, then? Air? For I have tried to live upon that, sir, and I can tell you it is not a pleasant experience."

"My uncle told me you were as grasping as your uncle, but I did not believe him."

"It is not grasping to wish to have a means of support for myself and my mother."

"Your mother? Your uncle provides for her."

"If we elope, he will throw her out. Oh!" Amy began to cry, large tears rolling down her cheeks. "My mother will learn of it if we do not go back to London soon, and it will kill her to know I am missing. You saw how fragile she is! Please, please, George. Do not do this. You say you love me. If you have an ounce of affection for me, you will turn back now."

George looked down into the large, tear-filled green eyes, and for a moment he wavered. Then he snapped, "Crocodile tears! Your eyes aren't even red. M'sister's eyes turn red and her nose runs when she cries."

"Well, mine don't! I can't help that. If you do not turn back, if you cause my mother one moment of anxiety, I will not only never love you, I will hate you!"

This gave Ingleworth pause. His jaw working, he looked ahead of him. After a few moments, he turned back to her. "Now, don't distress yourself. We will send word to her from the inn where I change the horses. She'll receive it before your uncle can know you are gone, and all will be right and tight. When we return from Scotland . . ."

"You'll never make it to Scotland. My uncle will pursue you like the hounds of hell." Amy folded her arms over her chest. "Doubtless he will challenge you, and I hope he puts a bullet through you, you unthinking, uncaring beast!"

"That old man match me for the ability to drive a team? I should like to see it. Now, Amy, you won't do without. I can live upon my expectations until I am twenty-five. It is only two years, after all. The money-lenders will be more than glad to frank me. And your mother can live with us."

Ahead, Amy saw a promising bit of dust being raised. A carriage was approaching. To distract George and make him keep his slow pace she lifted her eyes to him, letting a soft smile play upon her lips.

"She can? Really?"

"Yes, my beloved! I have a fine estate in Cornwall. We'll be able to live there quite economically, and what does money matter to those who love so deeply?"

"What indeed," Amy murmured. Then, more loudly, "But I do not love you that much!" She grabbed at the reins, turning his team so abruptly that the animals stumbled.

"Here, now!" He tried to recapture the rein she held, but she was tenacious. As they struggled, the horses continued in the direction her jerk on the reins had pointed them, which happened to be into the ditch on the wrong side of the road. Fortuitously, the approaching carriage drew near them just as George realized what was happening. He managed to stop the team before the phaeton overturned, but found himself athwart the road, with a fine black curricle with an equally black team slowing to a stop in front of them.

"Never suspected you of being cowhanded, Ingleworth," Lord Maxbridge drawled as he stopped his carriage. "Heard you were one of our best young whips. Up for the Four-in-Hand club, aren't you?"

Ingleworth darted a poisonous glance at Amy. "It wasn't my fault, my lord, it was . . ."

"Indeed it was not, and what an unkind assumption to make," Amy asserted, leaning in front of him to make herself visible to Maxbridge. "Some sort of creature darted under his leader's hooves and made him shy. Then I screamed, which only made the silly horses dart ahead, straight into the ditch."

Ingleworth grasped at the line she had thrown him. "Just so. Women and horses are too much alike, ain't they, Lord Maxbridge? Shying and kicking up a dust over the least thing."

Amabel frowned. "Not gallant of you, Mr. Ingleworth. An insult to our sex, and quite uncalled for."

Maxbridge lifted his left eyebrow, his expression remote. "It seems to me that instead of brangling in the roadway, you need to get your team turned back around. I am at a loss to know how they got in this position with London in the opposite direction. Do you require any help with them?"

Flushing with embarrassment, Ingleworth admitted that he required someone to stand at the leader's head while he backed them up.

"Perhaps Miss Armstrong will do it, since she contributed to this imbroglio."

"Oh, no, my lord! I couldn't, really. I am terrified of horses."

With a sigh, Maxbridge got down from his carriage. He spoke soothingly to his horses and tied the lead rein to a tiny shrub, then stepped around them to take his position at the head of Ingleworth's team.

Ingleworth gathered his reins and began to back his team.

While he was thus distracted, Amy slid down her side of the carriage, glad she was so tall, for it made the drop a little less disastrous. Still, she landed hard on her feet, then staggered back and fell. "Oof!" She could not help exclaiming.

"Amabel! My love!" Ingleworth abandoned his reins to swarm over the carriage to her side. He scooped her up, and tried to put her back into her seat, while she struggled with him. Maxbridge observed them for a moment, then put a strong, firm hand on Ingleworth's shoulders.

"Easy, there. Miss Armstrong may be hurt." He pulled the younger man back and assisted Amy in escaping his grasp. "Are you injured, Miss Armstrong?"

She could see suspicion in his eyes. Hopeful of avoiding a scandal, she laughed lightly. "Only my dignity, my lord. But I confess I would prefer not to be in the carriage while you are backing them up. Such unpredictable beasts, horses."

"I had not taken you for a fainthearted female, Miss Armstrong."

Amy shrugged and smiled. "When it comes to horses, I am." She went to the side of Maxbridge's carriage as the two men worked to back the nervous animals out of the ditch and get the carriage headed toward London. It took a bit of doing, and Ingleworth had sweat standing on his forehead by the time they had finished. Lord Maxbridge's windswept hairdo had begun to live up to its name, with long unruly locks falling over his forehead. Amy felt something pass through her, something sweet and warm and dangerous, as she took in this slight dishevelment in his otherwise impeccable appearance.

"You can rejoin me now, Miss Armstrong," Ingleworth called to her, eyeing her hopefully.

"Oh, I fear I cannot. Your poor leader has hurt his right foreleg. You will have to walk them very slowly, you know." She lifted imploring eyes to Maxbridge. "I hate to impose, my lord, but would you be so kind . . ."

"Injured!" Once again Ingleworth hastily left his carriage to examine his horses.

"Such admirable concern for an injured creature," Amy

muttered, willing herself not to laugh, though Maxbridge was grinning knowingly. "Pity he has more concern for a lame horse than a female."

"Doubtless thinks a posterior is not so easily injured as a pastern," Maxbridge said, winking at Amy.

"Lord Maxbridge!" Amy had to pretend objection to the impropriety, and sadly feared her eyes gave her amusement away.

"But I regret to say I will not take you up, my dear. I confess I have been wondering when you would make your move. This charming drama has taken me by surprise, but I must decline the gambit. You will have to be content with the wealthy but untitled Mr. Ingleworth."

"Wh-what are you implying?" Amy drew away from him.

"That you saw a chance to get my attention and took it. Even if I had no other objections to you, your willingness to endanger such fine cattle in such devious machinations would give me a disgust of you."

"Disgust! You speak of disgust! The arrogance of men disgusts me!" Amy stomped her foot. "One thinks I will elope with him, the other that I will wreck a carriage to throw myself at him."

"Elope? So that is why you were heading away from London?" Maxbridge's eyes narrowed; he turned to Ingleworth for confirmation.

"Just so, sir. And she was willing enough, until she realized I had trustees."

"Willing? Even if I adored you, would I be so cloth-headed as to elope, disgracing myself and bringing embarrassment to my family?"

"Why not?" Ingleworth asked. "Your mother did."

"She did it for love. Even if I loved you madly, which I do not, would I elope in an open curricle? Without luggage? Not so much as a bandbox? Lord Maxbridge, surely you cannot believe this of me?"

Ingleworth flinched. "You don't love me, I know. But you could come to love me, if only you would give me a chance.

Please, let me help you up into my phaeton. We will speak of this more when we are alone."

"You'll turn around and run off with me again." Amy gave Maxbridge a beseeching look, but he made no reply, and his expression was not encouraging. "Bah! Both of you have more wealth than sense, and are far too arrogant to love anyone!" She turned on her heel and began walking, glad she had worn half boots.

"Ingleworth," Maxbridge said in an ominous voice. "Did you abduct Miss Armstrong?"

"I . . ."

"You young fool! Miss Armstrong. Wait. I will take you to London." He chased after Amy.

She kept going, eyes straight ahead. "Thank you very much, my lord. I would prefer to walk."

"You can't walk to London, you idiot. You are being as silly as Ingleworth."

"I don't have to walk to London! I only have to walk to Wayside, where my mother lives, and it is but a mile or two down the road."

"A good five miles, I'd say." Ingleworth had come up beside them in his curricle. "Amabel, my love. Please forgive me. My ardor overcame my common sense. Do get into my carriage! I will drive you back to London."

"It's nothing like five miles, and I wouldn't let you drive me from one end of Hyde Park to the other."

"I begin to think Maxbridge has the right of it. You were after him all along!" Ingleworth snapped his reins, and when his cattle did not respond as swiftly as be wished, cracked the whip over them, leaving the two standing in his dust.

Amabel and Maxbridge stared at one another in silence for a long moment. At last Maxbridge sighed. "Miss Armstrong, I apologize."

"Why? As he said, I planned the whole thing. Knew you would be coming along that road, knew he would ask me to elope, knew he would abduct me when I refused! Impeccable timing, I'd say!" Amy turned her back on him and continued her march. It was a warm day for April, and the sun seemed unconscionably hot. She had the uncomfortable feeling that her upper lip was beaded with perspiration.

Maxbridge made a guttural sound in his throat as he hastened to catch up to her. "Harpy! Of course you didn't know that. You don't have to chew me up and spit me out, you know. I realize I've behaved foolishly."

"Yes, you have. Even supposing the rest of it possible, how you can have imagined I would set my cap for you, of all people, is beyond all reason," she said, stopping to confront him. "My family would never, could never be allied to yours, and you know it."

"I know it, but I wasn't sure you did."

Amabel thought he looked almost regretful. Certainly as she stood facing him, looking up into his flushed face, into his vivid blue eyes, she felt regret pass through her. *Ingleworth is not the only one given to air dreaming.*

She tossed her head. "I know it well, my lord. You are safe from my scheming ways."

He smiled then, a devastating smile, especially dangerous because tenderness lit his eyes. "Hornet. You won't let me forget that, will you? Perhaps I suspected you of doing what I hoped you would do."

"Abandon all hope . . ." she intoned.

"That were Hell indeed," he murmured, and started to reach for her.

Heavens! He would kiss me if I let him. Because Amy so very much wanted to let him, she turned away and began walking again, very fast.

To her surprise, he did not pursue her. After several long minutes of walking as fast as she could, she slowed her pace. Country bred, she could walk several miles if she had to, but she must pace herself. She heard the sounds of harnesses jingle, the whir of carriage wheels, and expected Maxbridge either to pull alongside her or simply to pass her and leave her in the dust as Ingleworth had. But instead, the sounds continued, very close behind her.

At last, unable to contain her curiosity, she looked back. A horse's head bobbed up and down just behind her. Amabel gave a little shriek and jumped to the side of the road. "Don't! I beg of you!"

"You really *are* afraid of horses."

She lifted her chin. "They are large, and unpredictable, and stupid. In my mind, a nasty combination. Like some men I know."

Maxbridge tried. He tried very hard to frown at her, but he couldn't. A deep, rumbling laugh began in his throat and he had to let it out. He threw back his head and guffawed. When he could stop, he wiped at tears in his eyes. She stood there by the side of the road, one hand on her hip, trying just as hard as he not to laugh, with more success.

"I can understand your disgust with my sex just now, Miss Armstrong, but perhaps you would put aside your prejudice for a moment and allow me to take you up. You really cannot walk five miles, you know."

"I can. Have done, many times. But I can't with a horse trailing me, so please just pass on by."

"And leave you alone on a public highway? Amabel Armstrong! If I have to come down there and throw you into this carriage, I am going to turn you over my knee first." He leaned down, holding out his arm.

"Brute!" Amy backed away from the carriage, determined to defy him, when a sound caught her ear.

Chapter Six

$\mathcal{W}$hen he saw the flash of fear in Amy's eyes, Max inwardly cursed himself. *Now I'll never get her in the carriage.* But before he could soothe her, she suddenly launched herself forward, grasping his arm and scrambling into the carriage with unseemly haste.

"I didn't mean that threat, Miss Armstrong, but I am glad—"

"Go! Hurry!"

"What . . . ?"

"There is a carriage coming. We must get away before they are close enough to recognize us."

Max did not need to hear anymore. If someone should see her standing in the road, they both would have a great deal of explaining to do. Scandal was society's favorite dish, and the less resemblance it had to truth, the more delicious. Though innocent of wrongdoing, Amabel Armstrong would find her reputation in question if found in such a situation.

He stood in the curricle and snapped the reins over his team's backs. More than glad to leave off their dull plodding, the two lunged forward, throwing Amabel back against the seat. She clung to it as they raced along at such a pace her bonnet, already askew, almost flew off her head. She caught it and held it with one hand while gripping the seat with the other.

"There. The turn is just ahead." She pointed to the side road Ingleworth had traversed earlier.

Max reined his team in slightly, taking the turn at a speed

that made Amy slide perilously close to the edge. She gave a little scream, and Maxbridge, transferring his whip to his right hand, swiftly reached out and caught her by the waist. The bumpy road gave them both quite a shaking.

"Are they following us?" he asked.

Amy looked behind them. "No. Or at least if they are, they haven't taken the turn yet."

He released Amy so he could control his team on the rough road. Immediately he felt bereft at the loss of contact with her. "Unlikely they will come this way. Did you see who it was?"

"No, they were too far away. I can only hope they have no better eyesight than I."

"And do you have good eyesight?" He looked down into those beautiful green eyes.

"A few minutes ago you certainly thought I could see you at such a distance and put Ingleworth in the ditch!" She lifted her chin and gave him a mock snub.

"You seem to like to distract one rather than answer a question, Miss Armstrong."

She laughed. "The truth is, I have fairly good eyesight, so I doubt the occupants of that carriage could have seen me. At any rate, I believe it was a barouche, which means the passengers likely couldn't have seen us, though the coachman might have."

"Good." Max slowed his team even more.

She busied herself restoring her bonnet to its proper position. They rode in silence for some way, each pondering the events of the past few minutes and wondering what to say to the other.

Finally Max cleared his throat. "Miss Armstrong, I beg you to believe I would not truly have put you over my knee."

She looked at him skeptically.

"I expect your uncle has given you a bad opinion of the male of the species, if he treats women as he did his soldiers."

"My uncle has been all that is kind to me and my mother since my father died." Amy looked straight ahead, hands clenched in her lap. Kindness had nothing to do with her uncle's treatment of her. The fib stuck in her throat with this particular man. She wondered how much of a sin it was to lie for self-preservation. Her uncle would be very nasty if he learned she had spoken against him.

"I am glad to hear it. At any rate, I doubt he told you the details of our quarrel. If you knew them, perhaps you would have less inclination to believe me capable of beating a woman."

"Just because a man objects to soldiers being whipped so severely they die, it does not follow that he believes women should not be controlled by physical force."

"He told you about it, then? I assure you, I find hitting a woman as bad as brutalizing a soldier."

"Actually, I had it from a newspaper clipping of many years ago. I know that it cost both of you your military careers, which is the source of our families' antagonism, but I want you to know that I greatly admire the stand you took."

He stared at her, willing her to turn her head and look at him. "I would not do physical harm to a woman," he said in a slow, precisely enunciated voice.

She looked into his eyes and nodded. "I believe you. And I am grateful that you took me up. I could have walked to Wayside, but it would have been most tiring, and I would have been so late . . . oh heavens!"

"What is it?"

"I am to attend the Merckles' ball this evening. I must be there, especially if Ingleworth starts any tale about me."

"Then we had best make haste. I'll turn back to the Highgate Road. We can be in London in an hour or less."

"And show up at my uncle's doorstep in your company? I think not. He will be sufficiently annoyed as it is. Please take me to Wayside. My mother will send a footman to London to get my uncle's carriage. I shall be late, but at least I won't have to explain being in your company."

He looked at her anxious face and clenched hands, and felt some powerful emotion he could not name sweep through him. "Tell me, Miss Armstrong, will you have the choosing of your husband?"

She glanced at him, then looked hastily away. "If he meets my uncle's approval."

"Ahh. That means if he is sufficiently wealthy. Perhaps titled?"

"Just so. I am exactly what you fear me to be, Lord Maxbridge. A fortune hunter. A scheming fortune hunter." She tilted her chin up defiantly. "But you and Christopher are safe from my machinations."

"You will have me believe you continue your association with Christopher out of friendship?"

"For what other reason?" she asked, frowning her perplexity.

"Never mind. I do hope you will be allowed to consider other qualities than wealth."

"I assure you my husband must certainly have more than wealth." *He must be willing to take my mother to live with us, away from my uncle and his ranting,* Amy thought. *He must provide for my dear little nieces, and if at all possible, find a way to remove my aunt from Uncle Victor's clutches, or at least secure her better treatment.* She had the strongest urge to tell her entire situation to the man who sat beside her. He obviously guessed a great deal. Pride and self-preservation both dictated that she must keep up the appearance of the dutiful niece and caring uncle. Victor wanted to improve his image in the *ton*, for the sake of his beloved daughters. He hoped his niece's marriage would enhance their prospects socially as well as financially. He would not like any gothic rumors that he was mistreating her to begin to circulate.

"Here is the turning into Wayside. I do thank you for taking me up. I hope you understand that I cannot invite you in. I must tell my mother and uncle I did not know my rescuer."

"I understand. I wish you well, little schemer." He drew up at the front steps and took the small gloved hand she offered him.

"And I you, my lord." She withdrew her hand reluctantly, something in her heart turning over at the look in his eyes, a look in which the masculine admiration she always received was mingled with something else. Could it be tenderness? Surely not. Maxbridge did not even like her, did he?

A footman stepped out of the house and hastened to assist her as she descended from the carriage. He was closely followed by Amy's little cousins, who dashed out crying excited greetings.

"Oh, Amy! Another beau!" Becky, the eldest at six, looked admiringly up at Lord Maxbridge. "This one's more handsomer."

"And he has pwetty horthseth," five-year-old Jane said solemnly. She started down the steps eagerly.

Amy's mother came out on the porch, just behind the girls' harassed governess, who grabbed the hands of her charges.

"I am sorry, sir. They escaped," the governess stammered, flustered by the tall, handsome man who smiled down at the children.

"Amy! Where is Mr. Ingleworth?" Mrs. Armstrong drew near and looked up curiously at her daughter's new escort.

"It is quite a story, Mother. Something of a . . . an accident."

"An accident?" Mrs. Armstrong put her hand to her chest. "Was Mr. Ingleworth injured? Were you?"

"Not at all. Do not be alarmed, Mother."

Her mother looked up at Maxbridge inquiringly. Amy sighed.

Yielding to the inevitable, Max got down from the curricle and took Mrs. Armstrong's offered hand as Amy made the introductions. He bowed over her hand, then looked into the sweet, fragile face turned up to his. "Very pleased to meet you, Mrs. Armstrong. And I see where your daughter gets her quite remarkable beauty."

"You are very gallant, my lord. But do tell me what happened, Amy."

"Lord Maxbridge kindly took me up when Mr. Ingleworth's cattle went into a ditch. No one was hurt, truly. But Mr. Ingleworth had to walk his cattle, so the earl conveyed me here."

"You are all that is kind, Lord Maxbridge. Won't you come in for a moment?"

"Oh, no, he can't. He mustn't. That is . . ."

"I should like that very much, Mrs. Armstrong." Maxbridge's expressive blue eyes twinkled at Amy's discomfort.

"I had not taken you for a fool, girl!" Her uncle loomed over Amy, his face red, his jowls quivering. "The idea of letting Maxbridge return you to your mother instead of going on with young Ingleworth."

"Victor!" Her mother's voice quavered. "Never say you would wish her to be enveloped in such a scandal."

"Why should *you* shrink from scandal for your daughter, madam? You did not shrink from it when you were young. *You* eloped, with a ruinously poor young man at that!"

Amabel watched her mother's face drain of color, and reached up for her uncle's hand, tugging on it to bring him down beside her on the sofa. "Dearest Uncle Victor! I know you mean well, but there is no point in raking over old coals, surely?"

"We have enough live coals, don't we! Why did you not elope with that young scapegrace? He is rich as Croesus!"

"I am confused, Uncle. Of what use would his wealth be, without the marriage settlements in place? Or do you feel I should have thought only of myself?"

"There would have been settlements! You know very well he could not have gotten you to Gretna Green without my catching you. A curricle and pair! No luggage! The young fool. I would have caught up with you, and extracted a rich settlement for us both out of him."

Amy bent her head. "I suppose you might have done, though he is one of the best whips in England, they say. But—"

"I have not known you to be so cloth-headed before. Fortunately, it is not too late! I will accuse him of compromising you . . ."

Her mother gasped in alarm. "And if he did not marry her? She would be ruined."

"I'd put a bullet through him, did he not."

"Very satisfying for you it would be, too, Uncle," Amabel said soothingly.

"Huh!" Uncle Victor looked down at the mild, calm face turned up to his. "Wouldn't help you much, though, would it?"

"No, Uncle. Nor your pockets. And you cannot want the scandal, after all."

He smiled grimly. "Awake on all suits. Which is why I don't understand why you didn't turn him up sweet and have him call on me, instead of being so cool toward him that he acted in desperation. I expect you can recover from it, though."

"Recover, Uncle?"

"Yes. Flirt with him, let him know you still consider him an eligible *parti*."

"He knew I considered him an eligible *parti*."

"Then what possessed the young chub to attempt an elopement? Why didn't he just call on me and ask for your hand?"

"I expect it had something to do with those tiresome trustees of his, Uncle. But you are right. I can doubtless bring him back to me. I shall set about it at the Merckles' ball tonight."

"Excellent!" Victor looked pleased for a few seconds before the import of her words hit him. "Trustees? Ingleworth has reached his majority, hasn't he? Parents dead, and from the way he lives it is clear he has a fortune at his command."

"He did say they were generous with his allowance. And he said if they cut it off, we could live on his expectations. It's only two years until he is twenty-five, after all. You are right, Uncle. I was very foolish not to go with him. But at the ball tonight . . ." Amy lowered her eyes, fearful she would laugh at the dawning concern on her uncle's face.

"Now, just a minute, missy! Tell me about these trustees."

Amy did. Victor turned almost purple when he heard the name Abernathy. "That would be Sir Tristram Abernathy, a pinch-purse and a demmed Jacobin, too."

By Jacobin Amy understood perfectly that her uncle meant that Sir Tristram had expressed some feelings of compassion for the poor or some sense that the landed interests were too powerful.

"Much chance we'd have getting a decent settlement out of that old skinflint."

"But once George reaches his majority, he will have control of his fortune and can make such settlements as we require. I shall encourage him, just as you say. I doubt not I can be wed in a fortnight."

"You'll do no such thing! A man pay for a gel he'd been married to already for two years? I'd like to see it! By that time he would be looking about him for a mistress, more like. You will not give this blasted Ingleworth any more encouragement, do you hear me, young woman?" He wagged his finger at her. "And from now on, you do not go unaccompanied for drives. A chaperon at all times! Not even in Hyde Park, and certainly not to Wayside!"

Mrs. Armstrong gasped.

"Not . . . not visit mother?"

"Only with your aunt or another suitable chaperon. You write Delia almost every day. You can stand another month or two without her company. Then you and your husband can have her forever!" Victor stood up. "Come along, then. We need to get you back to London for the ball. Better late than never. It is just that much more important that you meet as many eligible men as possible." He grabbed Amy's hand and started to drag her from the room. She broke loose, however, and ran back to her mother's side.

"Do not worry, Mama. All will turn out well. You just rest, do you hear? I will write you every day."

Her mother patted her cheek. "Oh, my love. I long to see you settled with a kind man."

"And so I shall be, and soon!"

Maxbridge urged his team into a brisk trot as soon as he left Amy. He had no idea what young Ingleworth might say of the day's events. Though he still had some doubts about Miss Armstrong, he did not wish to see her made the subject of scandal broth. *And that mother of hers. A strong wind would carry her off. A scandal and Brinker's wrath might do so as well.* He had been touched by Amy's concern for her delicate mother. Scheming minx she might be, but she was capable of deep affection.

As soon as he reached his town house. he called for Chris, expecting his nephew to know where Ingleworth lived.

"The young master has gone out, my lord," his butler informed him.

"Where?"

"I understood he was dining at the Clarendon with some of his friends, then going to Lady Merckle's ball."

Max had his carriage brought back. He hastened to drive to the hotel where Chris was dining. As he pulled up in front of the Clarendon, he saw several young men circled around a pair involved in a struggle or fistfight. He alighted and started to skirt around them, until he realized that Christopher was in the center of the group, facing off against George Ingleworth.

"What the devil is going on?" He shoved his way into the impromptu ring. "Christopher Ponselle, what do you mean, brawling like a street brat?"

"Ingle has insulted Miss Armstrong. Mean to make him take it back."

"And he's mine next," William Tremayne shouted.

"Then mine," Nathan Holmes chimed in.

"Told the truth. You know what happened. Tell them, Lord Maxbridge." Ingleworth turned to him, blood trickling from his nose.

Max grimaced. "Wish I had been the one to draw your claret, brat. Anything that happened today redounds to your discredit, not Miss Armstrong's. Should have kept your trap shut."

"What did happen today, Uncle?" Chris dropped his fists. "Ingle said you stole Miss Armstrong from him."

"What else did you tell them?" Maxbridge scowled at Ingleworth.

"I t-t-told them the truth. Miss Armstrong was eloping with

me, when she spied you and made my horses go into the ditch
so you could take her up."

"*Was* that the truth?"

"I . . ." Ingleworth wilted under Maxbridge's skeptical stare.

"Of course it wasn't," Chris shouted. "Miss Armstrong
wouldn't elope with him. Hasn't shown him a jot of preference." Other voices assented.

"You'll take it all back, or I'll . . ." Chris started for Ingleworth again, but Maxbridge pushed his way between them.
"Enough! We are attracting a great deal too much attention.
Gentlemen, I wish you all to come to my home and let us talk
about this calmly there. A young woman's future depends
upon not arriving at an erroneous conclusion about what happened today. And I want your word of honor that it goes no
farther until we have discussed it together."

Heads nodded. Slowly the group dissipated, leaving Chris
and his uncle to climb into the curricle behind Maxbridge's
weary team and return to his town house.

"How dare he abduct Amy? She must have been terrified."
Chris wiped at his eyebrow, where a small cut showed Ingleworth had given a good account of himself.

"Terrified is not quite the word for it. Miss Armstrong is a
rather intrepid young woman." He proceeded to tell his
nephew what he knew of the affair.

Chris's face was alight with admiration. "I say, she is game
to the core. But why were you so suspicious of her?"

"Wishful thinking, perhaps."

Chris looked in alarm at his uncle. "What do you mean?"

"Nothing. Nothing. Miss Armstrong is quite safe from me,
as I am from her. She assured me an alliance with our family
was as distasteful to her as to me."

"Oh!" Chris's shoulders drooped.

"The important thing now is to protect her reputation. I do
not think she meant to go with Ingleworth, but I am not posi-
tive. If I can get him to admit her unwillingness, then it would
be grossly unfair for her to suffer because of his wounded
pride. She must have a special care about this particular kind

of scandal, too. If this story gets out, in any form, her mother having eloped, some will see it as blood winning out, and brand her bad *ton*."

"I'll break that Ingleworth's jaw, see if I don't. Then he can't spread his tales."

"He already has."

"Only to the group that were around us. He started in as soon as he entered the club, and I dragged him outside."

"Excellent." Maxbridge looked admiringly at Christopher. The boy was becoming a man, a rather forceful man. "But Ingleworth's silence won't be guaranteed by violence. We must somehow contrive to make him tell the truth, whatever that is."

"Just what you know of it will be enough to embarrass him. I wonder if his pride will keep him from admitting the truth?"

"I think I know how to do it. I am going to speak with him privately before our little meeting with the others. Tell them nothing of what I have told you, if you please."

Chris nodded. His spirits considerably depressed by his uncle's comment about Amy's attitude toward his family, he rode the rest of the way to Maxbridge's town house with his head in his hands.

George Ingleworth glared defiantly at Maxbridge across the desk of his study. "I told them the truth. That they don't like it is none of my concern."

"The truth. Which part of it?"

"All of it. And if you tell the truth, you'll have to corroborate me."

"The part about you running your team into the ditch?"

"I didn't run my team into the ditch!"

"That's where I found you."

"She . . . that is . . . an animal . . ."

"Cowhanded. Inept. Nearly overturned the vehicle with the Season's diamond inside. Poor little thing, so terrified she feared to return to London with such an incompetent driver."

"Now, see here. You know she was just scheming to get in your carriage. You had the right of it, on that score."

"Mr. Ingleworth, my comments were intended to be jocular. I never really believed she was eloping with you, or fixing her attentions on me. She couldn't possibly have seen far enough to identify me when you went into the ditch."

"Still, she *was* eloping with me. Can't deny we were on our way away from London."

"In a curricle, eh, Mr. Ingleworth? No luggage in sight? Rather an impromptu elopement, I'd say. While you might be capable of such idiotishness, I shouldn't have thought it of Miss Armstrong."

Beneath Maxbridge's piercing stare George Ingleworth dropped his shoulders and hung his head. "No, she wasn't eloping with me. She wouldn't. I meant to talk her around, once we'd gone far enough to stop for a good conversation."

"You abducted her, then."

"Had to. Once she knew about my trustees, she wouldn't consider my suit." Ingleworth's chin came up. "Just as my uncle Tristram says, she is a grasping creature, determined to marry for money."

"Doubtless she deserved to be left standing in the road. I wonder if she ever made it home?"

"Made it home? Of course she did. You took her up."

"She refused my offer. There are gypsies near Hampstead. Perhaps they have her now."

Ingleworth gasped. "You left her out there by herself?"

"Why not? You did."

"But this is awful! I must go see what became of her!"

"Good idea. We'll just tell the others, and they can join the search."

"N-no." Sheer terror contorted Ingleworth's features. "Tear me apart, they will. You, too, shouldn't wonder. How could you, a gentleman, abandon a young lady in the country?"

"I wondered the same thing of you at the time."

"I knew—thought you would take her up."

"Oh, I tried, but by that time she was so disgusted with men, she declined my offer."

"You should have forced her into the carriage."

"As you tried to do?"

"You could have succeeded. I could have, too, if you hadn't been there to keep me from . . . that is . . ."

"To keep you from being really brutal with her? You are a fine specimen of manhood, Ingleworth. Shall we go tell the others now? Get this search started? Or do you mean to lope off to France to save your skin?"

Looking at Maxbridge's scornful expression, Ingleworth snapped, "Why so righteous. You did the same thing."

"Did I?"

Ingleworth dropped into a chair, relief causing his breath to whoosh out of him like a deflating hot-air balloon. "You took her up, didn't you? Took her safely home."

Maxbridge snorted and folded his arms across his chest. "The way I see it, you can recant your slander of Miss Armstrong, or you can admit to being a complete cad. Consider this, Ingleworth. A man can be ruined just as a woman can. Oh, some rakes and mushrooms will still acknowledge you, and some of the less attractive and well-connected young women may perhaps one day allow you to court them. But in society, you are going to be given the cut direct by most gentlemen. Mothers will pull their daughters out of your path. Fathers will forbid you to call. That is, if you survive after all of the young men waiting in my drawing room have done with you, once they know you first abducted, then abandoned the chit."

Ingleworth shuddered. "Tell me what to say. Our stories must match."

"Not such a gudgeon after all. Tell me first exactly what you have already said to them."

Christopher waited determinedly near the end of Lady Merckle's receiving line. He snagged Amy while her uncle was finishing his greetings with his host. Victor had, for once, decided to escort them to a society ball, so that he could "deal with that young man" if he dared to put in an appearance. He had ostentatiously loaded a horsewhip into the carriage.

Chris wanted to put her in the picture about Ingleworth's gossip, and the story he had concocted.

"Tell me what he said," Amy demanded.

When she had heard it, she sighed with relief. "That is a very good story."

"It isn't true?"

"Well, it is mostly the truth. It leaves out a few facts unpalatable to Ingleworth, is all."

Chris nodded. "But you should have heard the story he was spreading around before Uncle Max talked to him."

Amy put her hand to her mouth. "Once again, I am in your uncle's debt."

"Yes." Chris looked at her doubtfully. "Uncle said you don't want anything to do with our family."

"Oh, no! I didn't mean you and I couldn't continue to be friends." She smiled up at him. "Your uncle thought I meant to attach him, which my uncle would never tolerate. But as I told Uncle Victor, you aren't courting me, so there is nothing wrong with our being in one another's company. In fact, I quite rely upon you for a few minutes respite from all the foolishness I hear!"

Chris grinned down at her. "Just what I told Uncle Max. Now, he suggested you agree to dance with Ingleworth once, just so those sharp-eyed tabbies wouldn't notice any sudden coolness between you."

Amy frowned at this. "My uncle will likely cut up stiff about that. He was all for horsewhipping George."

"It is an activity he seems to favor." Chris laughed, but Amy looked even more serious.

"I shall have to explain it to Uncle Victor before they can come upon one another, else there may be a scene. Do take George away from here this evening, and tell him I shall dance with him at the next ball."

During that evening several people asked her about the incident with Ingleworth. Obviously the young men who had heard his story felt under no obligation to be silent about it. But thanks to Christopher and Maxbridge's efforts, the story rebounded to her credit. No hint of an elopement emerged, as Ingleworth had retracted that part of it, and admitted he had taken a wrong turn, then driven his curricle into the ditch while trying to turn it around. He had made up the elopement story, he said, to cover up for his stupid driving errors. The young men had thought this an ungallant bit of vanity, and had agreed not to repeat it, glorying instead in telling the tale of a bad bit of driving by one of the best young whips of the day.

Amy thought Ingleworth well deserved their derision, so she confirmed the story. Though it clearly had tongues wagging all over the ballroom, she neither heard nor felt any criticism of her behavior. She returned home that night relieved and grateful to Maxbridge. But when she attempted to explain to her uncle the favor his old enemy had done them, hoping to soften him toward Maxbridge, Victor had chosen to be angry at being under an obligation to the earl, and once again cautioned her against encouraging either him or his nephew.

"Yes, Uncle," she said, stifling the sigh that rose in her chest along with a lump of sadness. How she would have liked to confirm Maxbridge's suspicions that she had set her cap for him! Considering how decently he had behaved to her, how truly kind he had been to her mother, and how he had gotten Ingleworth to swallow his pride to save her reputation, she doubted that she would have much difficulty winning Maxbridge over. Her heart raced at the thought.

There would be a conquest worth the effort! But it was pointless to consider. Her uncle had made a threat on the way home from Wayside that had frozen her blood.

"If you marry against my will, even if it is against *your* will, I shall immediately take your mother into the wildest moor in Yorkshire and abandon her there to make her own way to whatever shelter she can find."

"Uncle! She'd never survive such a thing," she had cried out.

"Precisely. So don't get yourself abducted again, my girl, or begin air-dreaming about Maxbridge!"

Chapter Seven

"*M*r. Melchamp." Amy curtsied to her host, a friend of her uncle's from his days in India. "My uncle has told me so much of you." She smiled at him and his wife, a plump, pleasant woman in her fifties.

"I am pleased you came, my dear. I've been wanting to meet Victor's lovely niece for ever so long." He pressed her hand warmly before passing her along to his wife, who asked her about her carriage accident the day before. "Were you injured? I doubt you feel like dancing, which is a great pity, for I have hired some very fine musicians. From the king's own orchestra, they are." She looked anxiously at Amy.

"Now, dear, don't make Miss Armstrong feel obligated. . . ."

"I wasn't injured in the slightest," Amy reassured her hostess. "I look forward to dancing."

"Well, it seems you won't lack for partners," the older woman said wryly as a small army of men began to bear down on them.

Behind her she heard Mr. Melchamp say to her uncle, "A rare beauty, Victor. Lady Brinker, you must have your hands full, chaperoning such a magnificent creature."

Amy did not hear her aunt's reply, for Mrs. Melchamp was introducing her to a potential partner. He quickly secured the promise of a dance after dinner. Her aunt and uncle joined her, and while they chatted with some of the other guests, Mr. Melchamp approached her with another man, who she soon learned was the Mr. Braebarne she had been brought here to meet. He was, her uncle had assured her, rich as the Golden Ball.

"Lord Brinker, Lady Brinker, an honor it is, indeed," Mr. Braebarne said with a slight Scots burr to his voice. A not unattractive man in his late twenties or early thirties, he sported a neatly trimmed red beard. He stood half a head taller than her uncle, yet seemed to grovel to him as he bowed. "I've heard a great deal of you, my lord, from my friend Melchamp, all of it good. Discipline is to be desired whether in factory workers or soldiers, my lord. A shame it would be, if our army becomes soppy and sentimental over their treatment."

Her uncle looked as pleased with this encomium as Braebarne had expected. He then turned to Aunt Edwina. "Lady Brinker, Melchamp told me you were a lovely creature, one of the English treasures Lord Brinker carried out of India. I vow he had the right of it." Edwina, unused to praise, blushed and fluttered her fan.

Then Braebarne turned his attention to Amy. He drew a deep breath, as if suddenly stricken with awe. "And you are the famous Miss Amabel Armstrong. I had been told you were a beauty, Miss Armstrong, but that is what I hear of all young girls touted to me by interested relatives. For once such a claim was not an exaggeration." Braebarne looked her over with frank male appreciation, scrubbing his hands together exultantly. "May I lead you in to dinner?"

A quick glance at her uncle, who nodded, and Amy smiled as graciously as she could, considering that this man's manner set her back up. "Of course, sir."

They sat with her aunt and uncle. Mr. Braebarne dominated the conversation, inquiring eagerly of Amy, "And have you had your presentation, Miss Armstrong?"

"Yes, I have." Amy studied the dishes around her. *Such rich food!* She helped herself to some salmon in genevoise sauce. Mr. Braebarne urged on her a dish that he assured her was Laplander reindeer tongues in cream sauce. Even the potatoes were richly spiced and swimming in cream. On the table was a decoration made of marzipan, depicting an elaborate Indian scene of tiger-hunting from the backs of elephants. The Melchamps had spared no expense to provide for their guests. To her surprise, she found that her uncle was being treated as the guest of honor. It was a company of tradespeople and merchants to whom Mr. Melchamp had introduced them, and Amy had no objection to them per se, but found their intense efforts to toad-eat her uncle, her aunt, and herself tiresome. *Mr. Braebarne is the worst of the lot,* she thought as he waited with bated breath for her to enlarge upon her presentation.

"A grand to-do, I hear it is. Dressed all in white, were you? Hooped skirts and such?"

"Yes, and enough plumes that I am surprised I did not fly up the stairs instead of managing to wait on line until it was my turn to be presented."

Braebarne did not smile at her attempt at wit. "Worth it, though, wasn't it?" Though he did not physically do so, it seemed to Amy that he was once again rubbing his hands together, exulting over her position in society.

"Well, yes . . ."

"And have you met the prince? What is he like in private, I wonder? I've seen him, of course, from a distance, but . . ."

"I haven't exactly spent time with him in private. I was introduced to him at a drawing room, made my curtsy and then moved on."

"Oh, Amabel is too modest," Aunt Edwina interrupted. "The prince was most taken with her."

"Indeed, yes," her uncle chimed in. "My niece can turn the heads of royalty, never you doubt it."

"Oh, I don't, I don't." Braebarne chomped down a crab cake, never taking his eyes off Amy as he chewed. She ducked her head and devoted herself to an almond cream pastry, though so much rich food and Mr. Braebarne were almost nauseating served at the same meal.

"Go to Almacks, too, I don't doubt."

She lifted her head. "No, I haven't yet . . ."

Braebarne's eyes widened, then narrowed in disappointment.

"But she will! She will! Only a matter of time before one of the patronesses takes her up," Uncle Victor hastened to add.

"Of course. Of course. Hear they are devilish snooty." A sly expression in his eyes, Braebarne let his gaze drift down to Amabel's bosom. "Probably jealous cats, too. Still, you have the entrée to the *ton*."

Appetite deserted her, but Amy pretended to be preoccupied with her food as Braebarne continued to interrogate her aunt and uncle about their connections. It seemed to her he ran through Debrett's peerage, expressing satisfaction when they claimed acquaintance, and muttering when they admitted they did not know this or that lord. She darted a glance at her uncle. Though he continued to extol her virtues and answer Braebarne's questions, she saw lines of strain around his eyes and mouth.

He'd like to shout "mushroom" at the top of his voice and storm out of here, she thought, suppressing a smile. *I wonder if Uncle Victor can stomach him, even with his reputed riches?*

After dinner Braebarne claimed a waltz with her, and stomped on her feet twice before giving it up to promenade with her.

"Beg your pardon, Miss Armstrong, but I hadn't the advantage of a dancing master growing up. Too busy learning how to run my uncle's factories. Inherited several, you know."

"No, I didn't. Tell me where they are located and what you manufacture."

So he did, in loving detail. Amy had no ingrained prejudice against merchants or industrialists, but the picture that emerged as he described his mill system, with its hordes of children running the machines, disgusted her, particularly when he expanded on the high profits to be made when orphan children were employed.

Seeing that he had failed to impress her, he told her of his country estate, where he was building a fine mansion. "Everything of the best," he said. "Best furniture, best marble in the entryway. Italian marble, of course. I'm having a small river diverted to create a lake and waterfall. Antiques, paintings— I've agents scouring Europe even now. It'll make Coke's Holkham look like a cottage! A suite there fit for the Prince Regent himself. I expect he could be prevailed upon to visit us, for a sufficient loan."

Amy must have looked her astonishment. He misunderstood its cause, for he nodded sagely. "Oh, aye. That fine fat prince is an expensive fellow. Always in debt. Shouldn't doubt he'll give me a title, too, if I decide I want it. I'll count on you to see that I meet him, and soon I'll be a bosom beau of his, you'll see."

"I don't understand you, sir," Amy said frostily. "I think I had best return to my uncle."

Braebarne stopped and faced her. "Oh, you understand me well enough. You're for sale to the highest bidder, and the *ton* is not snapping you up, so your uncle is parading you here among the cits. I see how little he, or you, like it, too. I'll not offer for you right away. Let the pair of you see how hard it is for a girl with little or no dowry to snag a rich aristocrat. Then I'll get you a great deal cheaper. Oh, don't poker up so. I don't mean to be stingy with you, once I have you. I only mean that you and your lordly uncle shall truly appreciate what I bring to the marriage."

Amy felt a little faint. Saying nothing, she hastened to her uncle's side and told him she had the headache. Victor frowned and looked at her suspiciously, but after he allowed Braebarne to fawn over him a few more minutes, he escorted Amy and Edwina to their carriage, where she lost no time in repeating word for word what Braebarne had said.

Jaw working, Victor made no reply except to swear softly under his breath.

Edwina fanned herself, though the night was cool, and turned the conversation to the elegance of the Melchamps' home. "They've done such clever things with their Indian treasures, without looking barbaric, don't you think?"

Amy wanted to set her aunt at ease, so she took up the conversation. They reviewed the evening until they reached their town house. Then Victor sent Edwina upstairs with a curt bark of dismissal. "Got things to say to Amy."

"Oh, dear," Edwina twittered. "Hadn't it better wait until morning?"

"No, now." He pointed angrily at the stairs, and Edwina reluctantly left him with his niece. He led her into the library and poured himself a brandy, though he had already imbibed rather heavily at the Melchamps'.

"Now, missy, just what did you say to Braebarne after he made those statements to you? Did you antagonize him?"

"I said nothing, Uncle. I was too taken aback."

"Good. Hope it doesn't come to that, but you may have to swallow him. *We* may have to swallow him. Don't wish to alarm you, but the bills for those expensive gowns of yours are falling due, and . . ."

"Oh, Uncle," she said in a soft voice. "I know you are sorely pressed, but don't worry. The Season is yet young. However, even if I can make no more than an acceptable match in the *ton*, you truly do not want me to marry such as that dreadful man."

"My daughters must have a dowry."

"Better they have good *ton*, Uncle. Mr. Braebarne may be wealthy, but he is a cit. And not a genteel cit, either, like the Melchamps. They have made their fortunes in trade, but their money has gained them entry into the *ton* and they fit in with very little difficulty. He is not like that. He is a boorish cit, a pushy cit, an ill-mannered cit. Think of your daughters, Uncle. What chance would Becky and Janie have in the *ton* if I married such a man?"

Victor glared at her. "I mislike being contradicted and lectured to by you, missy."

"I am sorry, Uncle." She looked down, neck bent submissively, chagrined at her misstep. She knew direct opposition was the wrong way to go with Victor.

"Yes. Yes. Well. Mean well, though. Can't say you haven't the right of it. And how dare that man say he'll wait until you haven't received a good offer. As if you were merchandise to be knocked down when it doesn't sell!"

Merchandise is what I feel like, Amy thought. But she nodded her head vigorously.

Amabel's optimism about making a good match in the *ton* seemed well founded. Since Esmée's dancing party, her Season had truly begun, for there she had met well-connected young people, who invited her to various outings she might not have had entrée to otherwise. The strange incident with Ingleworth had made him a subject of fun, briefly, before the incident was replaced by some other *on dit*, leaving her reputation intact, to her vast relief.

In addition to balls and routes, and in spite of the freakishly cool, rainy spring they were having, she attended picnics and outdoor breakfasts at which muffs and fur-lined pelisses shielded their muslin-clad wearers. Often these outings ended in a dash for shelter, becoming house parties instead. On just such an occasion she ran into Lord Maxbridge again, quite literally.

They had gone to the Wilcombes' home on the banks of the Thames, an hour's drive from London, for a breakfast. As usual for a *ton* breakfast, it took place in the mid-afternoon. It was a warm but misty day that threatened to turn to rain at any second. The precipitation held off until after they had eaten, but afterward, while the young people were scattered across the grounds, the mist suddenly gave way to genuine rain, and Amy raced with several others for the shelter of the house. She charged up the steps and into the arms of Maxbridge, who had just stepped inside.

Once he had gained the entry hall, Max turned to watch the pell-mell flight of the other guests. He watched Amy race up the steps, the wind and rain plastering her clothing to her body and revealing her long limbs and shapely form.

Maxbridge felt as always an unusual mix of emotions as he beheld Miss Armstrong, composed of admiration for her beauty, which never failed to stir him to unwanted desire, and suspicion as to her nature. Chris and she were on the best of terms, he could see that, and it added another dimension to his complicated feelings. He still did not want his nephew and heir entangled with Lord Brinker's niece. Most especially since, as he admitted to himself as she raced toward him, he desired her so much for himself.

Her head down, using her bonnet to shield her face from the rain, she did not see him standing just inside the doorway. If the collision was not exactly planned on his part, he did not do all possible to avoid it. He absorbed the blow of her healthy young body easily, and put his arms around her to steady her and prevent her from falling. Swinging her around out of the path of the other young people entering the door in a rush, he looked down into her face, dewed with raindrops that clustered on her improbably long lashes. The laughter that had accompanied her headlong flight for shelter faded into something else, something much more than embarrassment. Max knew a deep satisfaction at the feminine awareness he saw in her wide pupils and full lips, which were opened in a surprised little gasp.

"Well met, Miss Armstrong."

"Lord Maxbridge!" She stepped away from him as the other laughing guests swarmed into the building and clustered around them. "I do beg your pardon, sir. I did not see you standing there."

"Obviously," he drawled, smiling. He looked around at their interested audience, including a scowling nephew. "You are all soaked. You will be chilled."

Mrs. Wilcombe fluttered around apologizing for the weather, quite as if she were to blame for its having rained. "There is a fire in the Charles II drawing room, and I am having hot drinks prepared. If you will all follow me?"

Maxbridge offered Amy his arm as politeness dictated, and they climbed the stairs to the first floor, followed by the others.

"I am surprised to see you here, my lord," Amy murmured.

"Thought me too old and stodgy to attend a country breakfast?"

"Not stodgy. Not old, either. How you do like to put me in the wrong."

"You are not wrong to be surprised to see me, however. Mrs. Wilcombe cajoled me into it to help her keep the infantry in line. She said that last year some of the young bucks got into a quarrel and very nearly came to a duel over some trifle, doubtless to impress the young ladies. From what I have observed, you will surely have a duel fought over you before the Season is out."

"Not if I have anything to say to the matter!" Amy tossed her head. "I would not have thought chaperonage in your line, my lord."

"Your hostess is my cousin."

"Oh. I didn't realize." Now that she thought of it, though, Mrs. Wilcombe had the same profile and chiseled features as Maxbridge. "Then you are related to Lady Phinea Marchant?"

Maxbridge nodded, his left eyebrow on the ascendant, doubting that she had not previously known the connection.

"Oh, she is a delight! We are become famous friends. I have never met anyone quite like her."

He couldn't help believing her enthusiasm. "She is one of my favorite people, too. But it is unusual to find friends with such a disparity in their ages."

She smiled, remembering that extraordinary conversation she had had with Lady Marchant. "We have . . . mutual interests."

Maxbridge wagged a warning finger at her. "Take care, Miss Armstrong. My aunt Phinea is a notorious bluestocking."

"You alarm me, sir."

He grinned at her mock-fearful expression. He would have liked to discover what interests she shared with his formidable Aunt Phinea, but they had reached the top of the stairs and the time for private conversation had ended.

They entered a large, sumptuously appointed drawing room with a blazing fire. A full-length portrait of King Charles II over the mantel indicated the source of the room's name. Christopher came to stand on her other side. Seeing her eyes on the picture, he informed her in a low tone, "Mr. Wilcombe is descended from one of the king's lesser-known mistresses. Odd, isn't it, how being born on the wrong side of the blanket in one's own generation seems scandalous, but a few intervening generations make it a matter of pride."

"Particularly if the ancestor is royal."

Max scowled at his nephew, bringing a rosy blush to Amy's cheeks, for she should not have treated an improper remark in a jocular manner. *He will think me quite a shameless baggage,* she worried.

Their hostess urged them to take hot chocolate, tea, or coffee to ward off the chills. While Amy accepted a cup of tea from Mrs. Wilcombe, a white-haired gentleman of some sixty years of age appeared at her elbow.

"Miss Armstrong! What a refreshing sight. I had hoped you might be here. I need your assistance."

Chapter Eight

"*L*ord Sunder! I should be delighted to assist you, my lord. Only tell me how." Amy's pleasure was genuine. Lord Sunder was as liberal-minded as he was kind, one of the few men of her acquaintance since the death of her father who understood that she was a thinking being, not merely a beautiful animal.

"I want you to reason with Mr. Wilcombe about the Catholic question. He will not hear me, nor his wife, and even Lady Marchant has not succeeded in persuading him. Perhaps your beauty may sufficiently engage his interest that he may listen to reason."

"Gladly, sir." Amy knew that her hostess's husband was a member of the House of Commons, and that every vote would be needed when Catholic emancipation was put to the test. She put down her teacup, took his arm, and left the disappointed group of young men hovering around her to go to the library with him.

"This I must see," Maxbridge declared to Christopher. "What can Amabel Armstrong know of the Catholic question? Or care?"

"Oh, Amy is interested in all things political, Uncle. It is most odd, isn't it? She tried to engage me in a discussion of the speech you made about the poor laws once. Accursed boring, it was."

"One of my speeches, eh? Was that before or after she learned I was her uncle's enemy?"

"Before. But I don't see what that has to do with it."

"I do." Maxbridge found confirmation that Miss Armstrong had had him in her sites all along. *She was preparing herself to*

*engage me in a discussion upon my interests, as any little
huntress will do who hopes to lure her prey into parson's
mousetrap. What a perfect little actress she is!* Once again,
Maxbridge's feelings were a confusing jumble. Miss Armstrong was no better than Bridget Gordon, he was sure of it.
He was torn between relief and disappointment at once again
having been confirmed in his original suspicions.

He, along with quite a number of the young men, joined the
group in the library and listened as Amy told Mr. Wilcombe
about a Catholic family in her Yorkshire neighborhood who
had sent three sons to serve in the war against Napoleon. He
had to admit she was most affecting in her narrative, telling of
their devotion to England and how much it had grieved them
when their youngest son had died.

"He was a handsome, lively young man of seventeen when
he went off to war. I remember him in his uniform, peacocking
in the village square. They were so proud of him, sir," she
said, leaning forward and gently touching Mr. Wilcombe's
arm. "And of their other soldier sons. They are loyal citizens,
sir, just as you are. Yet they cannot vote. Don't you think it
only fair that those who give their sons for England should be
granted the full rights of English citizens?"

Wilcombe sat looking into her eyes for several seconds, then
cleared his throat and straightened up. "I must say you make a
good case, my dear. I shall consider what you have said."

She smiled at him. "I know you to be a fair man, for I have
read your speeches on the need for compensation for our returning veterans."

She has read his speeches, too? Maxbridge frowned. *Perhaps she really has an interest in politics.*

Before he could pursue this intriguing possibility with any
questions designed to plumb her knowledge, Mrs. Wilcombe
bustled into the library.

"Miss Armstrong, please! You must rejoin my party. Lord
Sunder, I blame you for this! So many of the young men have
followed her here that the young ladies are quite discontent.

They wish to play at charades. Please do join them, Miss Armstrong, so the young men will do so."

"Oh, very well, my dear," Sunder replied. "If only I had several decades fewer in my dish, I should join you at the charades, Miss Armstrong. Indeed, I should join the throng of your admirers and cut them out, if I could."

"I make no doubt you could, my lord," she said, grinning up at him. What a pity there were no young men of Lord Sunder's ilk among her acquaintance.

Disappointed not to have the opportunity to probe Amabel's political interests, Maxbridge reluctantly observed the young people as Mrs. Wilcombe started them on a lively game of charades. After a while, he excused himself since he saw no sign of incipient riot. *I can't think what made cousin Julia insist that I come to this infantry party.*

He decided to go to the conservatory. Like himself, Mr. Wilcombe was an orchid fancier, and he wanted to see the latest addition to his host's collection. He lost himself for quite a while in the tropical garden. As he was studying a newly acquired Oncidium olivaceum Kunth, he heard a stir behind him, and turned to glimpse Amy through the foliage. She was being towed along by a young man whom Maxbridge did not know.

"Now! At last I have you alone."

"And should not! Please let go of me."

"Naughty girl. You know you separated yourself from the others so I could join you."

"I did not! I separated myself from the others because I was tired of the noise and the . . . oh! Do let me go!"

"Not before you allow me to tell you that I adore you and wish to make you my wife."

"Mr. Parmingham, you have only just met me this afternoon. You cannot possibly know . . ."

"But I do. One look at you and I knew!"

"Well, if love came so quickly for you, it did not do so for me, I assure you, nor is it likely ever to do so, if you do not let go of my wrist. I shall be bruised."

Maxbridge started to go to her rescue, but the young man released her.

"I had heard you liked to play coy. Tell me, do you enjoy making everyone mad with desire for you?"

"That is outside of enough! You should not have followed me here. It is most improper. Please go away and leave me to some peace and quiet."

"I shall call upon your uncle tomorrow."

Maxbridge saw from his leafy observation point that Amy was pointing imperiously, theatrically toward the entrance to the conservatory.

"Oh, very well. But I shan't give up. I warn you."

She made no reply. There came the sound of retreating steps and the slam of a door. Then Maxbridge heard a long, heartfelt sigh, and saw Amy move to the windows of the conservatory, where she leaned her head against the glass and looked pensively out at the rain-soaked vista.

Since he could not leave the conservatory without passing by her, he stepped out of his inadvertent hiding place. "I do beg your pardon, Miss Armstrong. I had no intention of eavesdropping on that touching scene, but . . ."

Amy whirled toward him. "Oh! You startled me."

"And you are wondering if you will ever have any peace. I shall leave you to your contemplations." He started past her, then noticed the sheen of tears in her eyes. He knew that an accomplished deceiver could call up tears at will. Hadn't Bridget proved that on many occasions? If Miss Armstrong was of that sort, as he suspected, he knew he should leave before the little schemer tried any more of her lures on him, but he found that he still wasn't armored against the sight of a female in distress. Especially a ravishingly beautiful brunette with green eyes.

"My dear Miss Armstrong. You did not let that young fool overset you, did you?"

"It is not just him. It is all of them. All of . . . *it*!" She gestured widely with both arms. "How shall I choose a sensible husband when all around me I am besieged by men—boys, really—whose wits appear to have gone begging? In love with me at one glance indeed! What kind of love is that? For all he knows I am a shrew, a hoyden, even an immoral creature."

He smiled down at her, touched and amused by her indignation. "Your beauty appears to be something of a curse to you."

"I had never thought it possible, but it begins to seem so." She frowned, wrinkling her nose. "Surely it is immature of them? Why is it that all I meet are unfledged chicks? Where are all the men?"

"I expect you had best go to Paris. Much of the *ton* has made its way there since the end of the hostilities with the French."

"Oh, yes. Mrs. Wilcombe did tell me that. She plans to take Georgianna there soon. I wonder you are not there."

"I did go over briefly early in the new year. Decided not to take Chris over until he had fledged, as you put it. Paris is a rather dangerous place right now."

"Oh? I had not thought it."

"Too many angry, resentful Frenchmen, former soldiers, looking for a fight with anyone English. Duels are fought daily over trifles, and while Chris is not terribly quick to take offense, I did not wish to risk his taking up a challenge before he had acquired sufficient skill to acquit himself well."

"Oh, no, of course not!" Amy shuddered. "Chris is such a dear. I could not bear to think of him being hurt. I think dueling is odious!"

"I agree with you, but sometimes it cannot be avoided."

She looked very grave at this. "I wonder if that is why my uncle did not want to go to Paris?"

"Perhaps." Maxbridge rather thought it was because Brinker would hate being in the company of the victorious army he had been forced to leave. He had always been one of Wellington's most vocal critics, and could hardly like to see Old Nosy in his triumph.

"Speaking of Paris, I have yet to thank you for your role in preventing Mr. Ingleworth from ruining me."

"On the contrary, you thanked me and your mother thanked me."

"For bringing me to her, yes, but not for stopping him from talking about it."

"Ah. Well, I hate to see a fool like that cause harm to the innocent." He looked down into the sweet face turned up to his and thought she looked the very picture of maidenly innocence—and was giving him ideas that were decidedly not innocent. He cleared his throat. "What about Paris made you . . ."

"Oh!" She giggled. "That must have seemed a non sequitur indeed! You see, Inglewirth has gone to Paris. Chris told me he tired of being teased about his cowhanded driving."

Maxbridge smiled. "I love your laugh," he said. Her eyes widened. For a moment it seemed gravity had increased in their vicinity, drawing them toward one another.

Amy gave herself a little shake. *This will not do.* "Did you tire of the romp, too? It is very quiet and peaceful in here, is it not?" She looked around her in appreciation. "How lovely these tropical plants are. I wish I knew their names."

He began to name them for her and tell her from whence they came. When they reached the Oncidium olivaceum, she clasped her hands up under her chin and stared at it like an entranced child.

"I had no idea orchids looked like this. How many blooms per stem does it have?" She began to count the tiny pink and purple flowers.

"Some have as many as fifteen," he said. "What do you think it smells like?"

She dipped her head over the spray of blooms, then lifted it to look at him in surprise. "Chocolate. At least a little. And something sweet."

"Does it make you hungry?"

She laughed. "Are they very difficult to raise, I wonder? I should like to have one someday."

"Not too difficult, really. They like a warm, humid environment, though, and are particular about the amount of light they receive."

"You know a great deal about them," she said admiringly.

"I am learning, at least. I have only a small collection. I am in daily expectation of receiving a new shipment of tropicals, however. I think I have commandeered every sea captain going to foreign shores to bring them home to me."

"How I should like to see them." She lifted shining eyes to his face, then colored up and looked away. "Oh, I think perhaps we should be getting back to the party."

Maxbridge nodded regretfully. *Go quickly, before I give in to the urge to kiss you.* "You go first. It wouldn't do for us to reappear together."

"Oh, my, no! My uncle would surely hear of it!" She hastened away.

Her uncle keeps her on a short leash, he thought, watching her go with regret. *I wonder if he mistreats her?* The thought of that brute laying a hand on Amabel Armstrong made Maxbridge physically ill. *I have been too harsh in my judgment of her.*

When he thought sufficient time had passed so that no one would connect his reappearance with that of Miss Armstrong, he rejoined the party. He found Chris and Amy standing together, apart from the others. Chris motioned him over.

"I think you should invite Amy to see your orchids, Uncle Max. She is quite taken with them, as I told her she would be."

"As you told her . . ." Maxbridge stiffened.

"He described your collection one day when we were visiting Kew Gardens," Amy said, wondering at his sudden change in demeanor.

"Then you knew, when you went to the conservatory, that you would be likely to find me there." He fixed Amy with an indignant glare.

"Uncle!"

"What are you implying, Lord Maxbridge?" But Amy knew. He thought she had somehow contrived the scene in the conservatory, just as he had suspected in the Ingleworth affair. Pain shot through her. Since he was strictly off limits, she knew it was quite irrational to care, but she wanted Lord Maxbridge's good opinion. She had never dissembled or pretended with him as she had done with potential suitors. Yet he suspected her of seeking to entrap him.

"Nothing, Miss Armstrong. Christopher, I think we should

make our way back to the city." *Not only did she have me in her sights before the Season began, she still does, in spite of the enmity between our families. And I almost fell for it!* Back stiff, face grim, Maxbridge curtly nodded to Amabel and motioned for Chris to come with him to take leave of Mrs. Wilcombe.

"If you don't mind, Uncle Max, I will return with William or Nathan," Chris said stiffly. After a long moment, Max reluctantly agreed. *Likely we will quarrel if he comes with me now.*

As he took leave of his cousin, Julia Wilcombe asked him archly what he thought of Miss Armstrong. "Isn't she a darling? Aunt Phinea was most taken by her. How did she like the orchids?"

"Julia, how did you know she viewed the orchids? And how did you know I was aware of the fact?"

Julia Wilcombe twittered nervously at his severe expression. "She was looking a bit peaked. So many young men vying for her attention. I took pity on her and sent her to the conservatory."

"And you knew I was there."

"Well, no, but I suspected as much. Did I do wrong, Max. Don't you like her? Such a pity. Aunt Phinea says she would make an excellent political hostess."

"Did *she* know I would be there?"

"Aunt Phinea? How could she? She isn't even here today."

"I meant Miss Armstrong, and you know it."

"Oh, no. She's a very proper young lady. She wouldn't have gone unaccompanied if she had known."

"I despise matchmaking, Julia, and you and Aunt Phinea know it."

"Oh, don't be such an old bear!" His cousin gave him a saucy grin and turned away.

The chink of glasses and silverware on china and dull murmur of conversation might at another time have been soothing to Maxbridge. But he found his interest centered on the wine and brandy rather than the food.

Quite a bit of brandy, as Mason Markingham observed with some surprise.

"Never saw you quite so determined to get foxed." Mason poured himself another drink also, and lifted the glass. "What are we forgetting tonight?"

"That I may have made an ass of myself this afternoon. That I may be losing my mind, in fact."

"Ah. Having made an ass of myself on many occasions, I can drink to the former, but as to the latter—no. I know few men as awake to all suits as you."

"Not lately." Max downed another glass. "Might as well just drink from the bottle, at this rate," he muttered, rising. "Let's go to my place. Don't particularly want to become a public nuisance."

Once comfortably settled in his library, with a bottle of brandy between them and two capacious glasses filled, Max stared gloomily at his friend.

"You may as well open your budget, Max. It'll make more sense now than when we both are totally cast away."

"It's the Armstrong chit."

"Oh, her! Damned disappointing, that. Loveliest creature I've ever seen, but poor as a church mouse. But that shouldn't weigh with you, Maxbridge."

"I suspect her of seeking to marry for money."

"Quite rightly, too. Greedy little witch, casting her lures at rich men."

Though Mason was only echoing his own sentiments, Max found himself annoyed by the comment. He held up his hand. "How can you censure her when it is what you are seeking to do?"

"I assure you I have no intention of marrying a wealthy man."

Maxbridge snorted. "Very funny! You know what I mean."

"Yes, but you do see my point? You do not despise me for seeking a wealthy wife, do you? So why are you so hard on her? You know it is the way of the world."

"You are a man of honor. You will not deceive a woman merely for her money. Miss Armstrong will pretend to love me. As Bridget did."

"It is not as if you are unlovable."

"Thank you." Max lifted his glass in salute.

"But I see your point. Better to marry with your eyes open—buy her if you must, but don't believe her if she pretends to love you."

Max considered this. "Possible, I suppose, if I took care not to let myself love her."

"You sound as if that last would be difficult for you, Max."

"That is what frightens me most of all. But this discussion is pointless. Even if I were willing to take her on such terms, there's Chris's infatuation with her. And her uncle's objections. He despises me. She has made it clear he would forbid a match with me or Chris."

"Then why do you think she is throwing her cap at you?"

"It's just that while she gives lip service to obeying him, she keeps turning up where I am, expressing an interest in what interests me, often to third parties. It occurs to me that her loyalty could be a sham—she pretends to care very much about her uncle's opinion, but if she has really been scheming to engage my affections, she must mean to make a break with him."

Mason gave a low whistle. "You certainly know how to distrust! But that means you'd have to elope. Quite a scandal that would be. Must run in the family."

"If I really knew that is what she was about, I could forget her. But at times she seems so genuine, so . . . sweet . . . I just can't believe it of her." Max rubbed at his forehead. "More brandy. I need to stop thinking about this before I get dizzy from going around in circles in my head."

"You'll never guess who has just offered for you." Amy's uncle sat behind the large desk in his study, looking quite pleased with himself, while Amy perched on a large leather wing chair.

"Who, Uncle?" She felt a little flutter in her heart and nervous moisture on her hands, which she smoothed down her dress.

"Mr. James Parmingham. You apparently did not succeed in discouraging him at the Wilcombes' breakfast yesterday."

"Oh! That dunderhead. Proposing the day after he met me! What did you tell him?"

"I inquired as to his situation, and if he has told me the truth, it shows some promise. He is very well heeled, and only six months away from his majority."

"I had thought him younger. He behaves like a schoolboy."

"I shall have to look into his age as well as his finances, but that is what he told me. Since you told me you did not like him, I made it clear that you would not come cheap, and he declared himself willing and able to pay the price."

How very considerate of you, Uncle, Amy thought, but did not allow her anger to show in her face. "What price did you name, Uncle?"

"Twenty thousand pounds! And the young fool did not flinch!"

Amy nearly fainted. "Surely not. You would not ask so much! Surely neither he nor anyone else would willingly pay it!"

"Amazing, isn't it? I don't understand it myself, for I was never in the petticoat line. Always thought the notion of a gel bringing something to the marriage made a great deal of sense. But I know some men have a madness for various gewgaws. For some it is horses, for another it is paintings or sculpture, and for many, it is beautiful women. You, my dear, are a rare beauty. I knew when first I laid eyes on you that someone would pay well for you. Never dreamed it would be so well. Still, don't like the idea of waiting for six months. He can't enter a legal agreement until he is twenty-one, and who is to say such an infatuation will last until then. Here is what you must do."

Her uncle then outlined a plan of coy enticement, to keep Mr. Parmingham on the string without letting him get close enough to feel himself accepted, and thus become complacent.

"Play him like a fat trout, my dear," he ended, smiling warmly upon her. "No fear of having to accept Mr. Braebarne when you land Parmingham! He may be a silly boy, but he is good *ton.* I can put my estate to rights, and pay off all of these debts I am incurring on your behalf. My girls shall have a fine dowry. I make no doubt I shall marry them off quite credibly."

Chapter Nine

*I*f Maxbridge had any doubt at all that his aunt and his cousin were matchmaking, it was dispelled two evenings later, when he went to one of Aunt Phinea's political soirées, to which she invited people of many different political persuasions, both in the *ton* and among the prosperous gentry and merchant classes. He ordinarily found these evenings fascinating. In fact, he had always admired his aunt's political acumen, and knew that she had been instrumental in keeping her late husband in the government, albeit in minor roles, even during the many years of Tory rule.

He was not surprised to see Lord Brinker there. Brinker, an arch-Tory of the worst sort, belonged to the foes of the Catholic emancipation movement. Aunt Phinea always hoped that such people could have their politics "improved" by their attendance at her soirées. Even if that didn't happen, their presence made the evenings lively and helped her Whiggish and liberal friends size up and understand their opponents.

What surprised him was that not only was Miss Armstrong also there, at the express invitation of Aunt Phinea, but that she was his dinner partner. She sat to his left, and to her left Phinea had placed Lord Dorringchase, a well-known roué who was also an arch-Tory very much like her uncle.

He felt acutely uncomfortable as they were seated, knowing he had been rude to her at the Wilcombe breakfast.

"Miss Armstrong, you must wonder at my behavior on Wednesday afternoon."

"Not at all." She lifted her chin and smiled at him pertly. "You think I am attempting to lure you into marriage. I expect a great many females have done so. My uncle's objections do not seem to soothe you, so you must judge me by my mother, and think I hope to induce you to run off with me."

Astonished at her quick perception, he stammered, "No, not at all. That is . . ."

"Be assured, my lord. I am deeply grateful to my uncle for taking me under his wing, and intend to marry to please him if I can. As for an elopement, I abhor the idea." She spoke in a dispassionate tone, neither begging for his trust nor angry at its absence. "Now, may we discuss something of greater interest to us both?"

Maxbridge could not but admire the way she met him head-on, and hoped her words were truthful. He inclined his head. "What topic did you have in mind?"

He expected her to bring up Catholic Emancipation, or the poor laws, or some other current political topic on which he had recently spoken in the House of Lords. She surprised him by tackling the question of French reparations.

"Do you think the French people, after so many years of war, can pay England and its allies for their expenses in defeating them? I do not ask about the fairness of demanding reparations, but about their capacity."

He considered a moment. "At the present time, no. I think the most likely way to trigger another round of revolutions is to squeeze the people financially."

She nodded her head eagerly. "That is what I think, too."

Let us try how she will respond when she finds herself in disagreement with me, he thought, still mistrustful of her. "However, in many ways, the French have emerged from the war in better financial shape than England."

She frowned. "How so, my lord?"

"Inflation."

She looked puzzled, so he explained, "Because of the huge

inflation in prices in France during these years of war, their national debt has nearly been wiped out. Bonds are worth only a fraction of their original price, in terms of the franc's purchasing power."

"Whereas England has borrowed heavily, and our currency's value has held up well."

How quick she is, Maxbridge thought. "Precisely. So what I think will have to happen is that the French government will have to issue bonds to repay us."

"In effect, to require future generations of Frenchmen to pay for the sins of their fathers."

"Biblical, and in this case necessary, I think."

She shook her head. "It doesn't seem fair."

"Life often isn't fair. Is it fair to ask the English taxpayer, now and in the future, to pay for France's sins?"

She shook her head, obviously reluctant to give up her position. "We are paying for some of our own sins, too, after all. I do not think we should have intervened once Napoleon had stabilized the revolution. We were determined to impose our views of government upon the French people."

"We shall disagree on this issue, Miss Armstrong."

She lifted up her chin in a gesture he was beginning to recognize. "So be it."

He smiled. "Was your father a radical, Miss Armstrong?"

"Do you think a female cannot develop a political opinion on her own?"

"If I say no, and you tell my aunt, I shall receive a wigging!"

She smiled in turn. "And deservedly so."

It was past time to turn their attention to the dinner partners on their other side, and Lord Dorringchase was clearing his throat loudly in a bid for Amy's attention. She turned to him reluctantly. When they had been introduced before dinner, he had eyed her bosom in a most particular way. She expected him to salivate over her appearance and flirt with her. He surprised her, and annoyed her, too, by showing that he had been eavesdropping on her conversation with Lord Maxbridge.

"More to the point, Miss Armstrong, are *you* a radical? And is your uncle aware of that fact?"

"My uncle doesn't pay much attention to women's political thinking, my lord, as he holds that they have no influence."

"Why did he bring you tonight, then?"

"Lady Marchant asked him to do so."

"Lady Marchant is a bit of a radical, if you ask me."

I didn't, Amy thought rebelliously, but she managed a tight little smile. "Why do you say so, my lord?"

"Oh, many reasons. Soirées like this being one. She had a tremendous influence upon politics in her day, through her husband, and seeks to continue it rather than adhere to a woman's role. I suppose you share with her the notion that women should have the vote."

Amy opened her eyes wide and pretended astonishment. "Surely Lady Marchant doesn't propose such a thing."

"Indeed she does!"

"It is very brave of her."

"You do not answer my question, girl. Do you think I do not notice it?"

Amy cocked her head to one side. "It is such a new idea to me, I shall have to give it some thought. I take it you do not agree with her?"

This gambit successfully launched Lord Dorringchase on a diatribe against women, expounding his own views of their place in the world. His tirade required no response from Amy, who occupied herself with her food until at last one of his remarks caught her attention.

"And it is women who are bringing this German music into popularity. T'will be the downfall of our moral system."

She lifted astonished eyes to him. "German music is immoral?"

"Tell me, do you like the music of Herr Beethoven?"

"I adore Mr. Beethoven's seventh symphony. It is so compelling."

"Do you indeed, Miss Armstrong? Is it not too . . . emotional for you?"

"But that is what I like about it. It just sweeps me along. I lose all sense of myself while listening to it."

"My point exactly."

"I don't understand."

Unexpectedly, Lady Marchant, who sat at the head of the table to Dorringchase's left, joined in. "He means a young lady should never loose all sense of herself. Never!"

"You, too, regard all German music as immoral, Lady Marchant?"

"Of course not. The cooler, more dispassionate music of, say, Mr. Mozart, might be allowed."

"Some of Mozart is far from cool," Amy objected. "At the opera last night's aria 'Dove sono,' by the Countess Almaviva, for example, I thought quite passionate."

"Ah, yes. *The Marriage of Figaro*. A woman singing of love." Dorringchase's tone was dismissive.

"If you ask me, that entire opera is improper for young unmarried girls to hear," one of the ladies across the table said. Amy noticed that several people nearby were listening with interest.

"I daresay you admire the romantic poets, too, Miss Armstrong?" Dorringchase's smile was patronizing.

"You mean Mr. Coleridge and Mr. Wordsworth? Indeed, I do. Why should I not?"

"Revolutionaries," he said in the tone of a cat pouncing upon a mouse. "Revolutionaries!"

"What, our wonderful lake poet? I thought him quite respectable."

"Did you know he went to France in 1791? Had a child there? Out of wedlock, I need not say. He expressed himself as approving of the revolution. The dawn of a new age and all that. In fact, there was considerable evidence that during the revolution he was a spy!"

"No," Amy said. "I didn't know that. How do you know it, if I may ask?"

"I had a minor role in government then, and have reason to

know he was observed quite carefully. He and that woman he lived with whom he said was his sister."

"Do you mean Dorothy Wordsworth?"

"So she called herself. A very common device for cloaking one's fancy bits with respectability—call them your sister."

"Oh!" Amy blushed.

"Too warm, sir." Lady Marchant lifted her quizzing glass and leveled it at him. "You should not have brought up such an unsuitable topic with young ladies present."

"Young ladies are not harmed by learning a bit of truth."

Though Amy felt embarrassed by the topic, she also felt strongly that young women were too sheltered, so she shook her head at the dowager. "I agree with you, Lord Dorringchase. How fascinating to learn of such things."

"There is a great deal more I would teach you, Miss Armstrong, if you would let me." Dorringchase's expression said the topic was no longer politics.

Amy colored up and lifted her fan, opening it too late to hide the blush that stained her cheek. She turned back to Lord Maxbridge, only to discover a look of disgust in his eyes that made her heart sink. She glanced across the table at Chris, and saw a frown on his face. The other nearby listeners were frowning at her. Lowering her head, she turned her attention quite seriously to her food.

"If you had any doubts of her real nature, this evening can scarcely have failed to dispel them."

Chris bristled. "What, that Dorringchase led her into dangerous waters? It only shows his wickedness."

"Led her? She positively fell over herself to flatter the man and lead him on."

"It shows her innocence. She had no idea he would turn a conversation about politics and music into unsavory matters."

"Huh! It is a very good thing you are not the direct heir. She'd already have your ring on her finger."

"I wish it were there! I could protect her from men like Dorringchase! God willing, soon it will be!"

"What, has she shown you signs of favor?" Maxbridge did not like the surge of emotion he felt, but he recognized it for what it was, jealousy.

"She saw who came to her and spoke to her after the dinner and smoothed her way when she was so embarrassed. The tabbies had given her a rare raking over while we were having our port! She was very grateful."

"I hope she may have learned deportment from it. But nothing can change a heart hardened to all but worldly gain."

"And nothing can change a mind made up by prejudice!" On this Parthian shot, Chris left the room.

While Chris and his uncle were arguing the matter in Max's library, Victor was giving Amy a severe trimming.

"How dare you! Flirt with Dorringchase, who is married, draw attention to your radical views, expose yourself to criticism for fast conversation! Do you deliberately court disaster? What if this gets back to Vendercroft, or Braebarne? Or Parmingham for that matter. Smitten as he is, he can hardly want a wife who will embarrass him in public."

Amy knew she had let her desire for equality get the best of her good sense in the conversation with Dorringchase, so she bowed her head and nodded and wept a little until her uncle was convinced she was truly contrite. Finally he dismissed her with a warning.

"No more politics for you, my girl. You keep your eye on your goal, d'you hear?"

"Yes, Uncle."

Mr. Parmingham proved to be a difficult young man in all respects. He took the point of view that he was her accepted suitor, and hung about her with a proprietary air, even going so far as to attempt to decide with whom she would and would not dance. He insisted upon a waltz at each ball they attended, and tried to insist upon the supper dance. He appeared at every function she attended, and cast her languishing glances when he could not manage to be her escort or partner. It began to be somewhat of a joke in the *ton*, the way he would stare at her and sigh at lectures or musicales, and follow her about in the park if she drove out with another man. Her attempts to snub him had to be tempered, as her uncle wished her to keep him on the line.

About two weeks from first meeting him at the Wilcombes' breakfast, she lost her temper with him when he told Chris that he must not expect to take her in to supper that evening. The occasion was the Villington's ball, and as usual, a crowd of young men hung about Amy before the dancing began.

"Already spoken for, you know," Parmingham told Chris with airy assurance, though she had studiously ignored all attempts by him to engage her that evening.

"Indeed I *am* spoken for, sir," she snapped. "Mr. Ponselle has already bespoken the supper dance this evening." He had done no such thing, but eagerly took her up.

"Do go away, Parmers. Miss Armstrong has given me her waltz this evening, too, so you may as well toddle off to White's and . . ."

"She most certainly has not given you her waltz. She waltzes with me and no one else!"

This was spoken in a tone loud enough to attract attention from others around them. Her aunt attempted an ineffectual remonstrance, but Parmingham, very red in the face, told her to mind her business.

"I should say Miss Armstrong is her business," Mr. Smythe-Amhurst protested.

"Come, Mr. Holmes," Amy said, turning to one of her quieter but more persistent suitors, "lead me out for the first dance, won't you?" She turned her back on Parmingham.

"Wait! You haven't told me which dance you have saved for me."

"None, sir." And she walked away.

Later Esmée told her Parmingham had looked as if he meant to go after her and tear her from Holmes's arms, but with Chris, Smythe-Amhurst, and several others blocking his way, he had changed his mind and charged from the room.

"He said you were promised to him," she told Amy. "I do hope that is not so, for he is a most disagreeable young man."

"Certainly not! Though I suppose I ought not to have been so . . . firm . . . with him, for he has much to recommend him."

"Oh, Amy. Coming it too brown. Nothing at all but a fortune," Esmée said, looking askance at her friend.

"Oh, I don't know. When . . . when we drive out together he is amiable enough. It is just that he is so jealous." Amy began to worry that she had been too obviously antagonistic. How embarrassing it would be if she had to marry him now, when so many saw how little she liked him. And she wondered whether his resentment might not serve her ill if she did have to agree to be his wife, for as yet no other suitor had presented himself who had a fortune sufficient to tempt her uncle to accept him. She did not count Vendercroft, who still hung about her, but whom she was sure her uncle would not compel her to marry.

Later that evening she managed to slip away from the ballroom. She had intended to go to the ladies' withdrawing room, but as she started to mount the stairs, she noticed through an open door a tiny room that appeared by its decor and furnishings to be the office of the lady of the house. Charmed by what she saw of it, she entered it and looked about. No one was in the room, and seeing the chance of some solitude, she shut the door behind her and made her way to the bow window at the front of her host's home.

There she sat in the embrasure, staring out at the rainy street scene. Her thoughts were as gloomy as the weather. Only one man had managed to capture her fancy, and he was totally ineligible because of their family feud. Moreover, he appeared to dislike her. She sighed and brushed at a fugitive tear. This evening the Earl of Maxbridge had merely bowed at her and moved on when their paths had crossed. How she longed to dance with him, to talk with him. She wondered if he had purchased any new orchids yet. She wondered if her behavior at Lady Marchant's soirée the other evening had given him a complete disgust of her.

"Peering wistfully out of windows again, I see. Ah, do not cry, Miss Armstrong. Surely the sun will come out in a day or two, and you will be able to go for a pleasant drive in the park."

She whirled to find the subject of her longings looking down at her with an expression half-teasing, half-concerned.

"Oh, how you do startle me, Lord Maxbridge. I collect you like to creep up on people."

"Only those who look to be in sad need of a friend."

She looked at the door; it was closed. "Where were you? Oh! That wing chair, I suppose. I swear I did not know you were here!" She rose to go.

"Please, Miss Armstrong. Don't run off. I'll leave you to your solitude. I just thought I'd . . . drop a hint. Men like Dorringchase . . ."

"Oh! Don't you start! I know I have quite ruined myself." The tears started in earnest. Amy put her hands to her face. "It is so hard to always guard every word I say! My uncle says I must give up politics, and I shall."

"No, you mustn't do that. It was the other . . . about Wordsworth and . . ." He put his hands on the distressed girl's shoulders. "Don't cry, Miss Armstrong."

She lifted her head from her hands. "Several people look at me as if I had tied my garters in public, and your aunt . . ." She passed her hand over her face. "Losing Lady Marchant's good opinion is what I regret the most. She is the first person who has made me feel . . . human . . . since I came to London. Well, that's not quite true. There's Lord Sunder, too. I suppose he will cut me now as well."

Maxbridge was surprised by the surge of protectiveness that swept through him. "Has my aunt actually cut you? I will speak to her."

She pulled away from him. "Not really. Just . . . looked at me so. I feel quite miserable at letting her down."

"I will try to make her see that you were . . ." Chris's phrase floated into his mind. *My nephew was right. Sometimes that boy has more insight than I.* "Tricked by a wicked man who took advantage of your innocence and your enthusiasm."

"Oh! You are so kind." She took his proffered handkerchief. "I am not usually a watering pot. Forgive me."

He smiled tenderly at her and took the handkerchief from her shaking hands to gently wipe her cheeks.

"At least you don't seem to see me as a siren bent upon your seduction this evening." She tried for a smile. "I think, my lord, that someone must have broken your heart at some time or another, by pretending to take an interest in matters important to you, in order to ensnare you."

This cut very close to the bone. Maxbridge looked away. "It is not at all uncommon for young women to do just that. Also, I do not like to think of Chris being used to obtain access to me."

"Chris! You think that is why I have been friendly with Chris? No wonder you have been so cold to me from the start."

"I have known . . . someone . . . to be very hurt in such a way."

Amy studied his expression. The grave, sad look in those blue eyes told the tale. Her anger was replaced by pity. She put her hand on his sleeve. "Someone I know?"

"Perhaps." Max fought the yearning to confide in her. If he let her, this young woman would be able to manipulate him even more than Bridget had. He decided to change the topic. He shrugged dismissively and stepped away from her. "Is that young fool Parmingham plaguing you again? Is that why you were hiding out by the window?"

Easily distracted by this gambit, Amy huffed, "He has never stopped."

"Surely your uncle can deal with him."

She bit at her lower lip and looked away.

"He wishes you to encourage him," Maxbridge surmised.

"Possibly."

Maxbridge muttered something that sounded remarkably like a curse. She smiled.

"My uncle says that sometimes, right out loud."

"A more honest gentleman than I."

"More honest, or less of a gentleman."

"Is there any way I can help you? Shall I speak to the young pup?"

"Would you? Just a friendly hint that his behavior is subjecting *him* to ridicule. For I do not think he would be in the least interested in how it is affecting *me*."

"I will gladly do this. A severe set-down from me might make him aware of the impropriety of his conduct."

"You won't let him know this comes from me, though?"

"Do not fear. A snub of his manners only, not a defense of you."

"Thank you!" She reached her hand out, and he took it and squeezed it lightly. Suddenly Amy felt the almost overwhelming urge to throw herself into his arms. They stared into one another's eyes for a long dangerous moment in which she thought he might well gather her up as she wished. Then he abruptly stepped back.

"I had best go. Bow windows and conservatories! Really, you will think me as bad as Parmingham, following you about so."

"You did not follow me either place. At least this time you do not accuse *me* of following you." She smiled up at him.

"No, I don't. And I owe you an apology for thinking so before. I have learned that my cousin sent you there. Miss Armstrong, I . . ."

But he stopped, not sure what he wanted to say. He looked out the window as if searching for an answer to the puzzle that was his feeling for Amabel Armstrong. But there was no solution there.

"I will take Parmingham in hand." He bowed to her and left her to another few minutes of solitude, during which she gathered the courage to return to the noise and clamor of the ballroom.

Snubbing Mr. Parmingham proved ridiculously easy. Christopher and he stood in the doorway to the ballroom, arguing, as Maxbridge returned from his brief tête-à-tête with Amy.

Maxbridge favored them both with a frosty glare, and Chris launched into an explanation. "He has driven poor Miss Armstrong right away from the ball, I declare. No one can find her anywhere. He follows her about, and tries to intimidate her other beaux, and pretends he is engaged to her . . ."

"*Are* you engaged to her, Mr. Parmingham?"

"Not yet, but her uncle has given me to understand . . ."

"I find it difficult to believe Lord Brinker would encourage a boy of seventeen to court his niece."

"Seventeen! Seventeen! I'll have you know I am twenty, and will attain my majority in December."

Maxbridge looked him up and down. He lifted his left eyebrow in his most disdainful way. "Astonishing. Your behavior is that of an unlicked cub in the throes of his first crush. You make yourself a figure of fun. And you, Christopher Ponselle, brangling with him in public, put me quite out of temper. Let the *ton* laugh at *him* if it will; I'll not have my nephew making such a cake of himself. Take care you don't bore me into sending you back to the country." He softened the reprimand by taking the boy's arm and leading him into the ballroom.

Chapter Ten

*J*ames Parmingham, fists clenched, watched Maxbridge and Christopher return to the ball. He was not a young man to hero-worship the elegant Lord Maxbridge, considered by so many to be top-of-the trees in sport and society. More likely to seek to tear down than to emulate such an admired gentleman, his mind immediately turned to revenge rather than reform. At just that moment Amy left the small room where she had spoken with Maxbridge. Parmingham's was a suspicious and jealous nature, and he instantly leaped to what was in this case the correct conclusion, that Maxbridge had just been there with her. She did not see him, as her goal was the stairway that lay to the right of the window and led to the ladies' withdrawing room.

The next morning he presented himself in Lord Brinker's drawing room, where Amy held court among her admirers. He stayed a correct fifteen minutes and made no special claims on her, which caused her to believe that Maxbridge's set-down had had a salutary effect on him. This and the fact that he held back at a ball the next evening, only soliciting one country-dance, caused her to believe he had learned to behave with more propriety. Thus it was that she agreed to go for a drive with him when he invited her a few days later.

She was accompanied by her maid Betty, of course. Since Ingleworth's attempted abduction she had always been chaperoned, in spite of the fact that it was crowded in a curricle with a maid along. Only the fact that both she and Betty were slender made it possible at all.

When she noticed the direction Parmingham was taking, she asked him if they were not going to Hyde Park.

"No, I thought we'd go to Green Park and walk around a bit, away from the crush. I do tire of the noise and distraction, don't you?"

Amy hesitated. Green Park was more rural, and might present certain opportunities for such an importunate gentleman.

"Come, Miss Armstrong. Give me a little time with you in private. I know I have rushed my fences with you. But give yourself a chance to know me better. You might find that you like me!"

Betty sat beside her; Parmingham's tiger Robert rode behind them. Amy felt there was little danger, so she nodded her assent. A few minutes' clever driving through the busy London traffic brought them to the edge of Green Park.

"Let's get down and walk, shall we? Betty and Robert will walk just behind us."

He helped her and her maid down while Robert tied the horses' reins to an iron ring. Just ahead of them stood an elegant carriage with six fine horses. An outrider was mounted nearby, a handsome roan hack on a lead at his side. Parmingham drew her toward the carriage, his eyes wide with admiration.

"Magnificent cattle, ain't they?"

"Indeed. One cannot but wonder why they require so many horses for town driving, though."

"There's luggage in the boot. Perhaps they are going out of town," he suggested, continuing to lead her toward it. "Matched bays. Four white stockings on each one. Quite a show when they are at the trot, I'd think."

Amy began to pull back as they neared the team. "Yes, but I prefer to admire horses at a distance," she said. She looked back, only to discover that neither Betty nor Parmingham's tiger were anywhere in sight.

"Where is my maid?" She tried to tug free of Parmingham's

hand on her elbow. Instead of releasing her, he propelled her
with great force and rapidity toward the carriage. Before she
could fully grasp what was going forward, he had opened the
door and was thrusting her inside. She attempted to prevent it,
but he was too strong for her and followed her in. When she
started to scream, he covered her mouth with his hand and
bore her back against the squabs.

Heart pounding in her chest, Amy struggled in vain, and as
she did so the other carriage door opened and her maid was
shoved in by Parmingham's cursing tiger.

"Keep your mummer shut," the wiry young man commanded her, slamming the door after her. Instantly, the carriage began to move.

"Get your hands off my mistress," Betty demanded.

Parmingham had considerably more than his hands on her,
literally lying athwart her so that she couldn't move. "Listen,
Miss Armstrong. I am not going to hurt you. If you will swear
to me that you won't scream, I shall let you up."

Amy glared at him over his hand, but after a moment's consideration she nodded.

"Good. Now, be calm. Shut up, you," he snapped in an aside
to the complaining maid.

"What do you mean by this, sir?" Amy rose quickly to a
seated position and shoved as far away from Parmingham as
possible.

"Miss Armstrong. My love. Do not shrink from me. I only
mean to free you from the slavery your uncle intends for you."

"Very kind of you, sir. I don't wish to be free." She reached
for the carriage handle, and instantly Parmingham grabbed her
arm and dragged her up against him.

"None of that! You promised me to stay put."

"I promised not to scream. Release me and my maid at
once, sir." She tried to glare at him, but at such close range her
eyes crossed, so she turned her head aside, holding her body
rigid.

"Yes, let us go!" Betty tried for the carriage door herself, but

Parmingham released his hold on Amy long enough to back-hand her sharply.

"You sit still and be quiet or it will be the worse for you," he snarled.

Shocked to her core by such violence, Amy could only stare at the man who now grasped her by the shoulders.

"Don't you see? He is selling you to the highest bidder. Not consulting your wishes at all, I daresay. Twenty thousand pounds! A king's ransom. I cannot, will not pay so much. But I want you, love you, adore you. I must have you. When you know me better, you will be very glad for this elopement."

A strong sense of déjà vu assailed Amy. "This is not an elopement, it is a kidnapping. If you think I mean to submit tamely to being mauled, my maid being slapped—look at her! Her lip is bleeding. You are a brute, and no gentleman. I will never consent to marry you. Now stop this carriage and let me go."

"Oh, you will marry me all right, once I have thoroughly compromised you! And your uncle be damned! Now be quiet. I am always queasy in carriages. I don't wish to quarrel with you."

Amy looked over at Betty, who lay back against the squabs, her arms wrapped around herself defensively and her eyes wide with alarm. A slight trickle of blood at the edge of her mouth was mute testimony to the kind of man they had to deal with.

"I've no wish to quarrel with you, either, Mr. Parmingham, but . . ."

"James. Call me James."

"James, then."

"My angel." He caught her hand to his lips.

". . . but I also suffer from carriage sickness. I will never survive a trip to Gretna Green."

"Nor will I. But we are not going so far, my love. A little country inn I know of on the Brighton Road will do nicely for us. Once we have spent the night there, your uncle will have to let us wed. You needn't fear scandal. He'll wish to hush it up, I am sure. I'll pay the old miser enough to make it worth his while to cooperate. But not twenty thousand pounds! Ah, my lovely Amabel. No matter how much I adore you, you must agree that that is too much."

"Indeed I do. I am excessively shocked at it. I had no idea he meant to ask so much."

"Why should he ask anything?" Parmingham screwed up his face like a querulous child. "More the thing for a young lady to bring a dowry to the marriage, ain't it? Instead of her relatives expecting to be paid to take her off their hands?"

"Indeed it is, sir!" Amy infused her voice with indignation, not a difficult task, as she agreed with Parmingham on this point. "Alas, I have no dowry, though."

"Then he ought to be glad of a decent offer for a settlement."

"I agree! He would have it that the costs of launching me into society must be paid by my husband-to-be, and I had to agree to that, for otherwise I would have been obliged to marry a rough farmer in Yorkshire."

"No!" Parmingham's eyes widened in astonishment. "A sacrilege."

"Yes, and it is to my uncle that I owe my rescue from that fate. So you see, I cannot in good conscience simply run away to wed, without considering . . ."

"It hasn't cost him twenty thousand pounds to fire you off!"

"No, I daresay it hasn't. And then, he hopes to have my little cousins make their come-out under my aegis. They are not likely to be beautiful, so they will need a dowry. He convinced me I should marry someone who would provide for them, and I admit I should like excessively to do so."

She spoke cajolingly, leaning toward Parmingham and widening her eyes. She even fluttered her eyelashes at him.

"Ah! Well, of course. No reason we can't bring them out. As for providing for them, why can't he?"

"His father and older brother ran the estate into the ground. He doesn't think he can bring it into good heart in time to accumulate a dowry for them. Are you not a very warm man, Mr. Parmingham?"

"I am that, or will be in six months," he declared proudly.

"Well, then, if you love me, will you not pledge to me to pay the debts my uncle incurred for my presentation and Season, and a dowry for my two nieces?"

"Ah . . ." Parmingham looked into the emerald-green eyes set in the most beautiful face he had ever seen. "Oh, my love, if it will make you love me and be happy with me, then of course I will."

She put her hand out. He clasped it tightly, then pulled off her glove and carried her bare hand to his lips, pressing fervent kisses on it. Amy hid her revulsion well, leaning toward him and murmuring encouragingly. "I am so glad you have agreed. I know we shall deal very well together."

He gathered her to him and kissed her full on the lips. She permitted it for an instant or two, then pulled away and hung her head shyly.

"I beg your pardon. Overcome, you know." He patted her hand awkwardly. "I apologize for alarming you . . . unnnnh." The carriage had turned rapidly, and he looked a bit pale.

"Do ask him to slow, James, dear. You'll be made sick at this rate. And I confess I am getting a bit queasy."

"Yes. Good idea. Since you have agreed to marry me, no need to do the thing at full tilt, is there?" He opened the little overhead door and shouted up to his coachman, "Slow down a bit, Jedson." Instantly the coach slowed, and Amy was as glad as Parmingham to have its swaying reduced. He sank back into the squabs and looked at her adoringly. "I knew you'd come around. Now, as to this financial arrangement, I should think the thing could be done for five thousand pounds, don't you think?"

"I have no head for finances, James. It shall be between you and my uncle. I know I can trust you to be fair."

"I shall, but I won't let the old robber hold me up."

"No, indeed!" She infused her tone with indignation. "After all, we must have something left for ourselves, mustn't we."

"Just so." Parmingham sank back farther, and closed his eyes. He looked green around the mouth.

Amy took this opportunity to look at her wondering maid, and winked at her. Then she motioned toward the door with her head, hoping the woman would understand she meant to escape.

After a moment Parmingham groaned again. "Are we stopping?" He peeked briefly out the window curtains. "We are just now reaching the first tollgate. Now I know you won't want to call attention to us, as you've agreed to marry me." At her nod, he relaxed. "I don't want your uncle to catch us until we've had time to spend the night together." He looked over at the maid. "You, behave yourself!"

"Yes, sir." She trembled and shrank back against the squabs.

"We'll make no fuss," Amy assured him. "Now that I know what my uncle is up to, I am heartily glad to be off the Marriage Mart. Where shall we live, James?"

Amy kept Parmingham entertained with plans for their future life of marital bliss until time for their first change of horses. He accepted her apparent acquiescence without question.

"Best get out and stretch your legs and such," he told her expansively. "And then I think if you don't mind I will ride for a while. Never liked being in a closed carriage so much as with you, but I still feel a bit queasy."

"I do understand. Perhaps I may doze a little when we start up. In the meantime, Betty and I will take your advice. Perhaps you would even be so good as to bespeak some refreshments for us? Tea and biscuits only—I could not eat anything more."

"I will do anything for you, my angel," he declared, kissing her hand fervently before helping her out of the carriage. She saw that they had stopped at a small but bustling inn. He escorted her inside and turned her over to the innkeeper's wife, who pointed out the necessary to her and assured her that when she and her maid returned they would find tea and biscuits in the parlor.

As soon as the innkeeper's wife had gone about her business, Amy took her maid's hand and led her rapidly through the kitchen, around the side of the inn away from the stables, and back out into the inn's yard. Though small, it had considerable custom. The day being fine, many people had decided upon a drive. Amy kept a carriage between herself and the door to the inn while she surveyed the bustle in the yard.

"There! The very thing," she said.

Betty followed her glance. "I hope you may be right, miss!" She followed as Amy hastened to a handsome barouche already turned to exit the inn yard. A pair of elderly women sat in it, parasols unfurled against the sun.

"If you please, Mrs. Ramsey," Amy began, stepping right up to the door of the carriage.

Both women turned to her, eyes wide with surprise.

"Oh, I beg your pardon. I thought you were my friend's mother. I do wonder if you might assist me, for I am in dire need of help." She wrung her hands and looked appealingly up at the two women.

"Go along wi' ye, doxy," the ancient coachman admonished her, and looked to be about to whip up his team.

"Stay, John," The older of the two women commanded him. Then the carriage's occupants studied her carefully, as if she were a butterfly on a pin.

"Very pretty," said the younger one.

"Dressed à la mode, but rather rumpled," the older one observed.

"No better than she should be," groused the coachman.

"I think I know the difference between a young lady of quality and Haymarket ware," the elder woman snapped. "What is it, my dear? How may we help you?"

"I have come to cuffs with my escort, you see, and was wondering if you would take us up. If you are not going to London, at least take us a little ways from here, and I shall send a message to my uncle, Lord Brinker, to come and get me."

"Lord Brinker, is it? Then you must be that niece of his that has everyone, including my grandson, all a-twitter."

The other woman added, "Said you were a diamond, and I see that you are."

"Thank you, ma'am." Amy made a pretty curtsy, and then, with an anxious glance at the inn door, asked again, "Would you consider taking my maid and me up?"

"Better not," advised the coachman. "Doubtless some robber's shill."

"Humpffh. Keep your opinions to yourself!" The older woman opened her carriage door, and Amy scrambled up, closely followed by Betty. They sat in the backwards facing seat. Amy hastily arranged her skirts and smiled at her rescuers.

"You may drive on now, John."

"Not what the master would have permitted."

"The master is dead these ten years!"

"No good will come of it, my lady. No good at all!" But the old retainer at last urged his horses to start. Their pace could only be described as stately, and Amy prayed he might move faster as they cleared the tiny village.

"I suppose we should introduce ourselves," the older woman said. "I am Lady Holmes, and this is Miss Scrimpton, my sister."

"Oh! I *do* know your grandson. Nathan Holmes, is it not? We first met at a party given by my friend Esmerelda Puckett."

Miss Scrimpton sniffed. "A little widgeon, that one."

"Now, Claire. Not everyone can be as blue as you." Lady Holmes smiled apologetically at Amy. "Please don't tell Mrs. Puckett of my sister's remark, I beg of you. An old friend she is, and I'd not hurt her for the world."

"I promise I won't, ma'am."

"What is wrong with your maid's mouth? Does she have a skin disease? If so, I beg she will sit with John Coachman and not with us."

Betty put her hand to her mouth. "Oh, no. It was that wicked man what done it. Hit me, he did, when I tried to . . ."

Amy put her hand on her maid's arm. She hoped to avoid
scandal by minimizing the incident, if at all possible. "My escort took exception to Betty's chaperonage. Well, she *is* a bit
of a dragon, but that is what my uncle hired her for, after all.
But she would insist that he not so much as hold my hand. I'd
no idea he would do such a thing as strike her, and as soon as
he did, I knew I could not ride back to London with such a
bounder."

"No, indeed," Miss Scrimpton said, clutching her spare
bosom nervously. "He sounds dreadful. Who is this barbar-
ian?"

"Mr. Parmingham. I do hope he is not a connection of
yours."

"By no means," Lady Holmes asserted vehemently. "His
grandfather and his father were both wretched men; I see he
but follows in the family footsteps."

"London," harrumphed the coachman. "Smoky. Too far by
half for an afternoon's drive."

"Ignore him, dear," Lady Holmes said.

"But he's right." Miss Scrimpton frowned. "This is much
too far for a drive from London. It would be dark before you
returned."

Lady Holmes nodded and looked into Amy's eyes. "Perhaps
you haven't told us the whole tale."

"Ruined her," called out the coachman.

"No, he never did. Oh, my dear, did he? You poor thing,
with your hair all mussed and your maid quite savagely
beaten." Lady Holmes put her hand on Amy's arm consolingly.

"Better take her back," Miss Scrimpton said. "He'll have to
marry her, and if she runs off, he might take a pet and not."

The coachman eagerly drew up the horses.

"No, no, ma'am. It wasn't like that." Hastily abandoning her
hopes of avoiding scandal, Amabel explained. "He certainly
would have done so, if I had not escaped. He hopes to force
me into marrying him against my wishes and without my
uncle's approval. Oh, here he comes. I do beg of you, ask your
coachman to whip up your team."

The coachman turned full around in the seat to see Mr. Parmingham riding toward them pell-mell on the horse she had seen the groom leading in Green Park, it seemed like ages ago.

"Never outrun him," the coachman said, looking quite satisfied.

"No, but do get underway. Now!" Lady Holmes leaned forward between Amy and Betty and gave him a sharp poke with her parasol's point.

Grumbling, the man gave his horses the office to start, but Parmingham was on them before they had trod more than a few paces.

"Miss Armstrong. What can be the meaning of this?"

"Go away, Mr. Parmingham. My dear friend Lady Holmes is going to restore me to my family."

"You lying little . . . ma'am, you can have no idea the sort of female you have taken into your carriage. It is easy for me to see that you are a respectable woman, both of you in fact." He half rose out of his saddle to bow to the two women. "You cannot wish to have a member of the muslin company in your carriage with you. The naughty creature has quarreled with me, but she shouldn't inflict her impure presence on ladies of quality."

The coachman instantly drew his team to a halt. "Told you," he growled. "Fine gentleman, blood horse. Can't take a frowsy female's word against such as he."

Chapter Eleven

"*T*hat's right," Parmingham said, nodding to the coachman. "Come here, Amabel. You've no business to be imposing on your betters."

"If she is a straw damsel, why do you call her by the name of Lord Brinker's niece? Why does she have a maid?" Lady Holmes waved her parasol menacingly at him. "You are a scoundrel, sir. John, drive on or I shall dismiss you."

"Oh, no you don't," Parmingham growled as the carriage lurched forward. Leaning out of the saddle, he grabbed Amy by the arm and began pulling her out of the carriage. Taken by surprise, she was dragged against the carriage door and felt herself being lifted up. Betty then grasped her by the waist, screaming.

Lady Holmes took her furled parasol and began beating Parmingham around the head and neck, but it was Miss Scrimpton who put her parasol to much better use. Leaning over her sister's back, she drove its point firmly into the flank of the roan, which was already tossing its head and sidling at the unusual behavior going on around it. Abruptly it kicked and twisted its hindquarters, dislodging Parmingham from his seat. He let go of Amy in a vain effort to save himself and fell to the ground as his horse galloped away. A bellow of pain and rage pursued them as the coachman, obedient to another poke in the ribs by his mistress, whipped up his team.

Amy was slammed against the side of the carriage in the

melee, and hung half out of it until Betty pulled her back. She stood to see if Parmingham was following on foot, for Lady Holmes's team seemed to have no other gait than a walk and a faster walk. The two women turned in their seats for the same purpose, and Miss Scrimpton crowed delightedly, "Only look how he is holding that arm. I do believe he has broken it."

"He is well served, then." Lady Holmes turned back around, cheeks flushed with triumph. "I haven't enjoyed anything as much since I pushed his father into a hedge when I was seventeen!"

Amy sat down, relief flooding her. Parmingham was indeed cradling his arm, which hung at an odd angle. He continued to scream with pain and rage at the top of his lungs.

"I am so grateful to you both," she gasped, clutching her bruised side. "I thought he had me. I do hope his servants don't pursue us."

"We must turn off the road before he can induce anyone to follow us. John, turn into the first lane you come to after we top this hill."

"Aye, my lady," the coachman said. "Never was so mistook. No gentleman would behave so."

"I'll horsewhip him. No, that isn't sufficient. I'll call him out. How dare he!" Uncle Victor raged and ranted for half an hour as they drove home in his carriage. Lady Holmes had, once they had reached her country home by a circuitous route, sent a footman to summon him. He had refused to leave Amy in their care even though they tried to convince him she might have a broken rib from her ordeal.

"No, indeed," he had said. "Can't leave her here. No telling but what that villain would track her down. Very much indebted to you, I am, but Amabel will be much better off at home. I'll have Dr. Gantry look at her."

"Oh, he is the best, I hear. But do you think she should travel so far before being treated, Lord Brinker? We have a country doctor here who could bind up her ribs."

"Mr. Gantry did wonders for my mother," Amy said. "And I

do think I should not impose on you further. I doubt any ribs are broken anyway. Just a nasty bruise." She hugged both women and kissed their cheeks. "How can I ever thank you?"

Lady Holmes patted her cheek and smiled. "You are a dear, as sweet as you are pretty. Lord Brinker, I hope you can find a suitable husband for this precious child soon. She is far too much of a temptation to men. Now my grandson, Nathan Holmes, is devoted to her and . . ."

"Quite! He is most welcome to call upon her," Lord Brinkton said, but his tone was dismissive. He had looked into Holmes's finances, and while the man had a competence, he was far from wealthy.

Now Victor sat next to Amy, alternately abusing the young man who had abducted her, and her for having allowed herself to be taken in.

"What am I to do with you? Lock you up? How shall you find a husband then, I want to know? Yet if someone steals you, and succeeds, all is lost. Indeed, I begin to wonder if you encourage these creatures in some way."

He eyed her suspiciously in the light of the carriage lamps.

Amy gasped and shook her head, remembering all too well his threat against her mother if she were carried off, whether against her wishes or not.

"Oh, no, my lord, she never did," Betty asserted, leaning forward earnestly from the seat opposite them.

"Shut up," he snapped, then thought better of it. "Tell me exactly what happened."

As the carriage rolled back to London, Betty told the tale as she had experienced it. Lord Brinker grunted or muttered indignantly through various parts of it, and even grinned at the way the two sisters had routed Parmingham.

"Old tartars," he said. "Your luck was in, my dear, to have run across them."

"I know, Uncle." Amy moaned a little as the carriage hit a rut.

"You hurting, girl?"

"A bit. I wonder if they will gossip about it? They said they wouldn't, but . . ."

"Ah, can't keep it a secret. Their coachman, whoever stopped to aid Parmingham, his servants. Parmingham himself. Devil of a thing. Even though he didn't get his leg over you, doubtless many will believe he did. He might even put it about, out of revenge. You're ruined, my girl. Through no fault of your own, I'll grant, but done in." Victor moaned. "Be lucky to marry you to a parson now."

They rode in silence for a while, then Amy straightened a bit in her seat. "I think the thing to do, Uncle Victor, is to go on the attack."

"Huh?"

"We must get the story out ourselves, as quickly as possible, and paint him in as bad a light as possible. Betty must spread the word among the servants." She leaned forward in her seat and took the maid's hands. "You may make yourself out to be the heroine of the story there, for you certainly tried to be. Tell how you succeeded in fighting him off and preserving my virtue. If that question is going to come up . . ."

"And it will," her uncle inserted.

"Yes! So we must answer it loudly and emphatically from the first. By the time Mr. Parmingham returns to town he will find that his villainy is known and none will regard whatever tale he may try to tell."

"If he dares to show himself in town, I will . . ."

"I know, Uncle. You will horsewhip him."

"I will! Minx, are you laughing at me?"

"Not at all. In this case a good lashing would be well deserved. If you put it about enough, he may decide to stay away for a while."

"You are a clever puss indeed! You'll do your part, Betty?"

"With all my heart, my lord."

"We must go over what you will say. I want it to be truthful, but dramatic. And it must jibe with what I will say. Oh, and I will pen a note to Lady Holmes and Miss Scrimpton. I am sure they will be glad to be allowed to tell their story, too."

"Of that you may be sure!"

It was not until after Dr. Gantry had examined Amy and bound her ribs that she had an opportunity to discuss her uncle's demand of twenty thousand pounds for her.

"Now, that is no matter for a female to concern herself with," he said, patting her cheek.

"Uncle, there cannot be three men in all of England able to pay such a sum, even if willing to do so."

"Now, puss, this is not for you to worry about. But I can tell you this. I set my figure high because I hoped to discourage Parmingham. Didn't like him above half for you, and it turns out I was right, wasn't I? Truth is, the amount is flexible. If you find someone who suits you to the ground, I shall be reasonable. Now, can't complain about that, can you?"

Amy studied her uncle's face. It was red, but whether from embarrassment, choler, or wine, she couldn't tell. She still didn't know if he really cared for her. Would he really accept less from a man she cared for? Did it matter, as there was no one she cared for? No one except . . . but useless to think of him, for that was hopeless. She sighed and closed her eyes.

"No, Uncle, I can't."

The campaign began that very evening in the servant's quarters. Betty, a cut lip and a purpling bruise on her face to back up her tale, figured as the heroine, though she asserted her mistress's courage to be considerable, first in calming the madman, and then in escaping from him. Off-duty footmen carried the story into pubs, and by morning it had begun to circulate through the *ton* via the servant-to-master grapevine.

The next day half a dozen callers appeared as soon as a decent hour had arrived for visiting. They were concerned because Amy had not attended a musicale in which she had been scheduled to sing. Amy's ribs hurt so much she had not been able to face dressing, so did not come down to receive her visitors.

Lord and Lady Brinker did not deny the abduction, but instead told it as a desperate struggle of virtue to preserve innocence, with the heroic maid figuring as the one who had tipped the balance.

Christopher Ponselle was one of the visitors, and he was ready to call Parmingham out on the instant.

"You leave him to me, my boy," Brinker growled. He did not like it above half that Maxbridge's nephew was there, though he liked the boy's readiness to take his niece's part. "I shall take a whip to him, for a gentleman he is not, and does not deserve a meeting for such an offense. If any of you know him and can tell me his whereabouts, I will greatly appreciate it. I have already tried at his lodgings, but he did not return home last night." All of the young men promised to tell Brinker as soon as they heard anything of Parmingham's location, and offered to help in the administration of corporal punishment.

Esmée and her mother spoke with Lady Brinker, and put their heads together with hers in a corner while the men plotted revenge. Mrs. Puckett wished to see and reward the maid who had done such a courageous thing; Betty, with her blackened face and split lip, came and told her tale to them. The result was all that Amy had hoped for. The storm of gossip that spread through the *ton* was favorable to her; any who might have wondered about her virtue daren't voice it in the face of such universal indignation at the villainy of James Parmingham.

Esmée came to call again the next day, and was admitted to Amy's room, where she was convalescing. Amy showed her the bruised ribs she had suffered, praised her maid's courage, and told a humorous version of the carriage incident, which had Esmée both laughing and crying.

"For it is ever so funny," she said, "and yet frightening. You were so brave, I can scarcely credit it, for I should have dissolved into a pudding when he first attacked me."

"Oh, no. It never does to give in, though sometimes a woman must seem to do so." She told how she had fooled Parmingham into believing she would marry him willingly, so that she could get away. This soon swept the *ton*, too. By the time Amy felt well enough to go about, she found herself a heroine, quite as much admired as before by the men, and now the darling of the women, too.

Unfortunately for Amy, Parmingham, who had retreated to his country residence to nurse his broken arm and bruised pride, wrote to friends of his, defending his actions. Few believed the report that Amy had gone with him willingly, but the news that her uncle expected twenty thousand pounds for her swept the *ton* like wildfire.

Stares and titters greeted her on her first public appearance after this news was out. Some cut her; others accorded her the barest courtesy. Worst of all, her avid court of admirers shrank almost to nonexistence.

It was at the Carmindales' ball. Her hostess greeted her and Aunt Edwina frostily, and as she crossed the room, people stepped aside for her instead of greeting her, so that it seemed she walked a cordon of hostile stares. Bewildered, she looked around her, seeking a friendly face to explain the problem to her. Esmée broke away from her mother and hurried up to Amy.

"What is it?" Amy asked. "Everyone is looking at me as if I had tied my garters in public."

"It is that wretched James Parmingham. He has put it about that your uncle expects your husband to pay twenty thousand pounds for you. It isn't true is it, Amy?"

Lady Brinker drew in her breath sharply and began fanning herself.

Amy sighed. She took refuge in what her uncle had omitted, rather than what she suspected: that he would sell her to the highest bidder. "My uncle would not discuss it with me. I don't have a dowry, though; everyone knows that." Amy's conscience twinged her a little at such sophistry.

"To ask money for your hand would be so crass."

"Indeed! I cannot but agree with you. But Parmingham is a villain. He couldn't ruin me one way, so now he tries another."

Esmée was not to be put off so easily. She turned to Amy's chaperon. "Lady Brinker, do you know?"

Amy's aunt plied her fan desperately. "Gentlemen never discuss finances with ladies. All I can say is that Mr. Parmingham has once again proved he is no gentleman."

"No proof of that was wanting, ma'am," Esmée said. "But the crassness of what he has suggested is making people cut Amy. It's so unfair!"

Amy felt a little faint. *What am I to do now? Oh, if I but had someone to guide me!*

At that moment Christopher and his uncle were announced. Amy turned to look at them. Her eyes first flew to Maxbridge's, and the hard look she found there did not encourage her. Then she looked at Chris, who hastened to her side, his eyes full of sympathy and curiosity.

"Oh, Amy! Tell me it isn't true."

"First you must tell me what I am denying."

He repeated Parmingham's tale. "I know you weren't seduced, and that you didn't go with him willingly, so all I want to know is if he lied about the sum of money your uncle expects to receive for your hand?"

Amy shook her head, though even more pained to have to deceive Christopher. "I asked my uncle, but he only said not to worry about it."

Chris took her hand and carried it to his lips. "If it is true, you are worth every penny of it!"

She looked at him curiously. *Oh, don't let him be in love with me,* she thought. For she knew how hopeless that was, in so many ways. But she only smiled and batted her eyes ridiculously at him. "You are all that is kind, sir!"

He laughed. "And all that is silly, too, I suppose you will tell me. Come, let us dance. Those tabbies shan't get their claws in you."

Never had Amy been more glad to have someone to stand up with. It was all too clear that she would not have her pick of partners this evening. In fact, when Chris returned her to her aunt, instead of the usual cluster of eager suitors, she found only one person waiting there, one who would not dance with her. Tall and thin, he seemed to her, in his austere evening

black, to lurk like some strange predator. Lord Vendercroft
bowed to her and smiled, a knowing, disagreeable smile.
Though her uncle would not permit her openly to reject him,
she had treated him with sufficient coldness that he could not
doubt her lack of interest in him.

"Your aunt tells me you will be able to promenade with me
at some point in the evening, Miss Armstrong," he said. She
wanted to slap the smirk off his face, but had no choice but to
curtsy politely to him.

"Indeed, Lord Vendercroft. As it happens, I am not engaged
for this dance."

"Fortune smiles on me." He offered her his arm. She had
promenaded with him before during dances, and it was dull
work. He had no conversation other than to sneer at the dress
and manners of those upon the dance floor. She supposed it
was jealousy that made him cast so many animadversions
upon his fellowman. This evening his conversation, while less
aimless, was no less distasteful. He tried to lead her onto the
terrace at the back of the Carmindales' ballroom. She held
back, lingering in the door.

"You are not so much in demand this evening as upon some
occasions, Miss Armstrong."

"As you see," she responded frostily.

"I see around me a pack of fools. Where are your many suitors? Suddenly nowhere to be found! A diamond cast in their
midst, and they haven't the courage to pick it up. Such teeth!
Such skin. Glowing with health and vigor, and all they can
think of is their precious reputations and terror of scandal. I
care nothing for scandal, Miss Armstrong. I have given them
fodder enough for their gossip mills from time to time myself."

"So I have heard." Vendercroft caused a murmur of disapproval wherever he appeared, though she did not know all that
lay behind it.

He looked down at her uneasily. "What tale about me has
sullied your delicate ears, I wonder?"

"Nothing in particular, my lord."

"No. Few would dare repeat some of my worst escapades to a gently bred female. But if ever they do, please remember from this experience of yours that the report is often much worse than the reality."

Amy had no wish to encourage this roué and so lifted up her chin. "In my case, I fear report is all too accurate."

"You eloped with that young fool?"

"No, not that. But . . ."

"He seduced you?"

"Certainly not!"

"He raped you?"

Amy knew her cheeks must be scarlet. She turned her head away. "By no means! I referred to the sum my uncle asked Parmingham for my hand."

Silence led her to turn back, hoping to see discouragement, even contempt, on Vendercroft's lined face. From him she eagerly sought it. But instead she found glee. "For the finest diamond, one must be prepared to pay, my dear. Believe me, I am able and willing to do so. Shall I offer for you tomorrow?"

Amy could not help letting the revulsion that these words gave her show upon her face. "I would prefer that you do not."

"I can see that. And yet, who else will do so? Will that rapacious uncle of yours take less? I will offer more, if need be. So learn to school those expressive features, lovely Miss Armstrong. I know you are able to do so, and will, if you know what is good for you. Now, let me tell you what delights await you as my wife."

Amy demurred when he tried to steer her farther out onto the terrace, so he turned back into the house and they walked around the edge of the ballroom while the dancers on the floor whirled by in a kaleidoscope of color and action. It was surely the longest dance of her life, listening to the raspy voice promise her the finest gowns and jewels, the richest furs and most luxurious carriages. If she had not found the conversation so distressing, she would have been amused, for along with these conventional trappings of wealth he reserved his greatest eloquence for describing the sanitary arrangements in both his town and country homes, which, it seemed, had a water closet and bathtubs with hot water on every floor.

"And drains. Such drains, Miss Armstrong! Never will you have foul odors rising through your home from cisterns under the house. My homes all drain the effluent far away, and with it the dangers of contagion that lurk therein."

"Really, Lord Vendercroft. This is not a pleasant conversation." Amy thought the topic peculiar, and his enthusiasm in enlarging upon it even more so. Was Vendercroft slightly unhinged?

He stopped and seemed to struggle with himself for a moment. "Very well. Suffice to say, I shall lay the world at your feet, Miss Armstrong. A diamond of your perfection and luster deserves the finest setting, and I mean to provide it. And you, in turn, will provide me with a bedmate of unrivaled beauty, and perhaps even an heir at last."

The thought of bearing this man's child almost made Amy gag. "I do not long for the things you speak of, Lord Vendercroft. My needs are simple."

"But your uncle's are not. And then there is your dear mama to think of, isn't there?"

"W-what do you mean?"

"Your mother is in poor health, as I understand it. And your brother, as her only male relative, has her in his keeping. What would be her fate if you did not marry to please him, I wonder?"

Amy stared at him. Whatever his faults, Lord Vendercroft had intuition. *What indeed?* But she again lifted her chin. "I do not need to marry a man of wealth to find one willing to provide a home for my mother."

"No, but you may find your uncle's spite prevents your so commendable desire to care for her. Ah, I see I have made a home hit. Now, as my wife, you may command for her the best of physicians, the warmest of homes in the most healthful of situations. Nothing shall disturb her peace or cause her the least distress, I assure you."

"Except knowing I had married such a one as you, my lord."

Amy took her hand from his arm. They were approaching her aunt, and she sketched him the briefest of curtsies. "I thank you for this most informative conversation. I hope and believe it will be our last."

His features twisted in rage. "You will regret those words, Miss Armstrong. I had not thought you a fool. Go your length in proving your contempt of me, as you please. It will only add a certain piquancy to my eventual victory." He bowed deeply to her, and stalked away, for all the world like some gaunt black vulture.

Chapter Twelve

*A*my found no one but Chris waiting for her when she returned to her aunt, who looked to be about to give way to
tears.

"Oh, my darling, I fear we should leave, for this is too, too
humiliating for you, to be snubbed so."

"I won't permit this," Chris stormed. "Come, dance with me
again."

"You're very sweet, but I cannot dance with you all
evening, Chris."

"You can dance with me once, though, can you not, Miss
Armstrong?" At the sound of that deep voice, Amy's heart did
a little somersault. She turned and looked up into Lord
Maxbridge's eyes. They weren't smiling, but there was no disdain there, either, only concern. She took his proffered hand,
and as he led her away he turned back to his nephew.

"Look about you for your special friends, Chris. I feel sure
you can find partners for Miss Armstrong in her hour of need."

The dance for which Lord Maxbridge had solicited her hand
was a waltz. For the first minute or so they danced silently.
Amy, eyes averted, was awestruck by the intensity of her
awareness of the man holding her by the waist and turning her
to and fro on the dance floor.

"You are very quiet," he said at last.

She lifted her eyes to meet his. "It's just . . . I never thought
to be dancing with you, especially a waltz."

"Is it distasteful to you?"

"Not at all!" She tilted her chin up. "You know better."

He fell silent, too. They danced without speaking, looking into one another's eyes. At last he seemed almost to shudder as he broke eye contact for a moment, then looked back down at her with a worried frown.

"Will you get into trouble for dancing with me?"

"Not when my uncle understands the situation. Surely not! He should be grateful for your kindness."

"I would be of further service to you if I could. Lord Vendercroft is not a man you should encourage."

"D-do you think I don't know that?" Tears came unbidden to Amy's eyes—tears of shame and sorrow that rolled silently down her cheeks.

"Oh, Miss Armstrong—Amy—don't! Not here, not now."

"I know. I won't." She struggled with herself. "I can't seem to stop it," she gulped. She could bring tears when she wished, but could not easily turn them off when they came unbidden.

He danced her off to the same terrace on which she had so recently begun her disagreeable conversation with Vendercroft. This time she went willingly as her partner led her down the steps and onto the lighted paths. Some distance from the house there was a bench that, though in full view of the terrace, faced away from it. He seated her there and held out his handkerchief.

She took it silently and swiped at her tears, then gave up and sobbed into it for a few minutes. This relieved her feelings sufficiently that she could gain control of herself, and she looked up at him, essaying a smile as she blotted her cheeks.

"You fear your uncle will sell you to Vendercroft, don't you? It is true, then? The rumored twenty thousand pounds?"

"I don't know the exact figure." She looked away. Even more than to the others, she disliked being less than honest with this man. "My uncle looks to my suitor to repay the expenses of my Season." She gave a half-hysterical laugh. "After tonight it seems they won't include the cost of my own ball."

"Is that all he asks?" Maxbridge said, relief in his voice. "It is not so very bad, after all."

She hung her head. "Not . . . not entirely. My little nieces . . . you see, he has no funds for their dowries. Naturally he . . . I hope to be able to help establish them credibly."

"Not an impossible expectation."

"And then . . . then . . . perhaps he hopes for something in the nature of a loan to help him put his estates in order." Amy bit her lip.

"Ah!" His tone and the look on his face hardened. "As Parmingham said, you in fact are to be sold."

"It is not as bad as Parmingham made it out to be."

"Meaning that your asking price will depend to some extent on your preferred suitor's pocketbook?"

She drew a deep, shuddering breath. "He says he won't force me to marry someone I absolutely detest."

"Poor little creature. Brinker is showing himself to be a true son of his father!"

Amy drew away, pride asserting itself. "I know you think him a villain, but he is not utterly cruel. He . . . he is devoted to his daughters and . . . and is quite fond of me. And he doesn't game or rake about or anything like his father and his brother, who left the estate in such bad heart that Uncle Victor is put to great shifts to manage. I do hope to be able to marry to please him."

Maxbridge took her hand in his and clasped it tightly. "I am glad to hear he cares for you, Amy. I wonder if . . ."

"So here is where you have gotten to!" Chris's voice startled them both, causing them to jump apart like guilty children.

"Miss Armstrong needed a few minutes to compose herself," Maxbridge said, giving her hand one more little squeeze before releasing it.

Chris peered at Amy in the dim light shed by the fairy lanterns hanging from the trees. "Oh, Amy, you've been crying. But I fancy I've just what will put a smile on your face again."

Though she wished with all her heart he had not interrupted

them at just that point, Amy knew it was perhaps just as well. She gave her eyes a final dab, blew her nose, and smiled bravely up at him. "What is it, Christopher?"

"A half-dozen partners lined up for you, that is what! You'll dance all evening!"

"Oh, Chris!" Amy jumped up and kissed him on the cheek. "You are the dearest friend in the world."

Chris took her hands in his and spun her about on the garden pathway, making her laugh. They skipped merrily away, leaving Maxbridge in the darkness to explore the newly opened hole in his heart gingerly, as one explores a tooth that feels loose in its socket.

"Was it terribly difficult to find someone to dance with me?" Amy asked as Chris escorted her back to her aunt. "Oh! They are almost all there!"

"Not difficult at all," Chris assured her. "Just needed to know it wasn't true. All a hum, and you still the same sweet girl they always thought you."

"Oh, Chris! I didn't say it wasn't true, only that I didn't know." It made Amy miserable to know she had deceived this kind, dear friend and so many others.

"Same thing. If it is true, they should snub him, not you. Besides, the fellows weren't snubbing you, they were just a tad intimidated. After all, none of us has that kind of blunt."

Amy danced every set that evening, though the crowd around her between dances was not quite what it had been at other balls. She let herself be teased, laughing along with her friends, who began calling her the "Tattersall Diamond."

When she repeated that sobriquet to her uncle on her return home, informing him of the near disaster that his greed had created, he was furious, and most unjustly but characteristically his fury was aimed at her and his wife for "managing the thing badly." Amy realized she must soothe him as well as try to impress upon him the necessity of reducing his expectations for her. He went to bed in a very bad humor.

Amy slept in the next morning, having tossed and turned for much of the night. Worry about her future mingled with disturbing memories of the dance she had shared with the man who could have no part in that future, indeed probably wanted no part in it, though he had been kind to her. She tortured herself with wondering what he had been about to say when Chris came up to them in the garden. *Very likely not anything like my romantic imaginings,* she scolded herself.

She breakfasted on toast and tea, and only ventured below stairs when told that her uncle wished to speak to her. It was with a heavy heart and a great reluctance to face the irate man that she entered his study. To her astonishment she found him grinning from ear to ear, in the best of spirits.

"Don't look so down pin, my chuck," he told her, pointing to his cheek to signify she should kiss him. She did so, then sat down in the chair facing his desk, more alarmed than relieved to find him in such a good frame of mind. Her fears were well justified.

"Thought you'd lost all hope last night, didn't you. Well, I knew my instincts were right. A diamond of your perfection and luster deserves the finest setting! You are to have it, my love. A title, riches untold, an adoring husband. And quite a generous settlement for your loved ones, too, I am sure you will be gratified to hear."

A diamond of your perfection and luster deserves the finest setting. Amy shuddered as she remembered Vendercroft's phrasing of the night before. But she schooled her features to innocent amazement.

"Why, that is of all things wonderful, Uncle. But who can it be, I wonder?"

"Surely titled, wealthy suitors are not so many for you not to have some idea? Don't play games with me, my girl. I know he would not be your first choice, but . . ."

"Oh, Uncle. You couldn't be speaking of Vendercroft, could you? I shall faint dead away if you suggest such a thing! But you wouldn't. You wouldn't. I know it! You care for me! You wouldn't force me to marry such a disgusting old roué!"

"Now, see here, Amabel. Get ahold of yourself. Sensible girl like you . . ."

She rose from her chair, shrinking away from him. "Sensible, Uncle, not insensible! He is disgusting. He is cruel! I can't, won't marry him." Amy's voice rose with each word until she was shrieking; her disgust was unfeigned, but she made no effort to check it, either. She had decided in her tossings and turnings last night that she would not submit tamely to any attempt to marry her to Vendercroft, and it was best to let her uncle know it.

She had retreated to the door by this time, and flung it open with a parting threat: "I would rather die than marry him. Indeed I would!" She ran from the room and down the hall to where her uncle's butler stood, mouth open, staring at her. She stormed past him and opened the outer door for herself.

"Miss. Oh, miss! You mustn't go out without cloak or hat. 'Tis a raw day," he called after her, but she did not heed him. At that moment the idea of catching her death of cold seemed attractive, and she raced down the square through a chilly mist, unheeding the stares of passersby, until she had to draw up because of a stitch in her side. When she looked around her, she realized she was but a block away from Esmée's home. What welcome she might receive there, she did not know, but decided to take her chances in preference to returning home just then. The mist seemed to have penetrated to her very bones, and the thought of dying of exposure had correspondingly become less attractive. She needed to get warm somewhere.

"Let him contemplate my words," she muttered to herself. "Let him wonder where I am, and worry if I'll get sick. He'd lose his investment if I died. Doubtless all he cares about, too." She lifted the knocker on Esmée's door, and to her relief was admitted immediately. The Pucketts' butler knew her, and put her in the front drawing room, where a comfortable fire warmed her while she awaited the results of his announcing her.

Esmée soon hurried into the room. "Oh, Amy! What has happened! You look a fright!"

"I know it," Amy said, eyeing her reflection in a mirror ruefully. "I apologize for appearing here in such a state, but I did not know where else to go."

Esmée drew her down on the settle nearest the fire. "Tell me," she said, and Amy caught her breath a little at the honest concern in the girl's eyes.

She truly is my friend, Amy thought. It had never happened to her before. She had always been too pretty to inspire anything but jealousy in other females of her age. Any hesitation about taking Esmée into her confidence disappeared; she poured out the events of the morning.

"Mother said Vendercroft would offer for you, after seeing him parade you about last night. I could not imagine that your uncle would accept, however. Oh, Amy, how dreadful for you, for where are you to turn?"

"I don't know. I have no other suitors who are sufficiently wealthy and independent."

"What about Lord Maxbridge?"

"What do you mean? He is not my suitor!"

"Last night he looked at you in such a way, as you were dancing, that I told Mama he must have a *tendre* for you. And I would swear you looked quite as spoony. Then the two of you went out into the garden together, and I hoped . . ."

Amy looked down at her hands, twisted in her lap. "Nothing of the sort. He was all that is kind last night. I don't know why . . . perhaps because Chris and I are such good friends."

"You are so beautiful. I cannot doubt you could make him your suitor if you wished. But it would be frightfully awkward, wouldn't it?"

"You mean because of my uncle's dislike for him? More than awkward, impossible!"

"I didn't know about that. I meant because of Chris."

"I don't understand."

"Oh, Amy, surely you know Christopher Ponselle is head over heels in love with you?"

"No!" Amy put out her hand, truly horrified. "No, do not say so! He is my friend, my dearest friend after you."

"Mama says there can be no such friendships between male and female. She says he adores you, and I believe she is right."

Amy bit her lip. "I hope she is wrong. I do like Chris, but I cannot love him. And even if I did, I could never marry him. My uncle wouldn't permit it, nor would his."

"Why ever not?"

Amy hesitated. Her uncle's past was no secret, but he had been careful to keep out of the way, to avoid any stirring of old coals. If he was not ashamed of his war record in the Peninsula, he obviously felt that bringing it to the notice of the *ton* once again could do her no good in her search for a husband.

"I don't understand it all. Something about a disagreement between them when they served in the Peninsula together."

"Oh, don't men just make one crazy, getting up grudges and holding on to them forever. So it was with my father and one of our neighbors. They were at daggers drawn over some trifle for twenty years, until he died. Not my father, I mean, but the neighbor."

Amy nodded her agreement. Seeking to change the subject, she asked, "How do matters stand between you and Mr. Smythe-Amhurst now, by the way."

Esmée sighed. "No better, and no worse. He still visits, and dances with me, but he still dangles after you and several other pretty girls, too. I do not believe I have succeeded in attaching him."

"You will! Only you mustn't hang on his sleeve, or seem to favor him. Flirt with others, and make him jealous."

"I wonder if it would serve?"

Both girls were diverted from Amy's problems by a strategy session concerning Mr. Smythe-Amhurst. Mrs. Puckett came downstairs, dressed to go out, and found them with their heads together, giggling.

"I did not know you were here, Miss Armstrong," Mrs. Puckett said, drawing on her gloves as she eyed her with some disfavor from the door to the drawing room.

"I beg pardon, ma'am. I just stopped by on the spur of the moment."

"So it would seem." Mrs. Puckett advanced upon her. "You look like a drowned rat, young woman."

"Well, I came out without my cloak, you see." Amy stood. "I expect I had best go home now. They will be worried about me."

"You walked?"

"Yes, ma'am."

"Ran is more like it. Mama, her uncle means to force her to marry Vendercroft."

"I *thought* he would offer for you. He has been looking about him for a wife for two years now. Well, I won't say that he has the best reputation in the world, but you would be a marchioness, you know, and rich as you can stare. If your uncle has his wits about him when making up the settlements, you'll be a wealthy widow someday and may do as you please."

"Mama! As if Amy would marry such an unpleasant old man for advantage!"

"No, won't you?" Mrs. Puckett looked hard at Amy. "Well, I am at a loss to know how you will get your uncle to allow you to marry any of your young suitors, for they either lack money or independence, or both. Whatever you decide, you must now return to your uncle."

Amy nodded. "I know. I've nowhere else to go."

"Come, then. I'll take you up in my carriage. I must go to the tooth drawer's today."

Amy shuddered. "Oh, how dreadful for you. Do you not go with her, Esmée?"

"I couldn't bear it!"

"Shall I accompany you, Mrs. Puckett? I am not in the least squeamish."

"Thank you," she said, her voice and manner softening. "You are very kind. But my maid is all the support I require."

Once in the carriage, with her maid facing them, Mrs. Puckett surprised Amy by pronouncing a comprehensive diatribe on her uncle, ending with the even more surprising statement that she would perhaps have done better to elope with one of her young suitors.

"Don't tell Esmerelda I said so. Wouldn't do to put notions in her head, but better by far than marrying Vendercroft."

"Oh, ma'am, do you truly think so? Even though I'd no love for either of them?"

"Might have learned. Never will learn to love Vendercroft. He isn't lovable! In fact . . ." She looked out the carriage window, obviously debating whether to say more. After a moment she shook her head. "No sense in raking up old coals. Know what I wish? Wish you'd take Dorwin Smythe-Amhurst out of Esmerelda's way!"

"Oh, no," Amy gasped. "You surely don't mean that? She adores him. And she's my very good friend."

"Yes, and it would be the kindest thing you could do for her, though I doubt she'd see it that way at first. Thing is, he's a weak, silly young man, and a bit of a gamester, I suspect. Skirt chaser, too. Esmée needs a man of character to guide her, for she's far from having your strong mind. You'd take Dorwin in hand, I've no doubt, keep him from ruining himself. Be well worth what it would cost him to get your uncle's permission, in the long run. And as for his skirt-chasing, well, it wouldn't bother you, for you don't love him."

Amy sat in appalled silence for a few moments. What a bargain Mrs. Puckett proposed. Yet compared to Vendercroft . . . "He is well to grass, ma'am?"

"Not so well-off as Vendercroft, but very nearly so. Seems besotted with you, too. And it isn't as if your keeping him at arms' length will help Esmée, for he doesn't see her. Can't! They've been raised together closer to sister and brother than friends, and her having no claims to beauty, either."

"I think Esmée is very pretty," Amy asserted.

"Generous. But only think, girl. He'd be a better husband than Vendercroft. Why not make a push for him? Doubt you'd have to do much more than crook your finger, at that."

Amy considered this proposition for a moment, almost tempted. But then she thought of Esmée's woeful countenance the first time they met, when she thought Amy would attach Dorwin. "I couldn't, Mrs. Puckett. Esmée would never forgive me, and she is my best friend."

"Loyal to a fault. Pity. But admirable, too. I knew your mother, and always admired her for marrying the man she loved instead of that nasty creature her brother had chosen for her. Apparently strong-minded women run in your family." Mrs. Puckett looked out her carriage window. "Here we are. Shall I go in with you, child?"

"Thank you, ma'am, but I shall do well enough." Amy impulsively leaned forward and kissed Mrs. Puckett on the cheek.

The second Amy alighted from the carriage, the door to her uncle's town house was flung open, and Aunt Edwina ran down the steps, her tears mingling with the steady rain that now fell. "Oh, Amy, Amy darling. We thought you'd run away and wouldn't come back. Come in, you'll catch your death of cold."

Amy raced up the steps with her aunt, and into the hall to find half a dozen servants standing about, gaping at her.

"I collect my uncle is from home," she said, knowing they wouldn't have dared do so with him there.

"He went out looking for you. In a rare temper he was, too, but worried for all that. Oh, Amy, what did you say to upset him so? He seemed to think it my fault, but he was so angry he made no sense at all."

"Let us go upstairs, Aunt Edwina. You have gotten as soaked as I have. We'll both change and have a cup of tea, and I'll tell you all about it."

By the time her uncle returned home, over an hour later, both women were warm and dry and Aunt Edwina was sobbing over Amy's fate. At the sounds of her husband returning, her aunt paled and shrank against the pillows, for she had taken to her bed.

"I shall go to my room, Aunt Edwina. Best you not say anything to him. Leave all to me."

Amy had put on a nightgown. She scrambled into her bed and urged Betty to take herself off. She then awaited the advent of her uncle with her heart tripping over itself from worry and fear.

Her fear left her the minute the man entered her room.

Forgetting her intention to look half dead, she sprang out of the bed, because that is exactly how Lord Brinker looked.

"Oh, my poor uncle. How miserable you must be. You are half-drowned, and shaking with cold. Oh, dear sir, I am so sorry, for I know you were looking for me! You must go straight in and change your clothes and have your valet pour some hot water for your feet."

Nonplussed by this solicitous treatment, Lord Brinker opened and closed his mouth several times before finding his voice. "What the devil do you mean, haring off into a rainstorm, missy? Trying to kill yourself, or me?"

"I confess, Uncle, I wouldn't have cared if I had caught my death, at that moment. However, I am never ill, you know. But you! Oh, how I regret my selfishness. Now, come, let me order you a tisane and a hot bath, won't you."

"But . . ." He sneezed. "Oh, the devil! I'm taking a cold. And Vendercroft due at any moment to pay his addresses to you."

"Well, he will just have to come back. I shan't leave you until I have seen that you are quite comfortable. And don't worry about my refusing him, for I shan't."

He gaped at her. "You won't?"

"No, indeed, Uncle. I've been thinking what a silly creature I'd be, to whistle down both a title and a fortune just because I find the man disgusting. But I don't think I will accept him right away, either. I shall explain all later. For now, we must make you comfortable."

She had pulled him along to his rooms all the while she talked, and once there issued orders for his comfort to his valet. "You must undress him immediately. Have you a warming pan ready for his bed? I'll send for hot water for his feet, and the hot posset. It won't do to have him ill."

Brinker lifted his hand to her cheek just for a moment, his eyes suspiciously moist. "You are the most amazing creature," he said. "No one else has ever cared for me enough to worry about me. Daresay Lady Brinker'd be glad if I kicked off."

"What a shocking thing to say, Uncle. She'd be a much better wife to you than you will let her be. Get those wet clothes off of him now, Mr. Throng. I'll return shortly."

When word came up that Lord Vendercroft was below, Amy was standing next to her uncle's bed, consulting with Dr. Gantry, whom she had called when Lord Brinker began to cough violently. She had put on her plainest, oldest dress, and tied her hair behind with a ribbon.

"Please go down to him, Amabel," her uncle pleaded. "You don't have to accept him just yet, but don't make him so angry he won't repeat his offer."

"Be quiet, you dear silly man. Didn't you hear Dr. Gantry? You are in danger of an inflammation of the lungs. Oh, of course I shall go talk to him, if it will make you rest easier."

Leaving Dr. Gantry to instruct Throng on the care her uncle needed, Amy ran downstairs, feeling torn between fear and elation. She had some more time! She had carried the day with her uncle because of his condition, yet knew the cause of his illness was herself, and that she would feel agonies of guilt if he were seriously ill. Yet how providential that illness was. *Oh, my, I don't know whether to send up a prayer of thanksgiving or beg for forgiveness,* she thought as she ran into the drawing room where Vendercroft stood pacing impatiently.

She curtsied to him, then approached him hurriedly. "Please forgive me for making you wait, my lord, but my uncle is very ill, and I was with the doctor." She looked up at him imploringly, not a hint of any dislike upon her countenance.

Vendercroft looked as nonplussed at her informal manner and pleasant demeanor as her uncle had done earlier when she had sprung to his succor.

"Very ill?" Vendercroft edged away from her a little. "He was in good health and better spirits when I left him this morning."

"Yes, well, be took a severe wetting and has caught a cold. I hope it may be nothing more, for Dr. Gantry fears an inflammation of the lungs."

"You look as if you have had a bit of a wetting yourself," Vendercroft surmised, looking at her kinky hair.

Amy put both hands to her head. "It is the moisture in the air. I daresay I look a fright, for I have been too distracted with caring for my aunt and uncle to think of my appearance."

"Your aunt?" Vendercroft's voice shook. "Sh-she is ill, too?"

"I fear it may be some sort of contagion." At his look of horror, she put her hands to her cheek. "Oh! I never thought of it, but I doubt I should have come down to you. I hope you may not catch it."

Vendercroft shrank farther away from her. "I hope not, too. Careless wench. I shall take my leave of you." He walked in a wide circle around her.

"I shall tell my uncle you called, my lord."

"Yes, do that." Vendercroft attained the door and from its safety looked back at her. "You did not expect me, then?"

"He said something about your calling, but I could not make it out." She opened her eyes as wide as they could go. "Was it something . . . particular . . . my lord?" She started toward him.

"Ha! I shall have something very particular to say to you in due time!" With a sour look, he hastened out of the room and down the stairs, leaving Amy both surprised and full of interesting surmise at his behavior.

Chapter Thirteen

*V*ictor's illness gave a brief reprieve from Lord Vendercroft's suit, but Amy could make little use of it to look
for a more desirable *parti*. Lord Brinker, having discovered in
her a sympathetic nurse, became a most demanding patient,
and she had to dance constant attention on him. Her aunt
would have nursed the invalid willingly, but he would not have
her, saying he did not wish her to catch the cold. Instead, he
packed her off to Wayside to be with her daughters. She went
gladly, and Amabel wistfully watched the carriage depart,
longing to visit her mother.

During those several days of Brinker's illness, Amy did not
receive visitors. Not a great many called, society having still
not quite made up its mind whether to cut her or not. But
Esmée called, and Christopher Ponselle, as well as a couple of
her most faithful suitors, Nathan Holmes and William
Tremayne. They were told she was not receiving. This immediately gave rise to chilling speculations. Esmée had told several people about Amy's panic-stricken flight from her home
after learning she must accept Lord Vendercroft's suit. It
seemed apparent to her friends that Miss Armstrong had either
been locked up in the attic with bread and water until she
should accept Vendercroft, or beaten until her survival was in
doubt, for refusing him.

Esmée did little to scotch these rumors, for when she first
heard of them she turned as pale as a sheet, put her hands to

her mouth, and began to cry. "I feared it might be so," she wept. Christopher was in her drawing room at the time she received this intelligence. He had gone there specifically to see if Esmée had heard anything of her.

When he tried to draw her out, Mrs. Puckett gave Esmée a quelling look and declared her daughter would not join in common gossip.

"Pull yourself together, daughter, or I shall send you upstairs," she admonished, and changed the subject firmly.

But that evening at a musicale, Christopher and Esmée managed to speak privately and shared their fears for Amy's situation. "We must find some way to save her," Chris declared.

Esmée agreed. "Her uncle is wicked as wicked may be. He means to sell her, and brave though she is, she is powerless. I called on her yesterday and was told she was not receiving. Neither was her aunt; indeed, their butler, that mendacious creature, said Lady Brinker had gone into the country. Doubtless Lord Brinker has locked her up, too, for coming to Amy's defense."

These revelations led Nathan, William, and Chris to a late night meeting over several bottles of wine at White's. Nathan had something to add to the alarming gossip. His cousin Elena had been Vendercroft's second wife. He told them intimate details of Elena's marriage to Vendercroft, which made them all shudder.

"She fled him and returned home, but she died in childbirth after my uncle was forced to return her to him," Nathan concluded the grim narrative.

"That is odd," William said. "I heard his first wife died in childbirth, too."

"We must do something," Chris declared. "The man is obviously mad. We cannot let him get his wicked, perverted hands on Amabel Armstrong!"

Thus it was decided that Amy must be rescued.

How to do it exercised them considerably. When Lord Vendercroft entered during their plots, Chris, somewhat well-to-go, approached him.

"Do I understand, my lord, that I am to wish you happy?"

Vendercroft raised his quizzing glass and tried to stare Chris down, but the boy was either too pot-valiant or too little in awe of the man to be put off by these tactics. He merely glared back.

Vendercroft had heard the rumors, and did not like figuring in them as the villain. "I collect you refer to Miss Armstrong," he responded repressively. "I have not seen her for several days. I understand her uncle is ill, and she is caring for him. Miss Armstrong is a girl of strong character and devoted to her family, you know. As for wishing me happy, I would, I own, delight to win the hand and heart of that lovely creature, but have not as yet spoken to her. However, when she is once again able to go about in society, I am sure these gothic rumors will afford her much amusement." He passed on, leaving Chris no less convinced that Amy was being pressured to marry Vendercroft.

The three young men continued their colloquy with yet another bottle, and someone, afterward no one could say who, suggested that the only way to save Amy from Vendercroft was to elope with her.

"Won't elope," Chris said, shaking his head. "Doesn't want to be like her mother. Have to abduct her."

"Won't like it," Nathan objected. "Didn't like it when Ingleworth abducted her. Certainly didn't like it when Parmingham abducted her. Won't like it if I do."

"You mean, if I do," William objected.

"I will do the abducting, I thank you," Chris growled. "I love her deeply."

"I love her, too."

"I also. Can't say I don't. Devoted to her."

"Neither of you dared to dance with her at the Carmindales' ball until I had done so first," Chris said.

"Would have dared," William insisted. "Didn't see there was any point in it, with such a price put on her. Mean to say, m'father's a warm man, but not that warm."

"Nor mine," Nathan agreed, nodding. "But Miss Armstrong

won't care for that. It's not she that hankers after a fortune, or she'd have married Ingleworth."

"Or Parmingham."

"Not Parmingham," Chris objected.

"No, not Parmingham. Clunch. Made a demned nuisance of himself."

"Not Ingleworth, either," Nathan said. "Rushed his fences."

"She didn't love either of them, so she wouldn't marry either of them. That proves she's no fortune hunter, no matter what my Uncle Max thinks." Chris tossed off another glass of wine.

"Then she won't marry you. Doesn't love you," Nathan said, grinning at this home thrust.

"Nor you," William said, wiping the grin from Nathan's face.

"Doesn't love any of us," Chris sighed. "But she likes me. She really does. Says I'm her best friend."

"Esmerelda Puckett is her best friend."

"I am!"

"Are not!"

"Am, too. Well, at least you can't deny I'm her favorite of the three of us."

This brought forth a fresh round of disagreement, which ended, however, upon a gloomy note of concord. "Doesn't love any of us. Probably won't marry any of us," Nathan summed up their plight.

"Love or not, she'd be better off marrying any one of us than marrying Vendercroft, though," Chris insisted.

"Draw straws for her," Nathan suggested.

This suggestion found favor with Nathan and William, but Chris objected. "What if the one who wins isn't her favorite of the three of us? Ought to give her some choice, oughtn't we? Tell you what. We'll all abduct her, then let her have her pick of us."

At first this scheme seemed flawless. "If she can't decide, *she* can draw straws," Chris concluded.

"Give her a choice, she'll talk us out of it all together,"

Nathan said. "Persuasive female. Give you one look of reproach from those big green eyes, and you'd melt."

"We all would," Chris agreed.

"Or she might run away from us, the way she did with Parmingham." William scowled at the thought. "Females don't know what's best for 'em."

"True," Chris said. "She can't know just how bad Vendercroft is. Stands to reason. Too innocent. Couldn't even enlighten her. Wouldn't be proper to speak of such things."

"S'right," Nathan said. "Can't tell her. Just have to save her."

"Tell you what," William said. "Have to tie her up, so she can't run away."

This drew loud objections from the other two. The idea of laying violent hands on the goddess!

"Every feeling revolts," Chris said.

"Couldn't do it," Nathan said. "The thought of the look in her eyes!"

"Don't look at her. Do it from behind. Have to gag her, too."

"Have you taken leave of your senses, Will?"

"But only consider. Talked her way out of being abducted by Ingleworth, ran away from Parmingham. Mustn't let her go to work on us. Only way is to tie her up and gag her. Use only clean linen, of course. And soft cords or silk scarves, not rope."

Chris and Nathan could not hold out against the logic of the idea, and fell to discussing how best to do it without hurting her if she struggled. In spite of the many distressing aspects of the situation, the three cavaliers agreed that their mission was just, that Amy would be better off with any one of them than with Vendercroft, and that she should have her choice of them once she was safely spirited away.

This drunken scheme might have been forgotten when the three sobered up, except for an encounter in the park a few days later.

Once Amy's uncle had sufficiently recovered to think matters over a bit, he tried to take command of the situation again, informing Amy that she was to accept Vendercroft's suit. She looked reproachfully at him

"I told you I would, did I not, if necessary."

"Yes, but it is necessary! You won't get a better offer, my dear."

"I have been thinking that we had better go to Paris after all."

"Paris! No, no, I told you. Not going over to be surrounded by Frenchies. Nor to be snubbed by Wellington's lackeys."

"It would be most unpleasant for you, to be among people who did not appreciate your abilities. But think, Uncle. If our whole future rests on it? Mrs. Puckett says almost everyone is there. That is why I have had so much trouble finding eligible suitors, I am sure."

"That's as may be!" Victor folded his arms over his chest in that way he had that told her further remonstrance would only result in hostilities. "Now, make up your mind to it that you must accept Vendercroft."

Amy drew a steadying breath. Keeping her voice low and coaxing, she tried again. "I am not at all sure of that. It is not, after all, just a matter of money, is it?" She looked at him out of wide, innocent eyes. "You wouldn't wish me to marry someone I find distasteful? I do think I might be able to bear Lord Vendercroft, but I am not sure. Let him court me. I will have the chance to know him better, and in the meantime someone else may turn up who is eligible."

"Hunh! Not so many of those about whom you would have."

"Well, perhaps I've been too nice in my notions. I must consider older men, perhaps. After all, if Vendercroft is eligible for me, then Lord Sunder is not so very much older. He pinched my cheek once and said if he were twenty years younger he would give the young bucks a run for their money. Oh, I know. Everyone laughs at him, such a doddering old man, always flirting with young girls. But what if he really would like to marry? He might be willing to pay."

Lord Brinker hemmed and hawed a great deal, but finally

allowed Amy to have her way. "Very well. Let Vendercroft court you, then. But take care what you are about! No more of these elopements or abductions, or whatever they might be! Remember what will happen to your mother!"

"I will, Uncle," she replied with conviction. Concern for her mother's safety and health were never out of her mind.

When Lord Vendercroft called the next day, she greeted him cordially. He stood somewhat tensely in the middle of the room, looking as if he might bolt.

"Your uncle is well?"

"Not entirely, my lord, but much better." Amy noted his posture with interest.

"And your aunt?"

"Oh, she never really became ill after all."

"Ah. And you, did you never take the contagion?"

"No. I thank you for your concern, but I have been quite well." *Concern for yourself,* she thought. His behavior confirmed her surmise that he desperately feared catching whatever her uncle had had. "Won't you be seated?"

Vendercroft visibly relaxed. He stepped forward and took her hands in his. "Then I may at last say what your uncle gave me permission to say several mornings ago. He has agreed that I may pay my addresses to you. I am sure he has told you this by now."

"Indeed he has, my lord. And I am very flattered by your offer."

"Ha! I see he has beat some sense in you, for you spoke from the other side of your mouth at the Carmindales' ball."

She pulled her hands away. "Please be seated, Lord Vendercroft. May I offer you some refreshments?"

"No, and I'll thank you to stop stalling. Flattered you should be, but eager you are not, as you made clear at the ball. Still, you've no choice but to accept, you know. I shall send the announcement this very day."

"I am surprised you have not already sent it, considering how certain you are of my acquiescence. But my uncle told me only that I might consider your suit, not that I must accept you."

Vendercroft glared at her, fists clenched. "How is this? That was not our understanding when he and I last spoke."

"I do think you must have misunderstood. My uncle would not be so gothic as to force me to wed a man I could not like. And you couldn't possibly want a bride so gained."

A gleam came into his eye. "You are mistaken. Adds a certain piquancy to the matter."

She cocked her head. "I don't understand."

"No, but I shall make you understand."

"Well, if this is how you mean to go on, it is extremely unlikely that you will find me willing to wed you."

Vendercroft sprang up, fists clenched. "Do you expect me to line up with all your other courtiers? To jostle with boys half my age, and dance attendance on you like a moonstruck halfling? No, indeed. I am the Marquess of Vendercroft. I'll not make myself a figure of fun courting you, diamond though you may be."

"Ah, I see how it is. You don't wish to force me to wed you out of cruelty, but out of diffidence, or pride. You much relieve my mind, my lord."

Vendercroft looked more puzzled than gratified. "Do I?"

"Indeed, yes. Now, then." She made her voice soothing, coaxing. "Don't you worry about being embarrassed or made a cake of. I only wish to know you better. Why, I understand you better just in this short little conversation. No need to be jostling with my other suitors, no need at all. Why do you not take me for a drive in the park, my lord? That would be unexceptionable, surely?"

"I wish to speak with your uncle first."

"He is still not quite up to coming below stairs. I doubt not you could speak to him tomorrow or the next day."

Baffled and frustrated, her unwelcome suitor tugged at his long nose. "Oh, very well. I suppose you may go for a drive with me, then."

Lord Vendercroft had a handsome team of chestnuts pulling

his high-perch phaeton, but when she praised them he only looked blankly at her and urged her up into the carriage. Since praising their cattle usually launched a conversation with even the shiest young man, Amy did not know how to proceed. She rode silently beside the stony-faced marquess as he threaded his way competently through the busy London traffic. When they had reached the park, his demeanor changed. He began bowing to this and that acquaintance, a look of smug pride on his face.

"You have insisted I bring you to the park," he growled at her. "Now, smile and look pleased with my company."

So she smiled and nodded to his friends. Soon enough she attracted a pair of her young suitors riding on her side of the carriage, but mindful of Vendercroft's dislike of vying with younger men for her attention, she was quite short with them. One of them was Nathan Holmes, who reined his horse away and went in search of William and Chris. The three of them watched in alarm as Vendercroft and Amy made their progress through the park, Vendercroft preening himself upon his companion, Amy smiling at his side.

"I called myself a jug-bitten fool for last week's scheme," Chris said, "but watching them now, I wonder if we hadn't the right of it."

"Know what you mean," William said. "He clearly thinks he's got her. Nor does she look too unhappy about it."

"You don't know her as well as I do," Chris said. "That's a false smile. She is miserable."

"Lud, yes. Blue-deviled. Would hardly speak to me," Nathan agreed. "But how shall we manage it, if her uncle means to shut her up unless she is with Vendercroft?"

While the plotters renewed their conspiracy, Amy plunged into a frontal assault against Vendercroft's impervious demeanor.

"Why do you want to marry me? You don't seem to like me, nor want me to like you."

Vendercroft turned cold eyes upon her. "I have been on the

town for longer than you have been alive, and have never known such a beauty before. I want to possess you, that is all."

"Beauty means so much to you, then?" Amabel studied his eyes, which seemed to her to contain little emotion of any sort, much less passion.

"It is everything."

She shook her head. "I don't believe you. There are other beautiful women in the world. There must be something else."

He stared at her for a moment, then turned the carriage onto a side path and slowed it down. "Do you wish me to compose sonnets to your eyelids to convince you? I haven't the skill or the desire. Smile at me a moment."

"Give me something to smile about."

"Don't be pert. I'll pay you back for it, if not now, later." He reached over and took her chin in his free hand. Tilting her head up, he scanned her features. "You have the most perfect skin I have ever seen. Close-grained as a child's. I doubt if you have ever thrown out a spot. Your teeth—what I can see of them—are perfect. Have you ever lost a tooth?"

She shook her head as best she could in his grip.

"No, I thought not." Suddenly his demeanor changed from cold dispassionate consideration to something more eager. "Do you have any cavities?"

"I see you would like to examine my teeth. Very well." She bared them in an exaggerated smile. "Very much in character with the way you are going about acquiring me, my lord, except that it is usual to examine the filly's mouth *before* you have made an offer on her." She laughed at her own joke, but Vendercroft was not amused.

"Answer my question, damn you."

"No, I have no cavities. What of it?"

"Have you ever been ill? I don't mean sniffles, but serious illness?"

Impatiently Amabel snapped, "Never. I am seldom sick, and never tired. And no, I never suffered from spots. But I still don't see . . ."

"There! That is it. That is why I want you. You are healthy!

The most perfect specimen in the world. Not for me the muslin company, I tell you. Nasty creatures, with spots they hide with cosmetics, rotten mouths, and doubtless rotting elsewhere in their bodies!"

Amy turned scarlet. "Lord Vendercroft!"

"You wanted to know my reasons! I have a detestation of disease in any form. I have kept myself healthy, and will have a wife who is perfection in skin, and tooth, and limb. Clean inside and out. And make sure, you will stay that way. How often do you bathe?"

"Really, my lord. The impropriety of this conversation . . ."

He put his hand around her wrist and gripped it painfully. "How often? Every day?"

Heart throbbing in alarm, Amy stared into eyes in which the light of fanaticism burned. "No, my uncle does not hold with bathing daily. I bathe several times a week, though."

"As my wife you will bathe daily. I have massive tubs in all my homes. Hot water, running water. It has been clear to me since first beholding you that in addition to being a most finished piece of nature you are also of a fastidious disposition, and have good habits of hygiene. You brush your teeth once daily?"

Beginning to be fascinated by his fascination, Amy nodded. "Every morning."

"You should do so more often. After every meal, in fact. You should use a different toothbrush every time. The red powder is best. I will instruct you on the best method of brushing. Have you heard of a Dutchman named Loewenhoek?"

This turn of the conversation utterly bewildered Amy. "A . . . a Dutchman?"

"He is the forefather of the microscope. He first found little living beings that cannot be seen by the unaided eye."

"Oh, yes. I have heard of that. I haven't had the opportunity to look at pond water under a microscope, but I understand there is a little world in there."

"What is worse, there is a little world in our mouth!"

Amy's eyes widened, both at this information, and at the tone of disgust with which he pronounced it.

"Yes. Horrible. Scrape the coating from teeth that are not brushed clean, and you will find living creatures swimming around in it. It makes me quite nauseous to think of it." Vendercroft turned away, looking a little pale. Just as Amy began to wonder if he was going to cast up his accounts, he turned back to her.

"But one can kill them! You can scrape them off, and you can kill them, by drinking hot beverages. As hot as you can bear! Salt in it helps. And rinsing with spirits. I have experimented with many solutions, and have found that salt and vodka kill them the best."

"Vodka? That is a Russian drink, I think."

"Yes. Vile stuff, but useful for hygiene. I have a theory. It is those little creatures that cause teeth to decay!"

"What an excellent notion." Amy's admiration was unfeigned. She began to think she was in the presence of a genius. A mad genius, but a genius, nevertheless. "You are something of a natural philosopher, indeed, performing experiments and such. You should write up your findings for the Royal Society."

Vendercroft did not take this as a compliment. "I do not consider it good *ton* for a marquess to publicly display his intellect in that way."

"But you may have an important bit of knowledge to contribute to the good of humanity!"

"I do not seek such vulgar notice as it must attract." He said it in a tone that warned her further efforts to convince him would anger him, which was not her intention.

"I daresay you are right," she murmured. "How disagreeable it would be, particularly if it should come to the attention of the *ton*. There are those among them who like nothing better than to laugh at the accomplishments of others."

"Just so! You are a remarkably quick-witted creature," he said approvingly. "Do you consider yourself to have been sufficiently courted to give me an answer to my suit?"

Amy reined in the impulse to tell him she was less inclined than ever to be the wife of such a peculiar man. "So impatient, my lord. I am far from plumbing your depths, I am sure. But I *am* pleased to have this opportunity to know you better. I hope you will make other such occasions. I begin to think we could deal well together."

"Humph." Vendercroft turned his horses' heads toward home, and said not another word to her on the way, in spite of her efforts to draw him out. He left her on the pavement in front of her uncle's house in token of his displeasure with her. But she was far from displeased by the drive. Though no more eager than before to marry Vendercroft, she felt herself to be more in control of the situation, having begun to take the measure of the man and how he might be manipulated. She felt no shame at the notion of manipulating him either, for women must use what weapons they had at hand, when men held so much power.

Her friends, not privy to her sanguine thoughts, despaired of her after seeing her out driving with the odious marquess. Chris saw his uncle across the park, and rode up to him.

"Uncle Max, did you see Amabel Armstrong with Lord Vendercroft?"

"Everyone in the park saw. They seemed to be on very good terms." Maxbridge scowled.

"Her uncle is going to force her to marry him."

Maxbridge shook his head. "She assured me he would not. It appears to me that Vendercroft is beginning to persuade Miss Armstrong to accept his suit."

"Rot! Anyone could see she was miserable."

"You are letting your emotions rule you. Miss Armstrong is a strong-willed young woman. If she marries Vendercroft, it will be because she has decided it is to her advantage to do so." Maxbridge put his heel to his horse's flank and rode away, unwilling to admit to his nephew how disgusted he had been by the sight of Amabel sitting beside Vendercroft, smiling and nodding like a queen on a throne. He had followed them at a discreet distance, wishing to see for himself what her reaction was when the marquess took her out of the main pathways. He had observed the marquess caress her, lifting her chin up, had seen her smile at him. The two had remained in intense conversation for several minutes, without the least sign of distress on her part. *Wealth and a title. That is what she wants. She'll sell her body for wealth and a title.* Maxbridge could not admit to his nephew that he felt sick to his very soul at this turn of events.

Chris called on Esmée, to see if she had been able to see Amy. When he learned she had not, he was even more alarmed.

"He took her driving in the park yesterday," Chris told her.

"I heard."

"My uncle said she was beginning to accept him, but I don't believe it. I know her, and that smile was forced."

"Oh, no. She would never accept him willingly. She told me so."

Chris then carefully exposed to her the plot he and his friends contemplated. Esmée thought it very daring, and very clever.

"I say, if you agree, perhaps you would help us with it, for how to approach her I cannot imagine."

"If I am not to be admitted to see her, I don't know how I can help."

"Try again, will you? Only, don't tell her what is up. Just see if you can get her to agree to go for a drive in the country with you."

Esmée's eyes widened. "You would take her from my carriage? Oh, Mama would never countenance it! And Lord Brinker would never let her go into the country without a chaperon. He is quite wary since Parmingham abducted her."

"Your mama wouldn't have to countenance it," Chris snapped. "It is to be an abduction, after all."

"Oh. To participate in such a thing has me all in a quake." Esmée's eyes were wide as saucers, and she fidgeted with her handkerchief.

"You don't have to do anything but tell us when and where you will go driving."

Though she hesitated some more, at last she allowed herself to be persuaded. It suited Esmée to have her friend married, not just out of concern for her, but because her beloved Dorwin Smythe-Amhurst still numbered himself among Amy's court, and had no eyes for Esmée at all.

"Very well. I will call on her again today, and tomorrow, and every day until I am admitted," she said. "I will do my possible for you."

"Good girl!" Chris shook her hand violently, and left to inform the other conspirators. A carriage suitable for the purpose, cattle, and money must be rounded up and held at the ready.

"And clothing," Nathan said. "Ingleworth made a fool of himself setting off without baggage. We will have to procure clothing suitable for her."

"And a toothbrush," William said. "Amy has such beautiful teeth. Must brush 'em every day, don't you think?"

Much struck with this observation, the others joined in praise of Amy's teeth, her smile, her hair, and figure, at which point Chris drew them up primly. "Won't have you speaking disrespectfully of the woman I mean to marry."

"Not disrespectful to say she's got a neat figure," Nathan objected.

"Not true to say you're going to marry her. Could be any one of us," William said, thrusting out his jaw pugnaciously.

Chris smiled knowingly. "It'll be me she chooses."

This led to a round of hostility that almost sunk the conspiracy, until Nathan brought them to order again by reminding them of Vendercroft's cruel treatment of his cousin. "She must not fall into his hands, not even if she prefers a groom to one of us," he asserted. The conspirators reluctantly set aside their rivalry.

Esmée and her mother called on the Brinkers the next day, determined to besiege the house until allowed to speak to Amy. They were admitted instantly to the drawing room, but

Lady Brinker was sitting with Amy, which made Esmée hesitate to raise the subject of Lord Vendercroft. She did ask why Amy had been unavailable for several days, and received the story of Lord Brinker's illness.

"And you, Lady Brinker," Mrs. Puckett asked. "Did you take the contagion?"

"No, my husband sent me to our estate just outside of London, to stay with my children for a while."

"And with my mother." Amy heaved a large sigh. "I do wish I had been able to go. I haven't seen her in an age."

Esmée seized the opportunity offered her. "Mother, why do we not take Amy for a drive on the next fine day, to visit her mother?"

When Mrs. Puckett quickly agreed, Amy clapped her hands in joy. "How very kind of you! I cannot wait!"

"And she said she had been nursing her uncle all of this time but I do not believe it," Esmée declared to Chris when he called on her at her invitation the next morning.

"Nor do I," Chris agreed. "Obviously they locked her up until she agreed to marry the man, then let her receive company again. Will she go for a drive with you?"

"Yes, but unfortunately Lady Brinker wanted to go along. Amy was in alt, for she hasn't seen her mother or cousins in ages."

"I cannot like it. Your mother and her aunt. So many people to overpower!"

"Ah, you can't mean to use force. Surely some subterfuge?"

Chris shook his head. "Tried and tried to think of one. Still, going to do the thing. We are determined! Send me a note around when you plan to go. I shall have all organized and be on the alert."

"I am so very excited to be visiting my mother," Amy said as she joined Esmée and Mrs. Puckett in their carriage. "It has been an age since I have been with her."

Her aunt seconded the thanks. "So very glad you suggested

this outing, Mrs. Puckett. Amy deserves a treat. London becomes so tiresome to one who has been country bred as she has."

With the exchange of courtesies, an account of Lord Brinker's illness, from which he had very nearly recovered, and discussion of the latest *on dits*, the four women passed the drive to Wayside pleasantly. Chris had agreed that the abduction should not take place until after the visit to Mrs. Armstrong, to avoid alarming Amy's frail mother, who would be expecting her.

Amy noticed Esmée's unsettled nerves and managed to get her alone for a tête-à-tête while the older ladies were enjoying tea.

"What is it, dearest? You are nervous as a cat."

"N-nothing. Oh, Amy, is your uncle going to force you to wed Vendercroft?"

"I don't know." Amy sighed. "What a good friend you are, to be so concerned. To tell the truth, I have begun to think I may have to marry him."

"I am amazed that you seem in such good spirits today if you think so."

"I am just trying not to think about it for a few hours. And I don't want Mama to know about it. She would worry so. I must marry someone who can provide her with a comfortable home and the medicine and treatment she needs. If that someone is less than desirable to me, well, I shall simply have to make the best of it. No one else who is eligible has offered. I'd prefer not to marry Vendercroft, but I think I can manage him."

"You do?" Esmée wrinkled up her nose. The three conspirators had not revealed Nathan's cousin's experience to her, as it wasn't suitable for female ears, but sufficient hints had been dropped to make her cold with fear for her friend.

"But wouldn't it be terrible if you couldn't?"

Amy gnawed at her lower lip, remembering Vendercroft's fanaticism. "Indeed, yes. But what else can I do?" To her chagrin, Lord Sunder, who had been her last hope among the *ton*, had gone to Paris a few days before.

Esmée had no answer for this, but decided that she could not reveal the conspiracy after all, as she had been strongly tempted to do when she had seen that Amy seemed in such good spirits. Now she knew her friend was just shamming it. *For her sake, I must be strong. I just hope my mother never learns my part in this,* she thought with a shudder, as the carriage drew away from Wayside later that afternoon, on its way to a rendezvous with fate.

Chapter Fourteen

"*T*hat was a pleasant visit," Mrs. Puckett said, shaking out her parasol as their carriage left Wayside.

"Indeed, yes," Aunt Edwina said. "So kind of you to take us. Amabel hasn't seen her mother in quite a while, and I always delight in visiting my daughters. Such a pleasant day, too. High time we had some pretty weather."

"The sun is almost hot. Esmée, get your parasol up."

Noticing that Amy seemed lost in a brown study, Aunt Edwina leaned forward and touched her hands, which she was twisting in her lap. "I thought Delia was looking well, didn't you, love?"

Amy nodded and attempted a smile. "Wayside agrees with her."

"I was surprised to hear her express a wish to come to London with us. But you did right to remind her that Dr. Gantry expressly forbade it. The London air would be so bad for her lungs."

Amy frowned and tugged at the fingers of her gloves, her mind revolving around the conversation with her mother, who had brought up the rumors that Vendercroft was courting her.

"I should not wish you to marry him, dearest," she had said. "Not a good man, not at all. And closer to my age than yours."

Amy had soothed her mother and tried to convince her that he was not so very bad. "I know he has been rakish in the past, but he is looking for a wife, so I am sure he has settled down.

And he has some interesting ideas about diseases and tooth decay. I really think he is something of a genius."

Her mother had looked skeptical and raised the notion of coming to London, which Amy had suppressed firmly. Not only would the London air be bad for her lungs, Victor's bullying would be very bad for her heart. Even worse would be her distress once she got to know Lord Vendercroft.

Lost in her thoughts, she had no awareness of the conversation among the other three in the barouche until Mrs. Puckett exclaimed, "Why is that carriage pulling across the road? Pull up, James," she called unnecessarily to her coachman, who had perforce to do so or crash into the larger carriage.

Amy turned around in her seat and half stood, as did Esmée beside her. "Why, it is Christopher Ponselle driving it. I did not know he could drive a four-in-hand."

"He doesn't drive very well, if that is his notion of how to go on," her aunt huffed.

"I expect he wants to speak with us. Show off his prowess, perhaps. Is that Nathan up beside him? And William riding alongside?" As she spoke, Nathan climbed down from the carriage and started at a run for the Pucketts' barouche. William, who was leading a horse, dismounted, tied both horses to the back, and followed his friend.

When Nathan reached their carriage, he greeted Mrs. Puckett and Lady Brinker courteously, but there was something very uneasy in his manner.

Mrs. Puckett returned his greeting frostily. "What is the meaning of this? Why have you blocked our path?"

"I do beg your pardon, ma' am."

"You'll do more than beg her pardon," the Puckett coachman growled, raising his whip menacingly. "Tell your driver to move that carriage on the instant, you scamp."

"In a moment, my man. The thing is, we wish a word with Miss Armstrong."

"Is . . . is something wrong?" Amy's heart rose in her throat at the way both young men were looking at her.

"No, not at all. That is . . ."

"Well, speak up, Mr. Holmes," Mrs. Puckett ordered. "The sun is hot, and we have to get back to London in time to rest before going out tonight."

"We need to speak to her privately," Nathan said. He had put down the steps and now opened the door and stepped up on the first rung, holding out his hand to Amy.

"Nonsense. Young man, I think you are foxed! Speak to her privately in the middle of the road in the middle of nowhere? Call on her at home, or talk to her at the rout tonight."

"It won't wait until then, I am afraid." Nathan stepped up to the top step and again held out his hand to Amy, who shrank back. The hairs were standing up on her neck at this odd behavior.

"Oh, do go with them, Amy," Esmée urged her. "Whatever silly bee they have got in their bonnets, best to find out so we can get moving."

Nathan looked offended by this comment. "Men don't have bonnets," he protested. "Can't say we do."

"I agree with Mrs. Puckett, Nathan. You are acting decidedly foxed." Amy looked back at the larger carriage blocking the road. "Is Christopher well to go also? He shouldn't be driving a four-in-hand in that state."

William stepped up beside the carriage. Without so much as a word of greeting, he gave his friend a shove. "Get on with it, Nathan. Get her down from there. If t'were done, t'were best done quickly."

This particular Shakespearean reference did not exactly soothe Amy or her aunt, who shrieked, "Murder! They mean to murder us!"

"Nothing like that, ma'am, I assure you," Nathan said, looking distressed. "Mean only the best for Miss Armstrong. The thing is, Amy . . ."

William tugged Nathan off the carriage steps and took his place. "Gudgeon! They'll talk you out of it," he said, seizing Amy by both arms. "Let's go!" He dragged her out of her seat. Before any of the carriage's astonished occupants could do more than voice their displeasure, Amy found herself pulled down the steps and thrust into Nathan's arms. He gathered her up and ran with her toward their waiting carriage.

"No. No, you mustn't." Amy began to thrash around, pummeling him with her hands. "Nathan, put me down. Nathan, if you have an ounce of regard for me . . ."

"I love you, Miss Armstrong. Love you to distraction." He set her down by the carriage door and opened it.

Amy saw Chris leaning over the edge of the box, watching the proceedings with a very uncomfortable look on his face.

"Christopher, help me. Don't go along with this. You mustn't . . ."

Abruptly she felt a silk scarf thrust into her mouth. William had approached her from behind. He tugged it taut and swiftly tied it so she could not speak.

"They're coming," Nathan said. "The coachman and Mrs. Puckett are getting down from the barouche."

"Help me tie her hands. Amy, don't struggle so. We mean it for the best." William and Nathan grappled with her and in spite of her frantic struggles, Amy felt her hands tied behind her back. Then she was lifted up and thrust into the carriage.

She heard Chris call out, "Be careful with her." Nathan climbed in beside her and uttered soothing words while holding her down on the floor of the carriage, which was thickly padded with silk cushions.

William swiftly tied her feet, then linked the cord to the one tying her hands, so that she could not rise. She looked imploringly at Nathan, who looked imploringly at William.

"Maybe we shouldn't . . ."

"Come out of there. Talk about speaking eyes. She'll have you setting her free if you stay in there with her." He jerked his friend out and urged him up into the carriage box. "Go, Chris." He untied the horses as the carriage began moving, and with the Puckett coachman's whip whistling around his head, mounted and raced after it.

"My word! They've abducted her!" Mrs. Puckett stood in the road, staring after the departing carriage. "I never imagined such a thing could happen."

Lady Brinker frantically called out to her, "Come. We must go after them. Quickly. Make haste!"

Nothing loath, the coachman hurried back to the barouche and helped the ladies in. Hastily taking his seat, he gathered his reins and took up his whip.

"Oh, Mama, don't go after them," Esmée begged. "They are going to marry her. It is for her own good."

"All of them?" Mrs. Puckett stared at her daughter. "Don't be ridiculous. Are you involved in this, Esmée?"

"Oh, no, Mother. It is just . . . I know them. I know they have been worried about her, and I am sure that one of them plans to marry her."

The carriage began to move. "Just a moment, James," Mrs. Puckett said as the coachman prepared to whip up the team.

"Don't listen to her, Mrs. Puckett," Lady Brinker said, clutching at her sleeve. "What can you mean, Miss Puckett? Let those young ruffians abduct your best friend? Three men and a closed carriage! What can you be thinking?"

"I expect she is thinking that Amy would be better off with any one of them than with Lord Vendercroft," Mrs. Puckett said. She was pale as a sheet, but had a determined look in her eye. "I do not think we should pursue them."

"You astound me. How would you feel if it were your daughter? Three men brutally snatching her out of her carriage, binding her, gagging her? What can they be thinking? I thought they were respectable young men."

"They are. But they know that your husband has received an offer from Vendercroft, an offer which he wishes Amy to accept. She'd be better off with one of them than with that evil man. I must say I think the less of you, Lady Brinker, if you support your husband in this."

"I don't. Oh, indeed I don't! But you don't understand. Whatever their intentions, Amy is in great danger. She is gagged."

"Don't be a goose. That is not a great matter. Uncomfortable, but not dangerous."

"In Amy's case it is very dangerous. She suffers severely from carriage sickness, you see."

Esmée gasped. "Oh, no!"

"Why did you not tell me this before. We have wasted too much time! James, you heard. We must pursue them."

"I heard, madam." He plied the whip and his team sprang into action. The carriage surged forward. Mrs. Puckett held on to her hat, for their carriage bounced fiercely as it traversed the rutted country lane. Lady Brinker gave a little moan and clung to the side of the carriage. Esmée began to cry.

"Did he tie her too tight? Is the gag too tight? I think the gag was unnecessary. Let's stop and take it off." Chris started to pull up on the reins.

"No! William is right. She'll talk us out of it. Just looking into her eyes almost had me giving it up."

"She fought so hard. Maybe it is a mistake. Maybe . . ."

"Maybe she should marry Vendercroft?"

Chris shook his head vehemently. He had beads of perspiration on his upper lip, and his stomach felt queasy from the sight of his beloved struggling with the other two young men. "If only there was another way."

"Well, there isn't. Here. Have a drink. It will steady you. Gave me courage. Never could have gone through with it without it. Good French brandy. Legal, too," he added as he saw Chris hesitate.

Chris regarded the flask Nathan held toward him warily. "Don't care if it's legal or smuggled, ninny. It's just that brandy never seems to steady me. Rather the opposite. And I'm not that practiced at driving a four-in-hand."

"All the mail coach drivers drink. Makes them more relaxed. Here."

Chris reluctantly took a short pull from the flask. He had no head for liquor, and knew it. But the warmth and numbness that spread through him convinced him it was just the thing for this situation. He took it out of Nathan's hands to prevent him from drinking the rest. "That's the dandy!" He took a long drink, and the world looked more cheerful. He grinned and leaned back on the seat.

"Doubtless she'll be thankful! Hug my neck when I take her out of the carriage."

"Or mine! Got just as much reason to be thankful to me, you know."

"Perhaps she'll hug William." Chris frowned. "He was the one who did most of the work. Got the carriage. It's his yacht we'll use to get to Scotland."

"Not William. Never would tell him so, but she'd never choose William. Too short, you see."

Chris agreed. "Besides, he gagged and tied her. Likely if she's angry with anyone, it will be him." *One rival down.* He smiled, beginning to spin air dreams about how grateful Amy would be when she learned she was to marry him instead of Vendercroft.

"Speed it up," William called up to them. "They are pursuing us."

"Right." Chris looked down pityingly at the rival he and Nathan had, in their own minds, defeated. He whipped up the team, and the carriage bounced merrily along the short distance from the country road that led from Wayside back to the Highgate Road. When he made the turn south, the carriage swung wide and rose up on two wheels briefly.

"Lord! A bit too relaxed maybe," Chris murmured. He looked questioningly at William, who had shouted out a warning as they made the perilous turn. "They still after us?"

William shook his head. "I don't know. Can't see them. They can't catch us, though, with just two horses. Keep going, but be careful, will you. Nearly overset her."

"Let me take the reins awhile." Nathan tried to take them from Chris.

"You don't know how to drive a four-in-hand." Chris batted at Nathan's hands, noting that his friend seemed a bit foxed.

"Good time to learn."

"Not while we're in the middle of an abduction, gudgeon." Chris smirked. Amy would never choose such a lack-wit for her husband. "No time to waste. Once we get her on William's yacht, they'll never catch us. They'll never guess we're not heading north. Everyone who elopes heads north. Who would ever guess we're off to the coast?"

"Not Brinker. Lord, I'd give a monkey to see his red face as he realizes we've given him the slip."

Both young men whooped with glee, and Chris snapped his whip over the heads of his leaders.

Chapter Fifteen

"*M*axbridge! Maxbridge. Do stop! I wish to speak with you."

Just on the point of entering his town house, Max slowed his steps and turned at the imperious summons. "Aunt Phinea! I beg your pardon. I did not see you." He assisted her down from her carriage.

"No, your head is in the clouds, to all appearances. Where is Christopher?"

"Why, he has just this morning gone into the country with some friends for a few days."

"With his friends indeed! With a particular friend, it seems to me, and not what I would have expected from such a young boy, and so well brought up, too!"

"What can you mean, ma'am?" Maxbridge offered his arm, and Lady Marchant leaned her by no means negligible weight upon it.

"Let us walk a bit. I don't want the servants to hear this. I have just come from my dressmaker, where I had a most interesting encounter with Christopher."

"Christopher? At your dressmaker?"

"Carrying out package after package. Enough feminine fripperies to clothe half a dozen Cyprians, I don't doubt. He and one of his young friends, Nathan Holmes, I think, were stowing them in the boot of a rather shabby traveling carriage. If they are going out of town, they mean to have company of the most dubious sort."

"You astonish me, Aunt. Christopher? And Nathan? Perhaps they were merely doing the pretty for some young female friend of theirs."

"Ha! Playing store clerk would be bad enough, but I'd gladly think it instead of what I *am* thinking. Nor was there any young female of any sort about."

"Perhaps . . . perhaps Nathan has a sister who is going on the trip with them?"

"If that is so, why were they both quite scarlet with embarrassment at being so caught out? And to my knowledge, Nathan Holmes has no sister."

Max thought a moment. "Nor William Tremayne, the other young man he is traveling with, as far as I know." He wrinkled his brow in deep thought. "And why a shabby traveling carriage? He has taken mine for his baggage and servant, though he of course is riding."

"Humpf. I think you are out of touch with your nephew, Maximilian."

"I have been rather preoccupied lately," he admitted.

"If I were you, I'd look into this party of his. An orgy, or perhaps an elopement, if you ask me. I saw into the boot as they loaded those packages in. There were bandboxes, hatboxes, and parasols, and I don't know what else."

"I shall, indeed, look into it, Aunt Phinea." He patted her arm. "Will you come in now?"

"No, I must be on my way. And you must be on yours. Put a stop to this, will you, Maximilian? It would break my heart to think that Christopher is beginning a career as a rakehell, and him not yet nineteen."

"I shall, Aunt. I'll set out after him as soon as I can."

Once inside his town house, Maxbridge stood frowning down at the tiles of the entryway, ignoring the butler who stood ready to take his hat and gloves. None of the three young men had ever shown any previous interest in Cyprians. "Perhaps an elopement," Aunt Phinea had said.

Who would the young makebate be eloping with, if not Amabel Armstrong? Christopher daily proclaimed his love for her, and loudly expressed his anxiety that she was about to be forced into a marriage with Lord Vendercroft. Maximilian had not liked the idea above half himself but he had seen Miss Armstrong driving with Vendercroft in the park. Her demeanor had convinced him that she had overcome her objections to the marquess. It hadn't convinced Chris.

"Put her out of your mind and enjoy the rest of your stay in London. The Season will soon be over," Max had urged him. It had been advice he had had difficulty following himself. He found that Miss Armstrong intruded on his thoughts constantly, to the point of madness.

"You are all on end about that girl," Mason had observed dryly one evening. "As well to admit you are hooked."

"She has made it clear she will throw me back." Maxbridge had changed the subject, for it was as pleasurable to him as a sore tooth.

A day or two later Chris had informed him he was going to visit his friend William at his coastal estate near Shoreham.

Elopement! Could it be that Chris's desire to rescue Miss Armstrong had led him to elope with her? Would she have agreed to such a thing?

"I shall be going out again," Max told his puzzled butler. "Send to the stables and ask that my curricle be prepared for me. Have it held in readiness. I have a short errand to run first." Max turned on his heel and hastened to Lord Brinker's town house. It was but a two-block walk.

When he asked for Lady Brinker, the butler, poorly concealing a knowing smirk, said she was not at home, and before Max could ask, said that Miss Armstrong was also unavailable. Clearly the servant thought Lord Maxbridge was joining the ranks of the beauty's many suitors.

"Are they together?" Max asked.

The butler raised his eyebrows. "I'm sure I couldn't say, my lord."

Max ran his eyes over the servant. His livery was shabby

and none too clean, and his attempts at a genteel accent were
less than acceptable. Lord Brinker might be spending a fortune
on Miss Armstrong's clothes, but he clearly wasted little of the
ready on his servants. Max reached into his coat pocket, took
out his wallet, and drew out a bill. The butler looked from it
into Max's eyes, and smiled.

"Miss Armstrong and Lady Brinker have indeed gone out
together."

"Thank you." Much relieved, Max passed the bill to the butler and left. But as he walked back toward his home, his mind
couldn't let go of Chris's worried face during their last discussion, when he had insisted that Miss Armstrong mustn't be
permitted to marry Vendercroft, even if she thought she
wanted to. Would the boy do something so shatter-brained as
to abduct the scheming minx?

Nathan had been with him at the dressmakers, Aunt Phinea
said. Nathan was to make one of the party at William's country
home. Chris, Nathan, and William were the most devoted
members of Miss Armstrong's court. Would they conspire together to abduct her?

The idea was so outrageous that Max laughed at himself.
Yet once in his head, the thought buzzed around like a trapped
fly, and he soon found his steps turning back to Lord Brinker's
house and another tête-à-tête with his butler.

"Where did Miss Armstrong and Lady Brinker go, do you
know? And with whom?" He already had his wallet out.

"I believe they went to visit their family at Wayside, my
lord. Do you know where it is?" At Max's nod, he volunteered,
"They drove in the company of Mrs. Puckett and her daughter."

Max placed a generous wad of bills in his hand and hurried
back to his town house, where he summoned his curricle.
Probably I am going on a wild goose chase, he thought, *but
better to be sure. I won't know a moment's peace until I see
with my own eyes that she is in the custody of her aunt.*

He made very good time on the turnpike to Hampstead, and
by mid-afternoon had turned onto the rutted country lane he

had previously taken with Amabel to Wayside. When he joined the smoother country road that ran in front of the Wayside property, his sense of foreboding grew, for he saw the Puckett's barouche bounding down the road toward him. Their unseemly haste slackened, then came to a halt as they recognized him.

"Oh, Lord Maxbridge," Lady Brinker wailed. "The most terrible thing. Your nephew and his friends have stolen Amabel. You must stop them, and right away! It is a matter of life and death that you catch up to them, my lord," Lady Brinker almost screamed. "Please, go!"

"Now, Lady Brinker, coming it too strong. I'd like to wring their necks, of course, but silly scamps that they are, they won't hurt her."

"Not on purpose, but she gets carriage sick, you see. Desperately, terribly so."

Maxbridge could not help but grin at Lady Brinker's histrionics. "Unpleasant, but hardly fatal."

"It will be, if she gets sick with that gag on." Lady Brinker broke into tears.

"Gag!" He looked to the other two for confirmation.

"Yes, gag!" Mrs. Puckett nodded. "They dragged her from our carriage, gagged and tied her, and threw her into theirs. None of them stayed with her, either. William is riding, and Chris and Nathan are driving the carriage."

Max felt a thrill of terror run through him. "I shall pursue them instantly. They headed for the North Road, I make no doubt?"

"I expect so," Mrs. Puckett said. "They aren't too far ahead of you. Perhaps fifteen minutes. I am surprised you didn't see them. I expect they turned north just before you turned off for Wayside."

"Wait! They aren't going up the North Road. They are returning to London."

All three adults turned astonished eyes on Esmée. "You knew about this?" Maxbridge glared at her.

"I did, and I'm not sorry, but I didn't know they'd tie her up and gag her, nor did I know she suffered from carriage sickness. William has brought his yacht there. They plan to sail back down the Thames and then make their way up the coast to Scotland."

"Why didn't I pass them, then? Oh! I collect there is another road to Wayside besides that cow path I just took."

"Yes," Lady Brinker said. "You turn left at that big elm just ahead, where the path you took joins this road."

"Don't fear, Lady Brinker. I will catch them. Wait for me here, if you please." He tipped his hat to the ladies and turned his curricle around, dashing off at a furious pace.

There was little traffic and Maxbridge made good time. He came upon a likely coach shortly after reaching the Highgate Road. It was weaving around a bit, evidence of an inexperienced coachman. Swiftly pulling alongside, he saw that William was riding ahead of the coach, leading a horse, and Chris was driving, dressed as a coachman and looking to be having a grand time tooling the team of job horses. Nathan sat beside him dressed as a footman, a flask held loosely in his hand. If the matter had not been so serious, Maxbridge would have laughed at their sudden change of expression from delight to chagrin at perceiving who it was that had driven up beside them.

"Pull that thing over," he shouted.

Jaw firming, Chris cracked his whip over his team's head instead.

"She suffers from carriage sickness," Maxbridge shouted.

It took a few seconds for the implications of this to sink in, but then with horror in his eyes Chris pulled up his team. William turned back with a shout of objection, but Maxbridge paid him no heed. He leapt from his curricle before it had completely stopped and raced for the carriage door.

He did not immediately see her in the dark interior of the coach, but instinctively reached for the floor, where his fingers encountered a dark blanket. He jerked this out and saw Amabel, lying on her side, eyes wide, straining to rise.

With an oath he untied the gag and jerked it from her mouth, then turned her and began untying her bonds. He quickly dispatched the cord that had linked her hands and feet to keep her from getting up.

Chris leaned into the door beside him "Is she . . ."

"I never could have imagined you could do anything so brutal."

"Please, I must . . . hurry . . . outside," Amy gasped. Without untying her hands or feet, Maxbridge pulled a decidedly green Amabel Armstrong from the carriage and held her as she began to retch. The three young men shrank back, appalled at the sight of their goddess casting up her accounts.

When her spasms had passed, Amy began to cry. Maxbridge leaned her against him and untied her hands. She clung to him, sobbing. He lifted her up and carried her to the side of the road, under the broad arch of an ancient elm.

"Shhh. Shhh. It's fine now. You will be better soon." He used his handkerchief to mop her face as the young men drew nearer.

"Nathan, untie her feet. Chris, get something to wash her face with. Is there anything to drink on that carriage?"

"Some ale, sir," Nathan volunteered. "We packed a picnic, you see."

"A picnic!" Loathing laced Maxbridge's voice.

"Well, yes, we did not exactly like to stop at an inn, sir."

"You thought of everything, in fact! Get me the damn ale," Maxbridge roared. Chris had already drawn a wicker basket from the boot of the carriage, and hastened to bring it to his uncle.

"Dip that napkin in the ice melt around the ale. Give it to me." Maxbridge cradled Amy in his arm and bathed her face with the cold wet cloth.

"Here, rinse your mouth with this," he told her.

"No, I c-can't." Amy struggled out of his arms and crawled a few feet away, where she retched again. When she had subsided, she took the cloth from his hands and wiped her face. "Th-thank you. Oh, my lord, I am afraid I have soiled your . . ." Embarrassment made Amy cry again.

"It is of no account." Maxbridge pulled her back into the circle of his arms. "Now, rest a bit. Shh. You're safe." He rocked her as a mother would a child, stroking her forehead and hair, and she subsided against his chest, sobbing softly into his shoulder.

The bumpy ride had been the most terrible time of Amy's life, for at every second she had been sure she would cast up her accounts and die of suffocation. Once her ordeal had ended, it felt good to give in to tears, especially with such a comforting shoulder to lean on.

After a few minutes Maxbridge looked up into the distressed eyes of his nephew, who held out his hand in supplication. He shook his head angrily. Chris turned and walked to where Nathan and William stood nearby, holding the horses. Together they awaited the peal that the older man surely would ring upon their heads.

"Meant it for the best," William said defensively when Maxbridge glared at them.

At this, Amy turned her head so she could look at him. "What *did* you m-mean by it?"

"Meant to marry you."

"So did I," Nathan said.

"I did, too," Chris declared, but in a very subdued tone.

She looked from one to the other in amazement. "All three of you?" Amy giggled, that little choking giggle that had first endeared her to Maxbridge.

"Keep you out of Vendercroft's clutches. Better off with me," William said.

"Or me," Nathan snapped.

"Or me," Chris said. "Give you your choice. You'd be better off with any of us than with him."

"Oh, my." Amy mopped at her eyes and struggled to keep from laughing out loud. She sat up and pulled away from Max, so he stood and then assisted her to her feet. "How very kind you are. If you had not very nearly killed me in the process, I'd be grateful to you."

"Grateful!" Max fumed. "Young fools!"

"Not kind," Chris responded urgently, coming forward to take her hands in his. "In love. Desperately, utterly in love. Please say you'll marry me. We can go on to Scotland right now, just as planned."

Amy pulled away from him. "I had no idea . . . I thought you were my friend." Betrayal rang in her voice.

"I am. Your very best friend. But I want to be more."

"I love you, too," Nathan said.

"And I," William hastened to add.

Amy shook her head and looked at Maxbridge again. He regarded her assessingly. "What say you, Miss Armstrong? You would be better off with any one of them than Vendercroft, you know."

"I know, but I cannot," she whispered, looking urgently, pleadingly into his eyes.

Maxbridge felt heat rising in him at that look, but something in him resisted what it seemed to say. The old wound still throbbed. Instead of encouraging her as he wished, he heard himself sneering, "None of them can afford you, can they? It isn't just a matter of satisfying your *uncle's* purse. *You* want Vendercroft's purse." He lifted her chin in his hand. "I can afford you, Miss Armstrong. Shall I offer for you?"

She jerked away from that hand, moments ago so tender and soothing against her skin. "How dare you make sport of my predicament?"

"I don't. I mean what I say. I am prepared to marry you. Against my better judgment, mind." He looked at his nephew, who had drawn in his breath sharply, then turned back to Amy. "But I desire you, I have to admit. You come rather dear, but I am sure you will be worth it. Your uncle will not like it, perhaps, but I shall offer enough to make it worth his while to overlook our long enmity."

"You, my lord, are insufferably arrogant and odious. I am as tired of your insults as I am of being abducted! I want a good deal more than to satisfy my uncle's purse, yes! But what I want, *you* can't supply."

"Ah, I see. You want to be a marchioness instead of a mere countess."

"You have the right of it, Lord Maxbridge. Why settle for less when I can have more?" Tossing her head, she strode away from him. He would have followed, but Chris confronted him, fists at the ready.

"Trying to steal her from under my very nose. And in so insulting a way! I should draw your cork for you!"

"I should like for you to try," Maxbridge growled. "It would give me great satisfaction to spill some of your claret right now. But I can't steal her from you, you looby. She isn't yours. Can't you see what she is?"

"It is you who can't see. For a few minutes there, I thought perhaps you actually cared for her. I could have borne that. But to offer for her only out of lust, and to hurt her feelings into the bargain! Your blind prejudice is disgusting."

"You are the one who is blind. She would rather marry Vendercroft than be poor."

"Why wouldn't she marry you, then?"

Max paused momentarily. *Why wouldn't she? Why had he even offered?* The proposal had surprised him as much as it had the others. "I expect she wanted it wrapped up in some sort of pretty declaration of love. Well, she doesn't offer love, so why should I or any other man pretend to it?"

"I wouldn't have to pretend." Chris looked as if he might attempt to challenge his uncle again.

"Wait!" Nathan started running toward the road.

To his utter astonishment Maxbridge saw that Amy had mounted his curricle and was turning his team. They had drifted to the side of the road to crop grass after he had abandoned them to go to her aid.

"Come back here with my curricle!" But she was underway, springing them.

Unsuccessful in chasing her down on foot, Maxbridge thrust his hand through his hair. "Little liar. Said she was afraid of horses!"

"Afraid of them, yes, but not of driving them. Gave her some lessons myself," Nathan said proudly.

"As did I," William chimed in. "Becoming quite the whip."

"Not with my team, she isn't!" Maxbridge grabbed the bridle of Nathan's horse, vaulted into the saddle, and took off after her.

"Shall I go after them?" William asked.

"No. Let us get that carriage turned around. We won't be needing it, after all, it seems." Nathan started for the road.

"Well, I'm going after them. He might do her an injury!" Chris reached for the bridle of William's horse.

"Better let them have it out. You had the right of it, Chris. For a while there, I thought he must have feelings for her. Mean to say, ugly moment, that. Couldn't have done it myself. And he dealt with her so . . . tenderly."

"Yes." Chris shuddered at the thought of what might have happened. "And the way she clung to him, the way she looked at him, makes me think she might have warmed to him if he hadn't said such ugly things. But now she knows his true feelings, and even if he meant it when he offered for her, she'll never have him. He has quite a temper. I'd better go after them, be there to assist her."

"Miss Armstrong is a match for him," William said. "Not gagged now!"

"Yes, she has a sharp tongue." Chris grinned, then his shoulders slumped. "Be glad she didn't give us the dressing down we needed. Never have any of us now."

"Never would have, willingly."

"Well, I don't want her unwillingly." Chris tugged the bridle out of William's hands. "I only mean to see she gets back to her aunt without my uncle hurting her further."

Maxbridge rode alongside his curricle and ordered Amy to stop.

"I won't," she shouted, looking at the road ahead. "Do go away. I am not experienced enough to drive and argue with you."

"You will!" He leaned down and grabbed for the reins. She

hit at him with the whip, and he jerked it from her, throwing it away. His horses became agitated at this unusual activity, and began to jib and rear. "Pull up or they'll run away with you," Maxbridge shouted.

"Then it will be on your head!" She gave the reins a shake, and the cattle bolted forward. He raced after her, and wasted no more time trying to get her to stop, but rode to the team's head and, leaning down, took the near horse's bridle close to the bit and brought them to a halt. To make sure she didn't get away again, he led them off the road and across a bumpy stretch of grass to where a small wood lay. He made sure that they were hidden somewhat from the road before letting go of the bridle. She tried to back them out but lacked sufficient expertise to do so before he had dismounted and dragged her out of the curricle.

Shaking with fury and a little alarmed at the expression on his face, Amy struggled vigorously with him. "Take me back to my aunt!"

"I will, momentarily. First I want to understand something. Do you really contemplate marriage with Vendercroft?"

"That is no business of yours, my lord."

"I am making it my business. Do you?"

"I would prefer not to marry him, but I would rather marry him than you!" Wounded pride gave her declaration a spiteful tone.

"Oh, you would, would you?" He jerked her into his arms and kissed her. At first it was a hard, demanding kiss, but quickly his lips softened against hers, and he began nibbling at her rigid mouth. "Come on, Amabel," he whispered. "Let me make love to you. Open your mouth."

"Certainly not," she said, unwittingly offering him access. The intimate kiss he forced on her at first frightened, then warmed her to her very toes. Before he pulled away, she had begun to melt against him, returning the stroke of his tongue with her own. She clung to him as he lifted his head and looked into her eyes. His eyes were smoky with desire.

"Ah, God, you are as passionate as I guessed you would be.

Now, let us have no more nonsense from you, my girl. You had far rather have my kisses than Vendercroft's, hadn't you?"

She struggled against him. "No, my lord. For his kisses would merely repel me. Yours would steal my soul and give me nothing but contempt in return."

Maxbridge groped for words, but before he could reply, he heard his nephew's voice.

"She is right, Uncle. You offer her a devil's bargain. Let her go." Chris gripped Max's shoulder and tugged on him.

"You are *de trop*, nephew." Maxbridge shrugged free of Chris's grip.

"I think *you* are. The lady is unwilling, you see."

Since Amy had taken advantage of Maxbridge's distraction to jerk out of his arms and move away, this statement had some credibility.

"She will think she has married the devil if she marries Vendercroft. I thought you understood that when you undertook such desperate measures today."

"*Do* you mean to marry him, Amy?"

"I don't know. But if I do, it will not be so very bad."

Chris's brow knit. "You should know his first wife died under suspicious circumstances, and his second left him, claiming he had tortured her."

"Tortured her?"

"Made her drink boiling water, among other indignities. Nathan told me. She was his cousin."

"Boiling water?" Amy laughed. "No such thing. That would defeat the purpose, you see. It would cause infection, not prevent it. Just very hot water, Chris."

Chris looked his astonishment. "How can you laugh at such a thing?"

"I shall know how to manage him, you see. Oh, dear Chris, don't worry so about me."

"Amy, please. Reconsider. I shall not be a poor man when I reach my majority . . ."

"*Et tu, Brute?*" She looked as if she would begin to cry.

"No, I didn't mean it that way. But I shall be able to provide

for your mother and your nieces, which is what you care for, I
know."

"No, Chris, I can't marry you. Especially not now."

"You won't forgive me for today."

"It isn't that. You, and the others, really did mean well. I
bear you no ill will. But knowing what I know now . . ."

"That I love you?"

"Yes, partly that." *And partly that I shamefully desire your
uncle.* "It wouldn't be fair, you see. For I don't love you, not
the way you deserve to be loved, not the way you would wish
to be loved." She put up her hand and touched his cheek tenderly. "Then, there is another thing. I have spoken to you of
the problems my parents faced as a result of their elopement?
The snubbing, the separation from family and friends, the
harm to my father's career?"

"Yes, but . . ."

"I won't do it. Not to my husband, not to my children. Or
rather, I would do it only if I loved the man I ran away with as
deeply as my mother loved my father. *And* he loved me." She
slanted a look at Maxbridge.

Chris sighed. "I think I understand. But you don't understand the depth of Vendercroft's cruelty. I can scarce explain it
to you, it is of so delicate a nature."

Amy frowned and gnawed at the tip of her glove. "I will tell
my uncle what you have said, and ask him to speak to Nathan
about it. He won't force me to marry a man who is truly
cruel." She spoke with more confidence in her uncle's benevo-
lence than she actually possessed.

"Then he won't force you to marry Vendercroft."

"Well, there you are, then." Amy tried for a cheerful tone.
"Will you drive me back to my aunt?"

Chris looked at his uncle, who nodded his head.
Maxbridge's expression was impenetrable as he watched Chris
assist her into the curricle and back it around. Amy looked at
him, trying to read something in his eyes. Not seeing anything
but blankness, she lifted her chin and looked straight ahead as
Chris drove her away.

Chapter Sixteen

"Oh, dear, do you think you have made the right decision?" Lady Brinker looked askance at Amy. "I don't wish to be selfish, my dear. Though their methods were deplorable, I cannot but agree with Mrs. Puckett that these young men had the right idea. You would be better off with one of them than Lord Vendercroft."

"That is just what I think," Esmée chimed in.

"Dear Aunt Edwina!" Amy leaned forward and gave her aunt a quick hug. "You know how it would enrage him. You would take the brunt of my uncle's anger. How could I do such a thing to you?"

"Well, I daresay I shall endure one more beating," she said, her voice quavering a little.

"Not on my account. I shall come about, never fear. Do you think your coachman can be persuaded to say nothing of this, Mrs. Puckett?"

"He is an old family retainer, and will do as I say. But I wish you would allow us to convince you. . . ."

"I hope that Christopher will persuade the other young men to be silent, as he promised. Esmée?"

"I would never do anything to hurt you. I shall never forget these last minutes, worrying if Lord Maxbridge had reached you in time. I would have felt responsible . . ."

"And rightly so." Mrs. Puckett glared at her daughter.

"But, Mother, you agree that Amy should have gone with them."

"It is one thing to endorse an elopement as a means of escape from an odious connection, quite another to aid in an abduction."

At Esmée's crestfallen expression, Amy reassured her, "I know you meant well, but I do hope you won't encourage any more such adventures." Before her friend could reply, she rushed on, "Esmée, did you see that fashion plate in the May issue of *La Belle Assemblée*? Such a hideous gown. I do hope orange will not become the rage. Oh, did I tell you I have chosen the dress I will wear to my come-out ball? It is a pale pink with a white lace overdress."

Amy directed the conversation carefully away from her marriage prospects, and was rewarded by seeing her aunt lose her pallor and cease trembling by the time they returned to London. But when they drew up in front of their town house, Edwina became agitated again.

"Oh, dear!" Her hands flew to her cheek. "It is that dreadful man's curricle, is it not?"

Amy turned around and peered over the side of the barouche. "Lord Vendercroft? Yes, I believe it is. What a mess I am. I had hoped to avoid being seen in this state." She thanked Mrs. Puckett for the drive, and gave Esmée a reassuring hug.

"I will run up the stairs as fast as I can when I enter the house. You will tell him I must change before going for a drive with him, won't you, Aunt Edwina?"

But her stratagem failed, for Lord Brinker and Lord Vendercroft were waiting in the foyer when they entered. "Where have you been?" her uncle demanded. "You should have been back here an hour since."

"Oh, I . . . we had a little problem."

Vendercroft recoiled from her. "More than a *little* problem, it seems. You are positively disheveled, Miss Armstrong. You look as if you had rolled on the ground and you . . . you reek!"

He plucked a handkerchief from his sleeve and held it to his nose disdainfully.

She hung her head. "I was ill, sir. Please, Uncle, if you will excuse me, I will go up and change."

"Ill? Why ill?" Vendercroft's look of disgust changed to alarm, and he put even more distance between them.

"Oh, the silly chit suffers from carriage sickness," Brinker explained to him, his voice too hearty.

"In an open carriage? Is this true, Miss Armstrong?"

"N-not usually. It may have been something I ate. I am quite sure it is not contagious, my lord. If you were wishful of going for a drive . . . ?"

"Not today, I thank you. I will send round to inquire after your health in a day or two. Your servant, Lady Brinker." Vendercroft sketched the slightest bow and made a hasty exit.

"Of all the ill luck," Victor exclaimed.

"Once you hear what really happened this afternoon, you may think it very good luck! I have learned that Lord Vendercroft is entirely ineligible."

Victor glared at her. "If you could see the mounting pile of bills, you would not think so."

"Let me change clothes, Uncle, and we will have a heart-to-heart talk."

Once she had explained matters to him, Amy could not tell if Victor understood or cared how dangerous Vendercroft was, but he at least understood with just what abhorrence others viewed the match. She took care to elaborate upon the effect this might have on his daughters' future.

This made him so distraught, he tugged at his hair with both hands. "The duns will be invading us before long! Once it is seen that no rich match is in the offing for you, my entire financial house of cards will come tumbling down."

"I had no idea it was as bad as that."

"It is! If you don't marry well, and soon, it will not be just you and your mother who will be out on the street! If it is not to be Vendercroft, it must be Braebarne. I am going to invite him to dinner before your ball, along with as many titled acquaintances as we can muster. He wishes to join the *ton*; we must convince him marriage to you will pave the way. I wonder if Prinny would come, in memory of my brother. They were great cronies, you know. I've not tried to trade upon that association, but now . . ."

"Braebarne!" Amy shook her head. "I thought we had agreed he would not do."

"Unless you have a secret suitor as rich as Croesus I don't know about?" Victor sneered.

Maxbridge's face flashed into her mind. Was he a suitor or not? It didn't matter, though. She knew that Victor would never agree, nor did she wish him to, after the insulting way the earl had treated her this afternoon. At least, so she told herself.

Amy sighed. "Very well, then, Uncle. Let us invite Braebarne. He is detestable, but at least I won't be in physical danger with him. I hope." *If, once we are married, he finds out how little influence in the* ton *my uncle truly has. I might be the one to feel his revenge,* Amy thought. But she saw no way out.

"And you won't cut Vendercroft, either. Not yet. Do you understand me?"

Amy sadly nodded. *I understand you'll gladly sacrifice me for your own needs.* They had been planning to go to a rout that evening, but Lord Brinker would on no account permit Amy to go out, in case she should be sickening for something.

"Vendercroft is something of a queernabs on the subject of contagion," he said. "Best for you to rest and try if you can head off any illness."

An evening in which to rest and reflect appealed to Amy, so she gladly complied. However, her reflections did not bring her any pleasure. Out of all the experiences of a wild and unpleasant day, two stood out. One was the kiss Maxbridge had given her, which had thrilled her and made her hunger for more. Whenever she recalled it with a shiver of desire, memory insisted on reminding her of the look of contempt with which he had pronounced those fatal words, *I can afford you, Miss Armstrong. Shall I offer for you?*

He thinks me a fortune hunter. Alas, that I have a heart. If I were the heartless, greedy creature he thinks me, it would not hurt so much to know that the one man I have met whom I thought I could love feels only lust and contempt for me.

She did not see any way out of marrying either Braebarne or Vendercroft now. She yearned to creep into her mother's arms and sob out her sorrows as she had when a young child. But her mother's fragile health demanded that Amy seem perfectly contented with her lot. She turned her head into her pillow, a poor surrogate for a mother's shoulders, but one which could take no harm other than came from a severe wetting.

Maxbridge had followed Chris on William Tremayne's horse as he drove Amy to rendezvous with her aunt. He wished to make sure no further misadventures took place with the all too tempting Miss Armstrong. He watched from a distance as the boy handed her down from his curricle and into her aunt's carriage. When the barouche passed by him, three of the four occupants had raised their hands in grateful salute, but Amy had looked away, pointedly ignoring his presence.

After a few moments Chris turned the curricle and drove up to him. "Shall I trade with you, sir? I need to take Will's horse back to him and drive that coach back to the hostel where we rented it."

"Let me ride with you a ways. I need to talk to you."

Chris's face took on a closed, forbidding appearance. "Not just now, sir, if you don't mind. I am in no mood for a scold, especially from one who treated the woman I love with so little respect."

"That is what I wish to talk to you about. It is time you knew why I feel the way I do about Miss Armstrong."

They tied the horse behind the curricle, and Maxbridge drove slowly while he recollected something he had spent a good many years trying to forget.

"When I returned from the Peninsula with my military career at an end before it had well begun, I was somewhat at loose ends. I applied myself to the art and science of being a man about town, and gave every promise of being a useless, expensive creature. So my older brother Matthew sent me to Scotland to manage his estate there. As you know, he was fifteen years older than I, and stood more as a father to me than a brother, as ours had died when I was quite young.

"I became acquainted with a local beauty, Bridget Gordon, as poor as she was enchanting to look upon. Not as beautiful as Amabel Armstrong, to be sure, but all of the local lads were mad for her, and one or two had much better prospects than I, a younger son, had. So I was flattered and completely taken in when she made up to me. Her mother took me aside and told me that she had no intention of permitting me to engage her daughter's affections unless my brother approved of the match.

"I thought I had already engaged her affections, so I arranged an invitation to our family seat in Kent for Bridget and her mother. I felt sure once my brother met her he'd be as enchanted as I, and approve the match. They went eagerly, and Matthew was indeed enchanted with her. She made a dead set at him and succeeded in captivating him. When I remonstrated with her, she laughed and asked if I had truly believed she would throw herself away on a younger son."

Chris swore. "She used you to get to him?"

"Precisely. With her mother's encouragement. Matthew was something of a recluse, due to a nasty scar he got in a duel. He was ripe for seduction by such an accomplished flirt. She was disgustingly proud of her conquest, and my representations to Matthew of her true character only drove a wedge between us, which she took care to widen in every way possible. He married her anyway. When she died in childbirth, he was so heartbroken he almost couldn't bear to go on living. From then until he died not long after, we were still estranged."

"I knew you and he were not on good terms, but I didn't know why. So you thought Amabel sought to meet you through me? That is why you suspected her originally? She isn't like that."

"Your loyalty does you credit," Maxbridge said.

"It's true. At any rate, you can hardly think she engineered this day's events?" When his uncle shook his head after a moment's hesitation, Chris pressed his advantage. "If she were the fortune hunter you think she is, she would have grabbed at your offer today."

"She wants to be a marchioness. You heard her! Vendercroft outranks me."

"Bosh! Choose an old man, a vicious one, over you because of that slight elevation in rank? Surely you cannot believe anything so preposterous."

"She didn't like that I saw through her. She wants me to love her."

"If she were what you say she is, would she care? Besides, you saw what was not there. You saw another woman, in another situation. I knew there was some reason for your suspiciousness. I shouldn't call it a reason, though, but an ungrounded belief, an unreasoning prejudice."

Maxbridge sighed. "You almost convince me, though there is little point in being convinced. You speak as if I am a suitor for her hand. I'm not, nor ever have been. I offered her marriage today on an impulse. Even if I should wish to pursue the idea of marrying her, her uncle will never let me court her, to know her better. Anyway, even if I found she is as good as you think, how could I marry her, when you love her so much? Chris, I don't want that kind of wedge between us. I don't want us to end up the way Matthew and I did."

Chris blinked a suspicious moisture from his eyes at this proof of his uncle's caring. "No matter how I feel about her, she doesn't love me, and to tell the truth I think she could love you, if you would let her. I want to see her happy."

Remembering the kiss they had shared, Max did not contradict this statement. As he drove back to London, he dwelt upon that kiss and her comment afterward. Something about his kisses stealing her soul. Then there was that look she had sent him, of mute appeal. And her declaration that she would never elope except with someone she loved deeply. Had she implied she would have eloped with him? Shame washed through him as he remembered the way he had treated her with such contempt. Or was he misreading the whole thing? Did he want her out of lust only, or did he truly admire her? *The truth is, you do admire her—if she is what she seems to be, and not another Bridget.* His nephew's scorn at last made him doubt his perceptions. By the time he arrived home, he knew he could no longer pretend he did not care about Miss Armstrong. His young nephew was the one who saw her clearly. She was not a cold, calculating fortune hunter. She was a young girl in the grips of a greedy tyrant, and her choices were dangerously limited. This new view of Amabel opened a floodgate of emotion he had so long dammed up. *I inadvertently lied to Chris today,* he thought. *I can't bear to see her marry anyone else but me. If he were to convince her to marry him, I'd be as distraught as ever I was when I lost Bridget. More so!* As for her marrying Vendercroft, the idea was preposterous. *Before I'd allow that, I'd abduct her myself,* he thought.

While Amabel cried into her pillow that night as she reflected upon Maxbridge's kiss and his contempt, the earl's mind ran much upon the same subject over brandy and cigars at White's, where he played cards with reckless abandon while trying to figure out how to court a girl he had deeply offended and whose guardian despised him.

The next morning quite early Esmerelda Puckett called on Amabel with an astonishing offer.

"Amy, I wish to give you Dorwin!"

"Give me . . . What can you mean?"

"I want you to let him court you. I know you keep him at arm's length for my sake."

Amy solemnly thanked her. "But why, Esmée? Have you quarreled with him?"

"No, I haven't. But it wouldn't matter if I had. You see, when I went to the Forbishers' rout last night, he showed no interest in me at all. He never does. He flirted with several others, and his one conversation with me concerned your whereabouts. When I went home, Mama and I had a serious discussion, and she said I should give up any hope of attaching him. So I have decided to give him to you. If I can't have him, you might as well. I don't say he will be the best husband in the world, for Mama says he likely will have a roving eye, like his father. But he'll be better, much better, than Lord Vendercroft. So you see, you must no longer keep him at arm's length on my account. I feel quite sure you could attach him in a trice if you just tried."

"Oh, Esmée. That is so sweet. But I really couldn't. I value your friendship too much to . . ."

"It won't cost you my friendship. It won't!" Esmée took Amy's hands. "You don't want to marry Vendercroft, do you?"

"Indeed, no! But Uncle now has his eyes set on a wealthy cit. You remember my mentioning Mr. Braebarne, the cloth manufacturer?"

"Oh, he is even worse, isn't he? You don't wish to marry him, either, do you?"

Amy admitted that she did not.

"Well, then, have Dorwin. He is as wealthy as he can stare, has control of his fortune, and won't ever beat you or anything gothic like that."

"You are sincere!"

"Entirely. You must dance with him at the Wormingtons' ball tonight. Promise me!"

Dorwin Smythe-Amhurst was far from Amy's ideal choice for a husband, but he was indeed a good deal better than Vendercroft or Braebarne. Her heart lifted with this new hope of deliverance. "Very well, if you are really sure." At Esmée's vigorous nod, she hugged her friend until she almost crushed her.

"I am very sorry, Dorwin, but I have no more dances. Why do you not dance with Miss Armstrong?"

"Essie, you know very well she never will dance with me. And you know why! Why didn't you save me a dance?"

"You will please call me Esmée!"

"I've called you Essie since we were children. Why do you

keep changing your name? And don't dodge my question. Since when do you not save me a dance?"

"Since I decided we would not suit. And now that I have decided that, I am sure that Amy will dance with you. Go ask her. Oh, stop looking like a backward schoolboy. I will take you to her!" And Esmée did just that. Dorwin followed hesitantly, and was more surprised than gratified when Miss Armstrong accepted his request for a waltz.

"You planned this between the two of you," he accused Esmée. "Otherwise she'd never have a waltz left."

"So? Excuse me, my partner for the next dance is waiting by mother's side."

Amabel looked up into Dorwin's petulant face in some bemusement. "Perhaps you would prefer not to dance with me, Mr. Smythe-Amhurst? Just because Esmée has decided to play matchmaker does not mean we have to fall in with her schemes."

"By no means. I mean, by all means. I mean, I should like very much to dance with you, Miss Armstrong." He led her onto the floor, but had little to say to her, and indeed kept looking in Esmée's direction during their dance.

Amy's hopes plummeted. Dorwin was not acting like a smitten young man.

"I think perhaps you are not as indifferent to Miss Puckett as you have pretended of late, Mr. Smythe-Amhurst."

He scowled. "Never was indifferent. Always meant to marry her, just not right away. Have some fun first, eh? But now she says we shall not suit!"

"Perhaps that is because you have taken her for granted."

"Well, I shan't from now on. Mean to say, you're a lovely woman, Miss Armstrong, and I'm sure you'll make someone a fine wife, but I do care for Esmée and, after all, our land marches together."

"If I were you, Mr. Smythe-Amhurst, I should not mention that last consideration in courting her."

He looked down at Amy, eyebrows lifted. "You think me mercenary? When you would hardly encourage me if I hadn't a fortune?"

She blushed furiously. "I didn't mean to criticize you, only to advise you on courtship." Amy realized that any time spent on Dorwin would be wasted. He had only sought her company for vanity's sake, to be squiring the reigning beauty. She put on an indifferent face, introduced no topics of conversation, and after they had finished the dance in silence, returned to her aunt's side resigned to marrying Braebarne.

. Chris was not at the dance, nor were Nathan and William. Esmée, on Amy's behalf, determined that Chris had gone to William's home on the coast near Shoreham for a few days. "I don't know where Nathan is. Doubtless they are all embarrassed to face you," she said. "Shouldn't be. They meant well."

"I know."

"I still think you should accept one of them," Esmée said plaintively.

"I do wish I could. But I have more than just my own wishes to consider."

"Your uncle does not deserve your loyalty!"

Amy sighed. She couldn't explain her uncle's threats against her mother, for she feared Esmée might speak of it to others. There was no way to escape her fate, so she must not indulge her desire for a confidante.

The next morning Esmée visited her, full of news. "Dorwin has declared himself, and I have you to thank for it!"

Amy shook her head. "Not at all. He just realized how much he loved you when he thought he might lose you."

"But you are so beautiful! If you had exerted yourself, you might have attached him. But you didn't. I saw how coldly you looked at him."

Amy pondered whether to tell Esmée what Dorwin had said about their land marching together, but decided against it. Esmée would still marry him, so why destroy her pleasure in the engagement? "Frankly, I think my beauty is much overrated as an attractant of serious suitors." She told Esmée of her decision of the evening before to marry Braebarne without further ado.

"I hate to think of you married to one who is such a mush-room!"

"A very wealthy mushroom, though. At least he is not repulsive looking. I daresay we shall deal well enough together. I shall just have to take him in hand and smooth off his rough edges." Having made up her mind to marry Braebarne, she knew she must begin paving the way for his acceptance in the *ton*. Only in that way could she hope for any sort of peace in the marriage.

Her uncle persisted in his idea of giving a grand dinner party before her previously planned ball, which she had originally intended to be a small affair. Indeed, he had rather hoped she might be engaged or married before the date rolled around. "Going to have to do the thing. Might as well do it right, impress Braebarn, what? Invite every titled person we can think of. He'll end up paying for it anyway."

Padding the guest list to impress Braebarne proved to be somewhat difficult. "I really have not made many friends among the titled, Uncle," she sighed as she looked at the scant few names.

"I can invite several," he said. "I'm being courted for my vote against Catholic Emancipation, so that will bring in Dorringchase and Merckle and Foster, at least. Still, none of them are single, so it's not likely that will encourage Braebarne to think he must bid high for you. Of course, we'll invite Vendercroft. That'll keep him on your string, as well as impress Braebarne. But only one marriageable lord. Too bad."

"Who is the marriageable lord?" Amy asked, pretending puzzlement.

"You just heard me say. Vendercroft."

"There's Lord Maxbridge," Aunt Edwina said, then shrank against the back of the sofa at the look of loathing her husband turned her way.

"Maxbridge! Here? Don't be ridiculous, woman." He muttered a curse, then shot her a suspicious glance. "He's not courting Amy, is he?"

"Well, no, but he might if he were encouraged. After all, didn't he ride to her rescue the other day?"

"The devil, woman. What will you say next? Encourage Maxbridge! I'd rather she married a tanner's apprentice."

Amy would have liked to back up her aunt, but this time she couldn't. "I fear he rode after me to keep me from marrying Chris, not out of any concern for me."

"B-but Braebarne won't know that," Edwina persisted.

Victor opened his mouth to contradict her, then closed it again. He rubbed his chin thoughtfully. "Might work, at that. A wealthy earl. That would make the cit take notice."

"I fear he would not come, Uncle."

"Perhaps, perhaps not. That nevvy of his would, wouldn't he? Maxbridge's heir, after all. Very eligible."

"Chris probably would, but he is out of town."

"Well, get him back into town! Top over tail in love with you, ain't he? Get him to come, bring his uncle. You can do it, girl! While you're at it, invite those other sprouts who are so mad for you. We'll surround you with suitors, let Braebarne see what he has to contend with. Between impressing him with our connections in the *ton* and the competition from other men, he'll have to come down handsomely for you."

"Very well, Uncle," Amy said, fighting off a feeling of nausea at the entire proceedings.

The next day, still bemused at her uncle's encouraging her to invite his longtime enemy to dinner, Amy wrote out an invitation to Maxbridge, though she did not believe for a moment that he would accept. Nathan, William, and Chris had long since been invited, but she wrote them each notes encouraging them to return to town for her ball.

To her surprise, Maxbridge sent an acceptance immediately. A flutter of pleasure in her stomach assailed her at the thought of seeing him again, though she tried to squelch it. For whatever reason he had accepted, it certainly couldn't be out of any regard for her. Moreover, once there, he'd see through their ploy and would be even more contemptuous of her afterward.

Chapter Seventeen

*M*ax could hardly believe his eyes when he opened the invitation to Amy's ball. What could have happened to cause Victor to invite him into his home? Perhaps he was grateful for the rescue of Amy from her most recent abduction, but Max doubted it. It seemed more like Victor to angrily blame him for his heir's misdeeds. Still, the invitation very much suited his wishes, so he accepted with alacrity.

I am wiser now than when Bridget caught me in her toils, I hope. I can tell whether Amy can feel a spark of affection for me, and if she doesn't, I won't wed her, no matter how much she appeals to me. Thus fortified, if perhaps uneasy that he was deluding himself, he attended the dinner and ball. He expected his first encounter with Lord Brinker to be a stiff, uncomfortable affair for them both, and was surprised and suspicious when Victor greeted him heartily, in a manner that implied they were intimates, and bosom beaus at that.

Then Brinker introduced him to a man he had met elsewhere, while investigating shoddy workmanship in military uniforms for the government. James Braebarne was as astonished as he that they were introduced to one another in a *ton* drawing room. Braebarne uneasily acknowledged the introduction, and Max, with a curt "we've met," passed on to greet Lady Brinker and Amabel Armstrong.

Amabel was, as usual, beautiful, exquisitely gowned and looked as finished a piece of nature as he'd ever seen. But something about her eyes alarmed him. She had an almost haunted look about her and would scarcely meet his gaze.

"Is . . . is Chris coming, do you know?" she asked him. "I haven't received a response to my invitation."

"I don't know. He is visiting William Tremayne."

"Yes, I know. I got his address from Mr. Holmes, and sent an invitation to both Chris and Mr. Tremayne. I suppose it hadn't time to reach them, or perhaps . . ."

"Perhaps he is a bit embarrassed just now." Maxbridge smiled down at her. "As well he should be. As should I be. I hope we will have an opportunity to speak privately at some time this evening, so I can apologize properly."

Aunt Edwina's eyes widened with astonishment. "I cannot see what *you* have to apologize for, my lord. Such kindness, such gallantry, to rescue my niece as you did!" She looked around to be sure her husband wasn't listening. "As to that, the young men owe no apology, either, for they meant it for the best."

Max shook his head. "Clumsily handled, and it could have had a tragic outcome. But you are most forgiving, as is your husband, to invite not only me, but them as well."

Amy blushed deeply and turned away. Her aunt stammered some sort of reply, and Max moved on to allow them to greet other guests, wondering at their response. He had thought the invitation odd, but had expected it to be meeting his host which would be awkward, not Miss Armstrong or her aunt.

Amy gave a glad cry as Esmée and her mother entered the drawing room, escorted by Mr. Smythe-Amhurst. As she embraced her friend she whispered, "At last, someone who is neither old, nor male!"

"There are certainly very few female guests," Esmée said after glancing around the room. "What is going on, Amy?"

"I will tell you later."

To Max's surprise, he was seated next to Amy at dinner, with Lord Vendercroft on her other side. Braebarne sat on the opposite side of the table, and looked at them so often it seemed his head must be on a swivel.

"So Mr. Braebarne is smitten by you, too, Miss Armstrong. That is easy to understand, but what is not, is his presence at such a gathering. The man is as far from being good *ton* as it is possible to be, and your other guests are the cream of society, with one possible exception." He looked just past her at Vendercroft to explain his meaning.

From the moment Maxbridge had entered the drawing room before dinner, Amy had been miserable. To use any man as a pawn to cause another to offer for her was disgusting; to use Maxbridge in that way pained her deeply, for it was him she wanted, in spite of his disdain for her. She decided to end the masquerade, even though it would justify once and for all his suspicions of her. If he got up and left during the dinner, she wouldn't even care. It would serve her uncle right.

"In a manner of speaking, Lord Maxbridge, he is the guest of honor," she said in a low voice, hoping no one else would hear. On her other side Vendercroft's attention seemed fixed on his other dinner partner.

"How so?" Maxbridge lifted that famous eyebrow.

"In fact, he is the reason you were invited."

"He is not, I promise, a special friend of mine."

"It was not done out of any consideration for you. You see, he is a potential suitor, but being of the merchant class, he seemed to wish to bargain rather sharply. He is socially ambitious. So we invited other wealthy suitors—at least, that is what he is supposed to think—in addition to as many other titled and aristocratic people as we could scrape together, to impress him with my worth to him."

"We, Miss Armstrong?"

She lifted her chin. "We, Lord Maxbridge. As you have known all along, I mean to make a rich marriage." She tried to stare him down as he glared at her, but could not maintain her gaze. In fact, she dropped her head and blinked her eyes fiercely to hold back tears. A long silence on her right followed, and she made herself nibble at a lobster patty that tasted like ashes.

Then Vendercroft turned toward her. "I find you in good health tonight, I trust?" He looked her over suspiciously.

"In excellent health, my lord. It was a short-lived illness."

"But an illness, nevertheless. That disappoints me somewhat, I confess."

Amy nodded. "I thought as much, as you did not call upon me again."

He laughed dryly. "Better safe than sorry. So, Miss Armstrong, I take it that the object of this gathering was to convince me that I had best act quickly or you would be snabbled up by some other man. I can understand Maxbridge, and even Smythe-Amhurst, though it looks as if he and Miss Puckett mean to make a match of it, but why Braebarne? Surely you do not think I would be jealous of someone like him?"

"I would not wish to inspire jealousy in you, Lord Vendercroft, nor any other emotion but revulsion. It has come to my attention that your interest in hygiene passes what is normal and approaches the bizarre, perhaps even the dangerous."

She had no trouble looking Vendercroft squarely in the eyes. Chin raised, she let him see her disdain.

"What can you mean, Miss Armstrong?"

"I mean Nathan Holmes's cousin, sir. Your second wife, I believe."

Vendercroft stopped his fork in midair to stare at her. "What has he been telling you?"

"I think you know."

He set his fork down. "Did I not warn you not to listen to gossip, Miss Armstrong? I hope one day to demonstrate to you the lying nature of that hysterical female's accusations."

Amy shuddered. "I hope not, my lord!" She turned her attention back to her plate, where an apricot tart awaited her. To her surprise, Lord Maxbridge addressed her, his voice conspiratorially low and caressing in tone rather than disdainful.

"So I am to be the means of raising your price, eh? Well, let us put on a good performance, then. If Braebarne can be brought to heel by my presence, my active pursuit of you

should have him emptying his purse. Will you save me two
dances, Miss Armstrong?"

She lifted her eyes to him, astonished. "Two?"

"One of them a waltz, if you please. And the other your supper dance. And . . . do you have a garden?"

"Oh, yes. Gardening is my aunt's passion. It is small, of
course, as most town gardens are, but charming now, with the
roses blooming and fairy lanterns everywhere."

"Good. We shall dance our way out into the garden. Who
knows, I may perhaps steal a kiss."

"No. Not a kiss." Amy looked away, unable to bear the heat
in his eyes, or the answering flush rising in her body.

"Coward." He chuckled. "But perhaps not a kiss. I don't
want to compromise you, or do I? Perhaps that is the answer to
your dilemma."

She turned eyes once more brimming with tears up to him.
"No. It wouldn't serve any purpose, my lord."

"Hmmmm." Max looked down at her. "I truly am not one of
your targets, then. How lowering."

"My uncle would never permit it. He said . . . he said he'd
marry me to a tanner's apprentice rather than let me marry
you!"

"Then I may be at ease as I aid you in your schemes, knowing I am not to be caught in your net." Though he kept his
voice cool, Maxbridge felt sharp regret. He wanted to be
caught in her net. He wanted *her*! More than any other woman
he had ever met. *Damn Brinker,* he thought. *Cruel, greedy, and
stupid. A formidable combination.* How he was to overcome
Victor's scheme to engage his niece to that disgusting cit he
did not know, but he did know that Amabel was not of her own
volition scheming to gain Braebarne's proposal. His conclusion of a few days earlier stood: *She is a beautiful girl in the
grip of an avaricious man. And I care for her deeply. I must do
something!*

He resolved that somehow he would rescue her, though he
had no idea how, short of abducting her. *I wonder if she would
go willingly?* She had told Chris and his friends of her dislike

of the consequences of elopement, and made it clear that she would never do such a thing unless she loved deeply. He still had no idea whether she held him in affection, though he knew enough of females to be confident she was attracted to him. *Why should she feel affection for me?* he thought ruefully. *I've treated her with such disdain, she would be justified to take me in dislike.*

As for Amy, much as she regretted his knowing her schemes and thinking badly of her, she looked forward to their time together. A few precious moments with a man she could love— no, the man she did love, she admitted to herself—were all she would have before a lifetime of servitude with Braebarne. *Better than no time at all,* she thought recklessly, promising herself that kiss in spite of the danger it represented to her reputation and her peace of mind.

"This place is a hotbed of anti-Catholic sentiment tonight, Miss Armstrong. Yet you do not share your uncle's views against emancipation."

"No, I don't."

"What do you think of the chances for passage of the bill any time soon?"

Amy tilted her head back a bit to look at Lord Maxbridge as he guided her expertly through the waltz. Conversation with most partners consisted of extravagant praise for her beauty, silly flirtations, or bragging about teams, races, wagers, boxing prowess, and other masculine interests. For any man, and especially this man, who had seemed so suspicious of her before, to consult her opinion on almost anything, much less upon such a political topic, was both novel and flattering.

"I do not think it will happen this year, at least. I wonder if it will happen, can happen, as long as our prince is opposed to it."

"It will be very difficult, to be sure. Eventually, though, I think we will wear him down. You follow parliamentary affairs with almost the same avidity as my Aunt Phinea, I understand."

"Indeed, yes. I find politics fascinating, and occasionally depressing. Why is it so hard to get any sort of reform passed? I particularly would like to see our legislators address the subject of working hours for children."

"Your prospective groom would not like to hear of such a thing—presuming you mean you would like to see them reduced."

"Most definitely! Children should play and learn, not slave away for a few cents a day. It is a good deal too bad for grown men to be out of work and supported by their children."

He smiled down at her. "Best not let Braebarne see that expression, Miss Armstrong."

"Oh, dear, did I have on my fierce face? My mother has warned me again and again not to let a suitor see me thus!"

"It would take a great deal more than that to put a man off a lovely, intelligent creature such as you."

"Oh, please, don't speak flummery! Let us discuss the Corn Laws, or even the weather."

"Let us speak of nothing at all," he said, dancing her out the French doors. "Ah, this is indeed a pleasant garden, although the fairy lanterns light it a bit too well for my purpose." He led her down the terrace.

"I told you there would be no kiss," she said, though she hoped there would be. "Why, if we were caught, you'd accuse me of trying to trick you into marriage."

"At this point, Miss Armstrong, I would be a willing victim."

Amy caught her breath. "You don't mean that."

"Let me show you." He pulled her into the scant cover of an archway covered with roses and without further ado gathered her against him. In spite of her murmur of protest, Amy found herself leaning into his muscular body and lifting her head for his kiss, which seared her very being.

When at last he pulled away, Maxbridge was breathing heavily. He looked about him. "Alas, no one has observed us. Step out into the light and I will do that again."

"No! My uncle wouldn't allow it. He'd see me ruined first. Please, Lord Maxbridge. This is hopeless."

"Then I shall abduct you. It is all the rage this Season."

She shook her head emphatically. "You cannot."

"You would prefer Braebarne and propriety to me?"

"No!"

"You told my nephew and his friends you would not elope unless you loved deeply. I confess I did not entirely believe it, for the look you sent me then. . . . No! Forgive me! I did not mean that the way it seems. I have put my suspicions of you behind me. Alas for me that you weren't scheming to attach me, for I sadly fear I have developed a deep affection for you. A feeling you apparently do not share."

"Oh, Maxbridge!" Amy's heart expanded within her at his adorably insecure look. She put up her hand and stroked his cheek. "I do have feelings for you."

He caught her hand and pressed a kiss into it. "Thank God for that, because, in fact, I love you!"

Amy caught her breath. "Can this be true? Because if it is . . . Oh! Maxbridge, I love you, too! I think I have for a long time."

He pulled her against him and kissed her once again, this time a deep, shattering kiss that left them both trembling.

"Amy, you must promise you will elope with me if your uncle refuses his consent!"

Amy shook her head, near tears. "Indeed, I would run away with you, if I had but myself to consider, but . . . oh! Uncle. I was just showing Lord Maxbridge the roses."

"He has seen quite enough. Come with me, Amabel. I want a word with you in the library."

Maxbridge moved to intercept them. "Lord Brinker, I have something very particular I wish to say to you."

"There is nothing—nothing—you could say to me that would be of the least interest to me, Lord Maxbridge. Now, if you will please let me pass?"

Max looked at Amy, whose eyes were averted, and reluc-

tantly stood aside. Victor grabbed her hand and towed her un-
gently up the path and back into the house.

While Amy and Maxbridge waltzed, James Braebarne had
stood beside Lord Brinker, watching. "I am surprised you
allow that, Brinker," he growled. "Thought you and he was enemies."

Amy's uncle was not best pleased to see his niece waltzing
with the man he hated most of anyone in the world. But he
knew Amy was just playing her part, and playing it well. With
those soulful looks she gave Maxbridge, and which he was returning with full measure, anyone would think them deeply in
love.

"Don't like the man," he agreed, "but he's an eligible *parti*.
Sometimes one has to compromise. He'll pay dearly for her."

"I'd give a lot to put a spoke in his wheel."

Brinker looked at him shrewdly. "Thought you showed a
lack of enthusiasm when you were introduced."

"He did me harm once. I'd pay him back if I could. Shall we
go into your library and talk for a few minutes?"

Thus it was that Amy was snatched from Maxbridge's arms
before she could explain why she could not elope with him.
Instead, she was led into the library, where she found Mr.
Braebarne looking like the cat that licked the cream. Her uncle
did not leave her acceptance to chance, but put her hand in
Braebarne's. "Niece," he said, "meet your future husband."

"And in the very near future, too," Mr. Braebarne declared,
taking her hand in a hard grip. "No need to wait, eh, Lord
Brinker?"

"None whatsoever. In fact, we'll announce it right now, if
you wish. That's right, isn't it, my pet?" He gave Amy a hard
stare, and after a moment she inclined her head in agreement,
though every fiber of her being shrilled with protest. Without
further ado, he led them both into the ballroom, where he
clapped loudly for attention.

The orchestra, which had begun the tune for the next dance,
raggedly halted, and everyone turned to stare at them.

"Friends, I'd like to take this occasion to announce something very special. My dear niece Miss Amabel Armstrong has just agreed to marry my very dear friend Mr. James Braebarne. I have asked for champagne to be served. I hope you will all join me in a toast to their happiness."

She looks like a frightened deer, Maxbridge thought. Seething, he elbowed his way through the crowd to confront the group. "I have reason to believe this engagement is contrary to Miss Armstrong's inclinations."

"That's not true, is it, niece?"

Victor had told her on the way up the walk that her mother would suffer this very night if she did not do as he wished. Amy drew a deep breath.

"I am sorry, Lord Maxbridge, if you gained a wrong impression, but I give my hand willingly to Mr. Braebarne." She spoke firmly, but could not quite meet Max's eyes.

"This is one toast I will not drink," he announced loudly, and stalked from the ballroom.

In a daze, Amy received the halfhearted well-wishes of her friends, and the more sneering ones from mere acquaintances. Esmée had no words for her, only hugged her close, tears in her eyes. Just behind her Mr. Smythe-Amhurst lifted his eyebrows ironically at her. Mrs. Puckett, tight-mouthed, offered her new fiancé as cold a greeting as she could give and still not cut him. This example was followed by several others. Nathan Holmes had recourse to several glasses of champagne in quick succession. As the milling, whispering company stood about, drinking champagne, a sudden stir at the door to the ballroom caught everyone's attention.

"William!" Amy's heart sank. She knew the news of her engagement, especially to such a man, would give pain to him, and to Chris, whom she expected to follow him into the room. But in the next second she saw that be was not dressed for a ballroom. He had on riding clothes, much travel-stained, and a wild look in his eyes.

"Where is Maxbridge?" he asked of the room at large.

"He has left," Amy replied, going toward him. "Is something wrong?"

"A great deal is wrong. Do you know where he went? He isn't at home."

"Young man, you should not be in a ballroom," Mrs. Puckett said, eyeing his attire censoriously. "You look as if you have ridden many miles. What can you be about, to come to Miss Armstrong's party in such a state?"

"Nonsense. Perfectly welcome," Lord Brinker said, a look of malicious triumph in his eyes. "Come, Mr. Tremayne, meet my niece's fiancé. Mr. Braebarne, I'd like you to meet William Tremayne, heir of Baron Tremayne."

To Amy's surprise, William barely reacted to this news. Instead he thrust his hand through his disheveled hair. "You'll have to excuse me, Lord Brinker. Can't stay. Have terrible news." He looked at Amy. "It's Chris. Chris has killed himself."

A collective gasp resounded in the room.

"Christopher Ponselle?" Amy felt the room sway beneath her. "Oh, no. Do not say so. How? Why?"

"How? He swam directly out to sea and drowned himself that is how. As to why, well, you know why." William glared at her.

"Wh-what do you mean?"

"He died because he loved you, and you thought of nothing but marrying a wealthy man. Well, I hear that Braebarne here is one of the wealthiest in England. You are nothing but a . . ."

Lord Brinker's hand closed on his shoulder in a crushing grip. "You'd best watch your tongue or I'll . . ."

"I know—you'll horsewhip me. Braebarne, I wish you joy of this family, though they've brought no joy to anyone in the last three generations." William turned on his heels and ran out of the room, closely followed by Nathan.

An appalled silence fell upon the group. It seemed to Amy as if somehow their guests had formed a hostile circle around herself, her uncle, and Mr. Braebarne, though few had actually moved.

"Hunh! A hussy, just as I've always said. Always eloping with someone, then changing her mind when she found out he was not rich enough. Be glad you escaped her clutches."

Amy could scarcely believe her ears. It was Mrs. Puckett, addressing Dorwin. Nose tilted in the air, she began to drag her speechless, stunned daughter from the room. Esmée pulled back, stammering and holding out a hand to Amy. Around them the other guests began to talk and draw even farther from their host.

"Just a moment." Braebarne blocked Mrs. Puckett's path. "What's this about her eloping?"

"I personally know of three young men she started to elope with," Mrs. Puckett said.

"Mother! That isn't true. They abducted her!" Esmée declared, then put her hands across her mouth.

Braebarne turned upon Victor, fist upraised. "What kind of trumpery goods have you tried to sell me? Elopements? Abductions? Good Lord, is she even a virgin? Look at how everyone is staring and drawing away. Why would I wish to ally myself with your family, eh? Tell me that? Thought you was good *ton*. Fat lot of good you'll do me now. You may consider our engagement at an end, Miss Armstrong." He didn't even bother to bow to her, just turned and marched out of the room, elbowing aside Mrs. Puckett as he did so.

Uncle Victor, mouth working like a landed fish, seemed nailed to the floor.

"Good riddance to bad rubbish," Mrs. Puckett said, and turned back toward Amy, looking very pleased with herself. But before she could say anything, Lord Vendercroft spoke up, his voice deliberately loud and carrying.

"You are well out of your engagement to that creature, Miss Armstrong. Can't think what your uncle was about, allowing you to engage yourself to him. As for your having anything to do with Mr. Ponselle's suicide, if such it was, the notion is ridiculous. Everyone knows you were just friends, and that you have not encouraged him at all. And this talk of elopement was mischief-making, was it not, Mrs. Puckett? I think you wished to scare Braebarne off, clever woman that you are. A kindness to the child, indeed. Everyone here knows what you were about. I think we can close ranks around Miss Armstrong now that the mushroom has left." He looked around the room challengingly. Amy did not know whether to be relieved or horrified to see that heads were nodding affirmatively. Vendercroft had saved her standing with the *ton*.

Lord Brinker looked as if he would embrace Vendercroft. Mrs. Puckett did embrace Amy, who stood stock-still, unable to take in all that had happened in the last few minutes.

"Of course I was," Mrs. Puckett agreed, nodding to Vendercroft. "Everyone in this room knows Amy too well to believe such a thing. That he would fall for such a tale about a carefully chaperoned girl proves that he is not only a cit but a dull-witted cit. Now, Lord Brinker, perhaps you will allow Amy to choose an eligible suitor from among the *ton*."

"Oh, indeed I will, Mrs. Puckett." Victor eyed Vendercroft greedily as he spoke, and had the satisfaction of receiving a stately bow in return.

A sly, triumphant smile on his face, Vendercroft turned to Amy. "Shall we go down to supper, Miss Armstrong? I am sure that your aunt has laid out a delicious repast for us." The marquess offered Amy his arm, and she, mechanically, took it. Too much had happened in the last few minutes for her to quite comprehend it all. Uppermost in her mind was the dreadful thought of Chris's death, and the fear that she might, indeed, have been responsible for it. *Maxbridge. Oh, what pain he will suffer.* Amy yearned to be with him, to comfort him when he received the news, then wondered if he would thrust her away. *He'll despise me,* she thought, and blinked back the tears.

Though there were many interested looks thrown her way, the other guests did not leave, but began to talk among themselves. Mrs. Puckett did not look quite as pleased with herself as she had a few minutes before, but shrugging, she led the others in following Vendercroft and Amy down to supper.

Chapter Eighteen

Maxbridge left the Brinker party with his mind in a whirl. He could still taste Amy. The sweet memory of her body pressed against him, her arms wrapped around him, warmed him and chilled him at the same time. How could she? How could she go from his arms directly into an engagement with Braebarne?

He went home, and with a curt dismissal of his servants, went into his library to drink brandy and try to sort things out. In his heart of hearts he knew Amy was not Bridget. Indeed, if she were, she would have taken him up on his proposal, eloping if need be, for he was much the better match, all things considered, than Braebarne.

"No!" Max shouted to the silent room, slamming his fist on the table and making the brandy bottle jump. "She cares for me, I know it. She wants to marry me, and not just for my wealth or title." Greatly relieved at last that he was able to put Bridget's treachery behind him and trust again, he turned his mind to the puzzle of Amy's behavior.

Why had she agreed to engage herself to Braebarne? *Clearly her uncle is forcing her into it. Doesn't she know that he can't really make her marry against her will? Does her dread of scandal outweigh any affection she might feel for me?*

Maxbridge decided that Amy was too intelligent and well educated not to know she could not be forced to wed against her will. It seemed to him she was also too strong a person to be ruled by fear of her uncle, especially with Maxbridge to protect her. So why insist on marrying to please her uncle? Maxbridge could not believe it was affection for Victor, or even a general sense of duty to her family. *He has some hold on her.*

What was it she had said? "If I had but myself to consider." Who else did she have to consider? He knew she cared for her nieces and Lady Brinker. And then there was her mother. Mrs. Armstrong's fragile features rose up in his mind's eye. *She looks as if a strong wind would destroy her. If Amy eloped, her mother would surely die if Brinker turned his rage on her.*

He had the answer! Putting his brandy glass down with a thump, he rose. Tomorrow he would take a trip out to Wayside, to call on Mrs. Armstrong. *I wonder if she would like to visit Aunt Phinea,* he thought, a grim smile tugging at his lips. *She is more than a match for Brinker, should he figure out where I have put Amy's mother.*

Once Mrs. Armstrong was safe, he knew he had to go to Brinker in person and force the man to listen as he asked for Amy's hand in a formal manner. Not until he had been refused could he justify clandestine action. But then . . . *Look out, Miss Amabel Armstrong. Your last abduction is at hand.*

As he started up the stairs, a loud knocking at his door made him regret sending his servants to bed. He opened the door to a distraught William Tremayne and Nathan Holmes, and his plans for the morrow abruptly changed.

"I don't believe it! Chris, a suicide? Did he leave a note?"

"No, sir, but you know he is an excellent swimmer. Like a cork, he is. Was."

"When did he take this swim?" Maxbridge mentally calculated how long it would have taken William to ride to London. "What time of day?"

"It was night, actually. Midnight."

"I haven't a tide table in my head, but . . . was the tide going out?"

"Yes, sir."

"A stupid time to go swimming," Nathan said.

"Just so. Which is why I believe he meant to do himself in."

"Had he been drinking?" Max studied William with narrow eyes, for he found it hard to believe Chris would intentionally drown himself.

William flushed beneath that stern scrutiny. "Yes, sir. We both had. Pretty well to go, actually. Drowning our sorrows." When the implications of that expression hit him, he turned away, pressing his fingers to his nose to stay the tears.

"Come upstairs with me while I change into riding clothes, and tell me the rest. Did he say anything before he went into the water?"

"Actually, I'd fallen asleep, didn't realize he'd gone swimming. Found his clothes on the beach."

Maxbridge cursed. "Folly! But not suicide, I'll vow. And excellent swimmer that he is, he may not be dead at all, but only come ashore elsewhere. Or perhaps a boat picked him up. I'll organize a search for him all along the coast."

Lord Vendercroft wasted no time in calling upon her uncle, and Amy could find no excuse for refusing to accept him. She did not hide her dislike of his proposal, but it seemed not to matter to him.

"You will soon be pleased with your choice, Miss Armstrong," he assured her. "A sensible, intelligent young woman such as yourself will in fact find other benefits in marrying me than being the wife of a wealthy man. I will not stint you on clothes, jewels, and so forth, of course, but more rational pleasures await you if you approach our marriage in the right spirit."

"What can you mean, my lord?"

"From what you said to me the day we drove in the park, I think you will find my researches into hygiene and health interesting."

"Experiments, you mean? Will you experiment on me as you did on your previous wives, my lord?"

"I have learned a great deal in the intervening years. And they were such silly, hysterical creatures. If you will assist me rather than resisting my efforts, I think you will find the results beneficial as well as intellectually stimulating."

The fanatical look she had seen in his eyes more than once had appeared again. Amy fought back a rising sense of panic. "Perhaps I will, my lord. Now, may I ask your assistance in something?"

"Of course."

"My uncle thinks to have a quick wedding, by special license, but I want a church wedding, with my friends and family present. Given that my mother eloped, it would not only be pleasant but socially beneficial for our union to be solemnized in the full view of the world."

Vendercroft left off contemplating her teeth, as he so often did while she talked, to look her in the eyes. "A stalling tactic?"

"Why should I stall? I am not one to fight the inevitable, my lord. I should think for your own consequence you would wish it to be seen that I am willingly and openly wedding you. A hurried, private affair might suggest . . ."

"Just the sort of gothic speculation I would detest." Vendercroft nodded. "Very well. I'll not subject myself to the crying of banns for three weeks, but we can put an announcement in the papers and have the wedding you wish. I should think two weeks would be sufficient to arrange it."

"I fear you will find the bills for my wedding gown and such laid at your door."

"You are not marrying a merchant or a cit, Miss Armstrong. I did not bargain with your uncle over his ridiculous demands, nor will I shrink from financing yours. Only do not attempt to escape the marriage once we are committed to it. I would be forced to be most unpleasant in such a case."

Amy nodded, and suffered his embrace and dry, hard mouth on hers in a betrothal kiss. Then her uncle and aunt joined them for a celebratory glass of champagne, and the two men went off to discuss finances.

Aunt Edwina embraced her niece and wept. "It is too bad,

just too bad of him. You are so clever, Amy. Can you not think of something?"

"I will try, Aunt. Don't trouble yourself. I can deal with Lord Vendercroft if I must." But she did not see how. Her other erstwhile suitors were all alienated from her. Maxbridge had given her up in disgust upon her agreeing to marry Braebarne, and she could not explain, because she knew without being told that Maxbridge had gone to search for his nephew. Indeed, if he shared William's belief that she was the cause of Christopher's death, he doubtless would never come near her again.

The thought of dear Christopher dead, for whatever reason, sent deep pain shafting through her. How could such a vibrant personality have been snuffed out? And so young, too. She wished for her father's counsel, for his faith had always been steadfast in the face of so many human tragedies. She knew he would have found some words of comfort for her. She was finding it difficult to think of them herself.

Amy's wedding preparations were a dismal affair. Whether the *ton* would cut her or not, she did not know, for her uncle had decided to take no chances of rebellion on her part, or rescue on the part of any of her admirers. He kept her close, only letting her leave the house with his escort. He admitted few callers, especially forbidding Esmée and her mother. Mrs. Puckett's transparent and successful efforts at ending her brief engagement to Braebarne had gained his enmity. When Amy begged to have Esmée for her attendant at the wedding, he flatly refused.

"Your mother and aunt will be quite sufficient female support for you at your wedding," he had declared. "Once Vendercroft has made you his wife, it will be for him to decide whose society you have. As for me, I care not, so long as this wedding occurs, and soon."

She had written as soothing a letter as possible to her mother about the Vendercroft engagement, which she knew would upset Mrs. Armstrong, who knew the man's reputation, though not the fact that he bordered on the insane. She asked her mother not to come to London until the day of the ceremony at St. George's, as London air harmed her health so much. She wished to spare her anxiety if she should meet and converse with Vendercroft. For all her frailty, Mrs. Armstrong could be quite determined when her motherly instincts were aroused. Yet she was not strong enough physically to stand up to Victor, so there was no point in risking a confrontation.

The wedding was set for the first Wednesday in June, and the announcement went out to the papers two days after her disastrous ball. In the ensuing days, she shopped unenthusiastically for a trousseau under her uncle's watchful eye, with the bills sent to Lord Vendercroft. She knew her uncle and Vendercroft had applied for a special license, to avoid having to have the banns cried for three weeks. Three days before the wedding was to take place, they had gone to Doctor's Commons to pick up the license they had arranged through the Archbishop of Canterbury. When she heard the door knocker sound while they were gone, she went out into the foyer, hoping it might be Esmée and she could convince their butler to admit the girl, for she longed to visit with her friend. To her astonishment it was Lord Maxbridge who stood upon her steps.

As luck would have it, Stuckey had not been told not to admit Maxbridge. Apparently it had not occurred to her uncle that his archenemy would be so brazen as to call upon her. Moreover, the butler recognized and welcomed the man who had tipped him so generously once before. So a haggard, road-weary Lord Maxbridge found himself in the presence of the beautiful girl he had hardly dared hope to see.

With a little cry she ran toward him. "Chris?"

He shook his head grimly.

Amy wrung her hands, tears coursing down her cheeks.

Stuckey cleared his throat. "Lord Brinker is not at home."

Maxbridge looked longingly at Amy.

Stuckey cleared his throat again as the pair stood gazing into one another's eyes. "Was Miss wishful of receiving this gentleman? Shall I send for Betty to attend you?"

"Oh. Yes, please. My aunt is laid down with a headache,

Lord Maxbridge. Won't you join me in the drawing room? Betty will be with us shortly to observe the proprieties." She said the last sadly.

Maxbridge turned to Stuckey. "By all means send for the maid." He leaned closer to the servant's ear. "Slowly?" He held out a coin.

At the glint of gold, Stuckey smiled. Palming it expertly, he nodded. "Indeed, I scarcely know where the wench may be. Have to search upstairs and down."

Maxbridge nodded, then turned to follow Amy into the drawing room. "Will he keep quiet about this?"

"For what you gave him, I should say so!" She seated herself on the sofa and, when he looked longingly at the space beside her, patted it invitingly.

"You look exhausted. How terrible it must have been for you." She swiped at her damp cheeks. "I can scarce believe he is gone. I had held out hope . . ."

"I searched every beach on the coast and every fishing village. I've put up a large reward for information about him. At this point, however . . ." He dropped his head into his hands.

His vulnerable pose suddenly swept aside all of Amy's inhibitions. She closed the distance between them and pulled him to her. He held her tightly, and she heard deep sobs gush from him. She rocked him back and forth like a child, murmuring words of comfort. At last he pulled away and mopped his face with his handkerchief.

"Forgive me. Ah, God, I don't know how to bear it," he said.

"Nor I. The thought that somehow I might be responsible has made it impossible for me to feel that I deserve comfort or forgiveness."

"Now, that is preposterous. William told me what he said to you, and I nearly thrashed him. Christopher did not take his life, for any reason, and least of all for you."

"Oh!" Amy grabbed the hand he held out to her. "If only I can believe that . . ."

"Believe it, my dear. Chris loved you, but he was not in any sort of despairing mode because of your rejection. He was quite worried about you, of course, as am I. I do not know how much of an improvement Braebarne is over Vendercroft."

She shook her head. "Braebarne cried off."

Relief swept his features. "Thank goodness. Perhaps that will incline your uncle to accept my suit."

"Your . . . your suit?" Amy's eyes widened. Joy thrilled through her. *He hadn't lost his regard for her after all.*

"Why do you look so surprised? Did you think I would give up simply because your uncle would not give me a hearing that night?"

"First the engagement to Braebarne, then Chris's death . . . I feared you'd never wish to see me again."

He shook his head vehemently. "I meant to offer for you the day after your ball, and in fact, to steal you away if Brinker did not accept, but I had to search for Chris." His features sagged again, but he drew in a deep, controlling breath. "When do you expect your uncle to return home?"

"Sometime soon, but alas, he will be unwilling to hear your proposal, Lord Maxbridge."

"Max. Please."

She lifted a trembling hand to his cheek and whispered, "Max. And you will call me Amy?"

"Amy. My love." He kissed her hand. "Surely if I offer him enough money, he will put aside that long-ago conflict. After all, there cannot be many more wealthy men . . ."

"I am now engaged to Lord Vendercroft."

His brows arrowed together. "That was fast. You acquire fiancés as quickly as abductors, it seems."

"I did not wish for any of it!" She started to rise.

"No, wait." He put a restraining hand out. "I have put my suspicions behind me. I know you have good reason for what you are doing." He pulled her into his arms and kissed her tenderly. "Amy, if he won't accept my offer—and it will be a generous one, I assure you—will you run away with me?"

"I don't care if it is generous or not! I wish I had a huge

dowry to give you. That you should have to pay for me infuriates me. I don't want you to give him a shilling!"

"Nevertheless, I will meet his terms. I do not wish to subject you to the kind of prejudice your mother suffered, my love. I will avoid an elopement if at all possible."

"I don't care for that. He doesn't deserve to prosper at your expense, especially the way he has used me! But run away?" She put her hands up to her face, covering her eyes, and sobbed, "I can't. I have . . ."

"I know. Someone else to consider. Your mother?"

She lifted her hands to look at him from tear-brimmed eyes. "Yes. He said if I eloped or even was abducted again, he would go straight to Wayside and take her out into the middle of the most inhospitable part of the Yorkshire moors and leave her there. She would not even survive the trip. Mother is quite delicate, you see. Her heart and lungs both are both weak as the result of a virulent fever."

"Which is why I mean to abduct her first."

"Wh-what?"

"Well, not exactly abduct. I am going to take her to stay with my Aunt Phinea. Victor will not look for her there, and even if he did, Aunt Phinea is more than a match for him. She'd never give your mother up to him."

Amy thought of the redoubtable dowager and nodded. "If only I thought it wouldn't frighten mother too much." She frowned down at her hands, twining them restlessly in her lap. "But she would surely not wish me to marry Vendercroft. Her last letter to me urged me to refuse him."

"So she will be eager to find a solution that saves you from him." Maxbridge put his hands over hers comfortingly.

"But there must be no pell-mell racing about in your carriage with her."

"I'll take the greatest care of her, I assure you."

"In that case I will elope with you."

"This must mean you love me." He smiled tenderly at her. "You told Chris and the others that you would never engage in a runaway match unless your affections were deeply engaged."

"So deeply I cannot think of life without you." She lifted up her face for his kiss. It was thus that her uncle found them. His bellow of rage broke them apart.

"What is the meaning of this? Get out of my house! Maxbridge, I'll call you out for this. Amabel, to your room. I'll deal with you later."

"Lord Brinker." Max put Amy behind him. "I have come to offer for your niece. We love each other and . . ."

"I am glad that you love her." Brinker advanced into the room with a cruel smile on his lips. "Seeing her wed to Vendercroft should cause you enough pain to partially avenge me for the harm you did me."

Amy slipped around Maxbridge. "Please, Uncle, listen to me. I love him, too. You cannot prefer that I marry a man like Vendercroft, cruel and half insane as he is, rather than Lord Maxbridge. If he can put aside his dislike of you for my sake, can't you do the same? If not for mine, for your daughters."

"My daughters? What have they to do with this?"

"Will you truly wish them to be brought into society by Vendercroft's wife? If I am even alive by then?"

"With his gold, I shall not need you to bring them out. A generous dowry will secure them husbands. Now go to your room and do not leave it. Else you know where I will go next, and what I will do."

Amy looked at Max. Their eyes met in understanding, and she turned back to Brinker. "Very well. At last I know how little affection you have for me. Three days from now I shall wed Lord Vendercroft. I hope you do not regret your decision, Uncle. I know I shall."

Maxbridge, tired as he was, drove to Wayside that very afternoon to visit with Amabel's mother. He found a woman worried about her daughter and receptive to his suggestions.

"I am so grateful to you, my lord," she said in her soft, almost whispery voice. "I knew Amy was marrying that dreadful man for my sake, and I scarce knew what to do about it. Are you quite sure you can keep me safe?"

"He won't find you before we are wed, and afterward, he'll have to go over my dead body to get to you. Not that I think he would try. His fangs will be pulled once Amy is mine."

Mrs. Armstrong sighed and leaned back against the cushions of the sofa they sat on. "I expect you think me a coward, sir."

"No, certainly not."

"Well, I would be, if I sought only my own safety. But it would break Amy's heart if she knew I had been injured on her account. Lord Maxbridge, I am fragile in body, but strong in spirit. I am not afraid of death, either. It is not my wish that Amy suffer the stigma of a runaway marriage. And there are logistical problems, too. A mad dash for the border in a carriage will result in a very sick bride. She suffers from carriage sickness, you see."

Maxbridge nodded, for he had very good reason to know this.

"Try though she might not to delay you, I expect Victor would catch up to you before you could make the border."

"In that case I should know how to deal with him!"

She looked at him narrowly. "Men, always so prone to violent solutions. That would make you persona non grata in your country. What kind of a life would you and Amy have then? And she has mentioned in her letters how proud she is of the stand you take in political and social matters. Your ability to affect government policy would end with the scandal of killing your bride's uncle, if not with having abducted her in the first place."

"Eloped, Mrs. Armstrong. If she goes willingly, it will be an elopement." Maxbridge folded his arms across his chest and glared at her. "Would you have me abandon Amy to Vendercroft just to avoid scandal?"

"No, but I would like to suggest an alternative, my lord, if you are willing?"

"I am listening, Mrs. Armstrong."

Morning dawned on a very tired Amabel Armstrong. She had spent the night worrying that Maxbridge had not under-

stood the reason for her submission to her uncle the day before. Had he abandoned the thought of marrying her? If he had
not, would his plan disturb her mother's delicate equilibrium?
And what would be her aunt's fate once she had decamped?
And her little nieces, if Victor in fact became bankrupt because
of debts he had run up dressing her for the Season?

Her mind had run back and forth between scolding herself
for being the most selfish person imaginable for putting her
happiness first, and bucking herself up with the thought that if
she did not marry him, her beloved Maxbridge would suffer
deeply. She did not know exactly what lay at the bottom of his
previous skepticism about her, but whatever it was, it had been
a deep scar, and he had overcome it to confess his love for her.

She alternately worried and prayed, at last falling asleep
with a sense of peace after submitting her fate to God's will.

She awoke with a sense of excitement. Would Maxbridge
come for her today? How would he manage it? She gnawed at
her knuckle as her maid combed out her hair. *Max was so
tired. Likely he rested last night and will go to Mother today.
How will I stand the suspense?*

She went in to visit briefly with her aunt, who was still very
much affected by her megrim. Something more, perhaps than a
megrim, if the bruise on her cheek indicated other such bruises
elsewhere from a recent beating. Amy's heart squeezed
painfully in her chest. She knew her presence had to some extent moderated Victor's abuse of his wife. What would happen
to Edwina when he learned that his ambitious plans had all
come to naught?

She tried to soothe Edwina's concerns, but told her nothing
of Maxbridge's possible actions. No need to add to her anxiety
or risk her fear-driven betrayal.

It was as she visited with her aunt over their morning chocolate that Victor suddenly bustled into the room. "Come, get
dressed, Edwina. Come downstairs, both of you, as soon as
may be." Not waiting for answer or argument, he left the
room.

Amabel assisted her nervous aunt into a morning dress.

"Now, dearest, it is probably Maxbridge, come to take me away. Uncle looked angry, and that is probably the reason."

They descended to the drawing room to discover Lord Vendercroft there, along with another man who was presented to her as the reverend Mr. Barclay. Mr. Barclay had the ruddy, veined face of a man who spent a great deal too much time worshiping at the altar of Bacchus. He seemed to have been at his libations already at eleven o'clock in the morning. He eyed her up and down and pronounced Vendercroft a clever dog for having snagged her.

Amy looked questioningly at her uncle, who deferred to Vendercroft. He took her chin in his and lifted it. "Your uncle has certain anxieties about another possible abduction. We have decided to obviate the possibility by proceeding with the wedding this morning."

She felt the world sway around her. "No! You promised me a wedding in a church."

"And if you wish it, you shall have it. We can be remarried two days hence, if you wish. I shall even invite all of your friends, including those your uncle no longer considers acceptable companions for you. Would you like Miss Puckett to stand up with you? It will be as you wish. But today we shall tie a legal knot which Lord Maxbridge will be unable to undo."

Amy steadied herself, fighting the feelings of panic that threatened to engulf her. "Very well, my lord. That is kind of you."

"Ah. Did I not tell you she would be an obedient girl, Lord Vendercroft. Shall we begin. Mr. Barclay?"

"Wait. I am not properly dressed. I should like to be married in the wedding gown you so kindly purchased for me. It is quite lovely, Lord Vendercroft." At her uncle's protest and Vendercroft's hesitation, she added, "I give you my word I shan't run away."

He nodded. "As you wish. I admit that shabby gown does not suit my consequence."

"Go with her, Edwina. If she does not keep her word, you will pay for it, I promise you."

Lady Brinker shrank away from her husband. "Come, Amy." As they went into the hall, Victor bellowed at Stuckey to summon Betty to Amy's room to assist her in dressing speedily.

Once in her room, Edwina took Amy's hands in hers. "Run, my dear. Go to Maxbridge. Do not worry about me."

But Amy shook her head. "I can't do that to you, Aunt. Besides, I gave my word that I would not run away."

"Your word! Amy, you cannot hold yourself to such a promise, given under duress."

"Calm down, Aunt Edwina. I have a plan."

At that moment Betty entered the room and Amy pounced upon her. "Betty, you must help me, and swiftly."

"Yes, miss," Betty answered stoutly. "I heard what is afoot. But how?"

"First, go down and get some of those strawberries that were left from supper. Pray to God the servants haven't eaten them," she muttered as an aside.

"They won't have," Edwina assured her. "I have strict orders from Brinker to see the servants eat only plain food. He had some of those berries for breakfast, but I know there were some left."

"Then go get them for me. Quickly. And when you return, I shall have a message for you to carry."

She ran to her writing desk and took out a pen and paper. A quick, urgent note to Maxbridge was all she had time for. She was sealing it as Betty returned with the fruit.

"But, Miss, don't berries make you break out?" Betty asked as she presented the plate to her mistress, along with some sugar and clotted cream.

She beamed at Betty. "Just so. Now, take this to Maxbridge, and impress upon his butler that he must have it at the earliest possible moment." She turned to her aunt. "Come, you must maid me while Betty is running her errand. The dress is at the top of the clothespress." She grabbed the bowl of strawberries, dashed some sugar over them, and began to eat them with more determination than pleasure.

Edwina, eyes wide, did as she was commanded, laying out also the shoes and gloves that matched the lovely dress. Amy finished gobbling down the berries and quickly rinsed the evidence from her mouth. "Hide the bowl," she said, beginning to unfasten the tapes of her morning dress.

By the time Victor stormed upstairs, she was dressed and Edwina was arranging her hair.

"What is taking so plaguey long?" he demanded. "Where is that maid of yours? She wasn't around yesterday, nor today."

"She is ill, Uncle. She has a most nasty-looking rash. I was afraid I might catch it."

"Ah, always thinking, clever little puss that you are. Vendercroft would not like that at all. Come on, though. That parson he has brought is guzzling my brandy and soon won't be able to stand on his feet. Besides, noon approaches."

Amy stood. "I am ready, Uncle." She bent to the mirror, ostensibly for one last pat at her hair, but in fact she scanned her face anxiously for the first signs of a rash. It had never taken very long for her to break out before.

On the way down the stairs she prayed that the effects of the berries, which she had often lamented, would now make themselves known with a vengeance, and just as she entered the drawing room, she felt the first flush of warmth along her neck that said her prayer was in a fair way to being answered.

Chapter Nineteen

"*H*ere she is now," Victor boomed jovially as he urged Amy into the drawing room. "Looks a treat, doesn't she?" He glanced down at her, then paused a moment. "The very picture of a blushing bride."

Mr. Barclay sniggered. "Blushing from head to toe. Must be anticipating her wedding night."

Vendercroft looked at Amy suspiciously. He was standing in front of the fireplace, and she started toward him. "More than blushing," he pronounced, holding up his hand to halt her. "Is that a rash?"

Amy put her hand to her face. "Oh, dear. I do feel so hot and itchy. I hope I haven't caught that maid's rash."

Victor spun her around and looked narrowly at her. "The devil," he said.

And then Edwina did something so courageous it fairly took Amy's breath away.

"Oh, dear. I hope it is not that dreadful recurring skin condition you caught last year in Yorkshire . . ." She put her hand over her mouth.

"Recurring skin condition?" Vendercroft stepped sideways, for his way out of the room was barred by Amy, who grew redder by the moment. Her eyes were beginning to swell, too. She could not resist scratching at the welts on her face.

"Recurring skin condition?" Victor tried to block Vendercroft's way. "Nonsense! I've never seen her like this before.

It's doubtless something she caught from her maid. Go away in a trice, it will."

Vendercroft maneuvered around the back of the sofa. "Will it, Miss Armstrong?"

"I don't know. I've never had it this bad before. Oh, my hands!" She peeled off her gloves to reveal red, blotchy forearms and welts on the back of her hands. She held them toward him. "But I am sure it never lasts for more than two weeks, my lord."

Vendercroft stumbled against a small gate-leg table by the door. "You have a recurring skin condition that lasts for weeks?"

Victor, with a blazing look at his wife, jerked Amy forward. "Nonsense. It is strawberries, that is what it is. You've eaten some of them, haven't you? Look, Vendercroft, she'll be right as rain in an hour or so."

"Oh, dear," Edwina said, scratching hard at her cheek. "I fear I have said something I should not have. I am sure Amy never had a rash before in her life, Lord Vendercroft."

"You'd say anything to get me to go on with this wedding," Vendercroft snarled.

"No, no, that isn't true." Edwina scratched at her neck.

Vendercroft lifted his hand to his neck and scratched in the same place. "My God, man. It is an epidemic." He picked up the table and held it as a barrier between himself and Amy, whom Victor had thrust in his direction. "Keep away. I want out, Brinker. Out, do you hear? I want a healthy wife!"

Victor thrust Amy aside and charged the retreating earl. "You can't cry off," he shouted. "What about my debts? I'll sue you for breach of promise." He grabbed the marquess's sleeve and hung on.

"Get away from me. You might have the contagion on you." Vendercroft grabbed his hat, which an interested Stuckey held out to him.

"Contagion or no contagion, you are not going to cry off because the girl throws out spots. I'll make a laughing stock of you in the *ton*, see if I don't."

"I'll pay," Vendercroft shouted. "Send the bills to me for her trousseau. I'll settle with you." With a mighty tug, he freed his arm from Victor's grasp. "Keep away. Will five thousand pounds content you?" Not waiting for an answer, he charged down the steps.

Victor, tearing at his hair, returned to the drawing room to find Amy gasping for breath, lying back in a winged chair. Her aunt stood over her, fanning her and weeping.

"Don't die, Amy. Don't die. Oh, please, don't die."

"Die?" Victor leaned over and jerked her half out of the chair, then dropped her upon seeing her swollen features and hearing her rasping breath. "Die? Oh! I am dying, too." He staggered toward the sofa.

Maxbridge was smiling as his carriage pulled up in front of his house. He had spent the night at Wayside and brought Mrs. Armstrong back with him. A few minutes before, he had delivered her to Aunt Phinea. A change of clothes, and then he would go beard Victor in his den. He chuckled at the thought of the man's discomfit once he learned he held losing cards in his hand.

As he descended the carriage steps, he noticed a maidservant leaving his town house. She looked distressed. Spotting his carriage, she hastened toward him.

"Are you Lord Maxbridge?" At his nod, she took his arm and began to tug on it. "Oh, my lord. Your butler has the note, but you must come quickly. That awful man is there, with a parson and one of them special licenses. Miss Armstrong is to be wed this very morning. She may already be."

Maxbridge turned and looked up at his coachman. "Come to Lord Brinker's house on the instant. I can run there faster than you can drive these crowded streets." He clapped the footman who had opened the door for him, on the shoulder. "You, too, Ben. I may have need of your strong arm."

"Yes, my lord." He jumped up onto the box of the carriage as Maxbridge sprinted away.

"All our plans for naught," he thought as he ran. "If Vendercroft has wed her, by God, I'll kill him if he doesn't give her up for an annulment." He thought an annulment would be possible if he could prove that Amy had been coerced. But what if the ceremony had been finished and they had already driven away, to who knows what destination? He ran even faster, propelled by desperation.

He charged up the steps of the Brinker town house and slammed the knocker down. Stuckey admitted him instantly, and his first sight was a cluster of servants standing around in the hall, looking very grave.

"Am I too late?" he asked.

"I don't know, my lord. It be bad," Stuckey said.

Frowning at the wording, Max dashed up the stairs and into the drawing room, where it took him a moment to comprehend the scene before him. Vendercroft was not in sight. A boozy-looking man in a clerical collar was staring owlishly at a crumpled form in a chair, and on the sofa Lord Brinker was stretched out, moaning, while his wife stood between the chair and the sofa, wringing her hands and crying.

When he realize the figure in the chair was Amy, he thrust the parson aside and gathered her in his arms. "Darling girl, what is wrong with you?" He scanned her face, swollen and covered with welts.

"If you have beaten her, Brinker, I shall kill you," he shouted at the man on the sofa, who had come up on one elbow.

"Get out," Brinker said, weakly. "Haven't I suffered enough today?"

"Nothing to compare with what you will suffer. Amy!" He gathered her up. "I'll take you home with me and call a physician."

"Not necessary," she gasped. "Only a few minutes more. Water?"

At his baffled look, she whispered, "Strawberries."

She looked too miserable for him to laugh, but relief made him almost giddy. He sat her down, and demanded of the butler standing by, "Get her some water to drink, and a bowl of lavender water to cool her." Then he lowered her back into the chair and, leaning her forward, began to undo her gown.

"Here, now. Leave off, I say. I don't give my permission, shall never give my permission . . ."

"But I don't need your permission, Lord Brinker," Maxbridge said, glancing cursorily at his old enemy. "I have her mother's permission and that is enough." He pulled the garment away from her red shoulders, leaving her shift in place to preserve her modesty. "Poor darling," he whispered, pressing a kiss into her hair.

"Her mother! I am her guardian!"

"She says you never took legal steps. Didn't want to spend the money, did you, Victor? Thought you had Amy well in your power, through your threats on your own sister's life."

"Carry them out, too," he said, rising. "Amy, send this man away or I leave now for Wayside."

As Victor rained down his threats, Maxbridge took a glass of water from Stuckey and offered it to Amy, who sipped it with difficulty through a swollen throat. Then he applied a cloth soaked in lavender water to her face.

"Go, by all means," Max said once he had finished. He slanted a disdainful look at Victor. "An excellent idea. Depart immediately."

Amy pulled the cloth away, sputtering a protest.

"See. She won't let me. She knows what's what. I've got you, Maxbridge. Now, leave."

"As I said, you may go to Wayside with my best wishes. You won't find Mrs. Armstrong there." He smiled down at Amy, who relaxed and replaced the cloth.

"Not find her?" Brinker stood right beside him now, his eyes bulging.

"No. I have abducted her, and now I am abducting Amy." So saying, he lifted her up and started toward the door.

"Not abducting," she murmured. "Eloping."

"Actually, not either. I'm taking her to stay with her mother, at a friend's house. We are going to announce the engagement in the papers, have a lovely wedding, and then a wonderful life together." He kissed her on her red forehead.

"Wait. Wait. Don't! What will I do? I've spent a fortune on that girl. Amabel, you can't do this to me."

Amy looked at her uncle coldly. "You are well served if you lose money on me. I never agreed to be wed to a man I found disgusting. Vendercroft is giving you five thousand pounds. With that you must be content."

Maxbridge should have felt triumph, but at that moment he happened to look at Lady Brinker. She had dropped into a chair, and her pinched, frightened face spoke volumes.

"Perhaps . . . perhaps we could come to some sort of accommodation," he said, lowering Amy to the floor and holding her against him.

"What do you mean?" Brinker's bellicose expression had been replaced by one of despair.

"I mean that though I am deeply flattered that Amy will throw over her family for me, I know it will grieve her to do so. She and her mother have grown quite fond of her aunt and nieces. For a certain consideration, I will agree to provide you sufficient funds to cover your debts and make some of those improvements you wish to make to your estate."

Brinker's eyes widened, his mouth opened. "You will? What sort of consideration? You already have Amy, and seem to think you may simply carry her off at will. Though I will call you out for it." The threat came in such a weak voice it was clear to Amy that Victor would never have the courage to carry through with it.

Maxbridge looked down at Amy. The adoring look in her eyes told him he had made the right choice.

"You are feeling somewhat better?" he asked.

She nodded. Indeed, though she still itched all over and felt as if she had been dipped in fire, she could feel the swelling going down in her throat. She knew her hives would subside quickly now. It was the worst reaction she had ever had. *A near run thing,* she thought, promising herself never to eat strawberries again.

Maxbridge helped her back to the chair, then went to Lady Brinker. He knelt beside her and gently touched the bruise on her cheek.

"Here is what I wish in return for generous settlements, Victor. You will sign a legal document agreeing to a separation from your wife if you ever strike her again. And you will permit her and her daughters to live with us in that event."

"My daughters! Give up my daughters? Never!"

"Uncle." Amy struggled to her feet and went to Victor. "Do as he says. You must learn to curb your temper anyway, or sooner or later you will strike Becky and Jane when they displease you. You only strike out when you are angry or frustrated. Surely you can find some other way of expressing yourself?"

"Strike my daughters?" Victor's voice was pregnant with awful realization. He stood looking down, face muscles working, pondering what had been said, while the other occupants of the room—and the interested servants clustered at the door—waited with bated breath.

At last he lifted his head. "You *are* fond of them, and their aunt, aren't you? But your old uncle Victor, I guess you hate him now."

Amy frowned. "Not hate, Uncle. My father taught me that hate is a corrosive emotion. But for what you tried to do to me, it will be very difficult to forgive you. If I can, someday, can you forgive my beloved? Can you end this enmity between you?" As she saw hesitation in his eyes, she lifted her hand and placed her palm along his cheek. "Please, Uncle? You will be a happier person for it."

Victor grabbed her hand as if it were a lifeline. "I will. I will. I only hope . . ."—he turned to his wife—"I only hope you can forgive me someday, Edwina." Then he rounded on Maxbridge, full of bravado. "If you ever lift a hand to my niece . . ."

"I know. You will horsewhip me." Max went to Amy's side and embraced her. "Never, never will I strike the woman I love."

"I hate that you have to pay anything for me," Amy said pensively, looking up into his dear eyes. "I promise you I will be a most economical wife. I will live contentedly in the country. I don't care for furs or jewels, and I don't need all these expensive gowns, you know. I can sew quite well, and . . ."

Maxbridge laughed and pressed a quick kiss to her lips. "Nonsense. The wife of a future prime minister must dress the part."

"Oh! I hadn't thought of that." Amy looped her arm around his neck. "Will you take me with you now?" she asked, not entirely trusting her uncle. "I know I look quite hideous, but . . ."

"You could never look hideous to me, sweetheart." He lifted her up and carried her out of the house. By this time his carriage was waiting at the door. "Your last abduction, my love." He placed her tenderly in the carriage, then climbed in beside her.

"Then I had best make the most of it." She wrapped her arms around his neck and kissed him.

Epilogue

"*H*ow is Mama this morning?" Max waited for Amy at the bottom of the stairs, smiling up at her.

"She is well. She is up and working on that christening gown already." It was Amy's mother's habit to remain above stairs in the mornings, giving her daughter and son-in-law some time alone together.

"I don't need to ask how you are, because you are glowing from within."

When Amy reached the step that allowed her head to be on a level with her husband, she stopped and put her arms around him. "They say that is what increasing does to you." They kissed deeply; then he lifted her gently and swung her around, depositing her on the floor beside him.

They walked out onto the terrace of Maxbridge, Max's principle seat in Kent. It was a fine spring morning, and they stood side by side contentedly listening to the birds calling out their courtship songs.

Max looked around quickly to see if they were observed, then put his hand on her slightly rounded stomach. "How is my heir this morning?"

"Busy. Ever since I realized what that little fluttering sensation means, I have learned he is a very active child. Has the post arrived yet? I am anxious to hear from Aunt Edwina."

"There is a large stack of mail in my office. Shall we go through it together?" They walked into the comfortably cluttered room that was not only Maxbridge's sanctum, but hers, and sat on a sofa side by side. He picked up the stack and began sorting, handing her letters and keeping some for himself.

"Ah, here it is." Amy opened her aunt's letter. "Oh, Uncle Victor is such a bad patient. She says the doctor does not think the stroke was very serious, yet he is become quite the invalid. Poor Aunt Edwina!"

"Ha! Edwina is probably glad to have him quiet and dependent upon her, rather than bullying her around."

"Probably." Amy continued perusing the letter until she felt her husband suddenly stiffen beside her. "What is it, love?"

"This letter. It . . . it looks like Chris's handwriting."

Amy's eyes widened. "Oh! Open it, do."

With trembling hands Maxbridge broke the seal and opened the folded piece of paper. He gave a shout of joy.

"Alive?" Amy pressed against him, trying to read the letter for herself.

"Yes! Alive and well. He is in France. It seems he was taken up by a smuggling ship as he was swept out to sea. They rescued him, but with a navy cutter in hot pursuit could not bring him back, so they carried him over to France. He's in a fishing village on the coast of Brittany."

"Oh, Max." Tears of joy coursed down Amy's cheeks, tears mingled with her husband's as she pressed her cheek against his. Then she straightened up.

"Why has that wretched boy taken ten months to write us?"

"He says he took a blow on the head from an oar, and did not know who he was until very recently."

"Is he ill? Is he coming home? I'll bet you need to go to France, don't you? You'll want to tell him about us yourself."

Maxbridge continued perusing the paper. "Too late. He read about it in the English papers. He had been studying them, hoping to find a clue to his identity. He wishes us happy. He says he plans to stay in France. There is a girl . . . Oh, Zeus take him! A smuggler's daughter."

"Oh, dear. Now you will have to go." Dread filled Amy's

voice. She couldn't bear to be parted from Max just now, yet the very thought of going on board a ship to accompany him made her nauseous.

He smiled down at her, encompassing her in his arm and pulling her close. "I suppose if I were a truly responsible uncle, I would go. But we are still newlyweds, after all, and you are increasing! Leave my beloved to chase off to France, just to keep my scapegrace nephew from marrying an unsuitable bride? I find I am not such a dutiful uncle as that."

The eager, lengthy kiss she gave him showed her approval of his lapse.